The Water Will Catch You

Chase Potter

CHASE POTTER BOOKS
www.chasepotter.com

Chapter One

Curtis

"How do you always manage to screw things up?"

I flinch at Celia's words, but actually I deserve this. Not that I cheated on her or anything, but I've been a lousy boyfriend.

"I know that the, uh… weekend in Montreal was important to you," I begin, struggling like so many times before to put together an apology that will save this relationship.

Her eyes narrow, and I know I've said something wrong. "I don't give a shit about that," she snaps. "Were you even going to mention that you were at risk of losing your job?"

My cheeks burn red, and there's nothing I want more than to get the hell out of here. At least for a few hours. "Do we have to discuss this right now?" I fight to hold my voice steady.

Celia crosses her arms, and with that action, my chance for escape disappears. "That's what you always do," she spits out the words. "I'm not going to put this off. You can't run away every time there's a problem. That's not how a relationship works."

Frustration pours dangerously into my chest, breaking down my inhibitions. I'm supposed to apologize and tell her that I'm going to stay and work through this. But I don't think I will. "You know what?" I say, gaining confidence as I speak. "Maybe I'm done working on this relationship. I've hated being together almost since the beginning." Every word tastes so damn good.

Silence fills the room. Celia opens her mouth, then shuts it. Seconds tick past and my heart thunders. *Has being with her really been that bad?*

"Fine. We're done," she says, and her voice is strangely empty of emotion. "Pack up your stuff and get out. It's my apartment. Good luck finding a place to stay with no job."

Oh, shit. "You're serious?"

She stares me down. "Yes. But if you do need a place…"

I raise my eyebrows. "Yeah?"

"There's a homeless shelter on Victoria street. Now pack your shit and get out, you asshole."

Sixth Grade

School let out a couple hours ago, but I don't want to go home. I don't actually know if Dad is drinking tonight or not, but I don't want to risk it. So instead I'm here, in the park.

I stare at the cover of the Spider-Man comic I picked up earlier, savoring the crisp and colorful ink as I cradle it with gentle hands.

A breeze picks up, bringing relief to what has to be one of Ontario's last hot days before autumn really sets in. Wanting to cool off, I keep walking through the park until the community swimming pool is sprawled out in front of me. Hot sun washes over everything, painting the afternoon with amber tones as I let myself through the fence of the gated pool.

Some kids are tooling around in the water, but otherwise it's quiet. *Perfect.* Just enough activity that no one will care about me relaxing at the edge of the pool.

Kicking off my shoes and socks, I approach the tile and concrete edge and stare down into the water. From nowhere, a boy's voice yells. "*Hey!*"

My head snaps toward the sound, but as I turn, my heel slips on slick tile and I flail backwards. My balance lost, the comic falls from my hand and flutters toward the water. I only have a fraction of a second to regret that before my head cracks against the concrete and the world winks out of existence.

My eyelids are slow to open, but the light forces its way in anyway. My vision adjusts as I blink, and in the newfound clarity appears a boy's face staring down at me. His eyes are this special kind of blue.

A color that an artist would kill for. Not brilliant and not dull, but something in between. A living shade that isn't like anything I've ever seen before.

I can't look away.

"You okay?" he eventually asks, backing off a bit to give me more room.

Vaguely aware of the pain in the back of my head, I finally sit up. But I still don't look away from him. "Why did you shout?"

"Sorry," he says, and concern flits around his expression. "I thought you were someone else." He seems taller than me, skinnier too, and he has short blond hair.

He's only wearing swim shorts. They have sharks on them, and they look new. I wish I had ones like that.

"Well?" he prompts again, and his question dislodges my attention from his appearance.

"My comic," I say, scanning the pool frantically. It's floating in the water, pages splayed.

He tries not to grin, but I can tell he's amused. "You're kind of weird."

Refocusing on the boy, I ask, "What happened?"

"You smacked your head on the edge of the pool. Then you fell in, face first."

I glance at my soaked clothes before giving him a long look. "You pulled me out?"

"Yep. So are you okay or what?"

"I guess so."

"Great." He reaches a hand out and tries to ruffle my hair, but it's too wet, so it just sort of gets tangled around his fingers. He grins wider now. "You're soaked," he says.

Up until now, I've been on the fence about what I think of this kid, but at that moment I decide I like him. "What's your name?"

"Danny. You?"

"Curtis. Do you live near here?"

Danny nods and points behind us. "Just a block from the other side of the park."

"I've never seen you before."

"We just moved here a few weeks ago." After a moment, he adds, "I have to get home for dinner."

"Okay. I'll see you around."

"I hope so," he says, and I feel like he actually means it. His eyes flash over me one last time. "It was nice to meet you, Curtis."

"You too," I say as he turns.

I watch as he walks away, wondering whether I'll see him again sometime. He's a little bit scrawny, and maybe a little pushy too, but I can't help but want to get to know him better. Maybe we'll even become friends.

Chapter Two

Curtis

It's been seventeen years since the day at the pool, but I've never forgotten the image of Danny's face hovering over me. Stunning blue eyes, pokey wet hair, and the hint of a smile tucked into the corner of his mouth.

We became best friends, more or less from the moment he hauled me out of the pool. The interests we had in common aren't worth remembering, and that we found it so easy to laugh together doesn't really seem to matter much anymore, either.

The important part is that he saved my life. At least I'd like to think so. Whether or not he actually dragged me back from the jaws of death, I'm not quite certain. In all likelihood, some passerby would have stepped in had Danny not been there. But it was Danny's face above me when I regained consciousness.

Regardless of everything that happened after that, the image of eleven-year old Danny staring down at me will never leave me. That's what happens when someone saves your life, I guess.

But even when we were best friends in high school, I never kept Danny's number in my phone. Thinking back, I'm not sure why I did that. Maybe it was because I could never figure out how Danny fit into my life, or maybe I just didn't truly appreciate what we had. That we even met was pure happenstance, and somehow our friendship never really managed to make sense in my mind.

A couple times at his house, I almost ran out the door because it always felt too good being around him, like I didn't really deserve it.

The ironic truth is that Danny was the one to finally disappear on me, and not the other way around. Not that Danny actually disappeared – not at first, anyway – because I knew where he went to university.

For good or for bad, I still have his number memorized, just like I always had. Taking a deep breath, I lean back in the driver's seat of my aging car and dial the number.

My fingers tighten around the worn leather steering wheel as the line rings.

"Hello?"

After years of not hearing Danny's voice, it sounds surprisingly familiar. For all our time apart, it's like he never changed.

"Hey, Danny," I say after a tense pause.

"Who's this?" he asks, the confusion in his tone grappling with curiosity.

Oh, right. My own number has changed half a dozen times over the years. I'm lucky that his is still the same. I hesitate, then admit, "It's Curtis."

"Holy shit."

That's about what I expected. Danny never did well with surprises. I give him a moment to let it sink in.

"Um, so," he begins, "how have you been, man?"

"Pretty good," I say, even though that's a complete lie. I'm about as far from *pretty good* as you can be. My eyes scroll to the white box sitting beside me in the passenger's seat, the box that's filled with everything from my desk at work. Dark blue letters on the side spell out *Select Commercial Services*. They also spell out the end of a career, if an assistant closer job at an unknown title company can even be called that.

"Actually," I correct myself, "things are kind of shitty."

"Oh?" His tone is guarded, almost like he's afraid to ask.

"I, um..." I practically have to kick the words off my tongue. "I kind of need a place to stay."

I wait for his response, straining to hear any subtle emotion buried in his words. After a moment's pause, he states, "So you called me."

He doesn't sound upset, and I breathe a little easier.

When I don't answer, he asks, "You're still in Thunder Bay, right?"

I'm surprised he knew that, but maybe it was just a guess. "Where else would I be?"

Danny sighs, and the sound scares me. It's a mix of conflicting emotions that I don't understand. And Danny used to be so easy for me to read. I hold my breath and wait for him to speak.

"Sorry to tell you, Curtis," he begins, "but I've been living outside of Victoria for a few years now. I'd definitely let you crash with me if I was still around."

"Victoria as in... British Columbia?" I say, the last glimmers of hope winking out silently inside my chest.

"Yeah."

For what it's worth, he does actually sound sorry.

"So what's going on?" His question is open-ended, and I can tell he's looking for more than just the reason I called him today.

I'm not going to explain how the years since graduating college have been one disappointment after the next, so I opt for the simplest answer. "I lost my job."

"I'm sorry to hear that," Danny says carefully. "But that doesn't explain why you need a place to sleep."

I grit my teeth, annoyed that Danny never lost his insatiable desire to ask questions I don't want to answer. But if I'm going to share this with anyone, it might as well be him. It's been years since we've talked, but we used to be best friends, and despite the passing time, he still knows me better than anyone else in the world. I've made other friends since then, of course, but none of them were ever like Danny.

My gaze shifts from the box beside me to the duffel bag stacked on top of more boxes in the backseat. "After I got home, my girlfriend broke up with me. It was her place, and she pretty much told me to leave."

"Jesus," Danny says. "So you really are in a tough spot, huh?"

I'm thankful he doesn't suggest I stay with my dad. Not that Danny would, because he knows what it was like for me in high school.

"Feels like it," I say, drumming my fingers on the steering wheel. I want to ask Danny what he's been up to the last several years and how he ended up across the continent from where we grew up, but I can't waste time right now. I need to be looking for a job, and an apartment...

"Come out to Victoria," Danny says abruptly.

"Huh?"

"You said you lost your job and you don't have a place to stay, so nothing is holding you there," he reasons. "Stay with me for a few weeks. I've got a spare room, and you can take some time for yourself while you get back on your feet."

"Yeah, right." I try to laugh off his suggestion, but actually I'm frustrated that he's giving me false hope. I can't afford to fly out to the west coast, and while I might not be afraid to call Danny up and ask to stay with him for a while, I would never ask him to pay for a plane ticket. I don't want handouts from anyone, not even Danny.

"Why not?" he presses. "It would be fun to catch up. And Vancouver Island is beautiful this time of year."

I glance out my window at the snow piled up on the street outside, crusted with rocks and dirt kicked up by passing cars. I pause, biting my lip. "March is beautiful? It's freezing."

"Not here." He hesitates, like he doesn't trust himself to say what he really wants. "Seriously, you should visit."

"Maybe," I say finally, "but I can't afford to fly out there."

"So drive," Danny counters. "It's not *that* far. You do have a car, right?"

"Of course I do," I say through clenched teeth, wishing he would just stop.

"So drive out here."

"Thanks for the offer, but I can't."

He sighs, and the sound echoes with every one of the years we've spent apart. When he speaks again, his words are hollow and layered with untruth. "So I, uh, have to go. But good luck figuring your stuff out."

"Okay," I breathe. The phone feels heavy in my hand, and in that moment, I can't wait to stop talking to him. "See you later."

"Bye, Curtis."

And like that, the line goes silent.

I stare out the window past the frost creeping up the glass, and a bitter feeling touches the back of my throat. Suddenly I can't stand to be in this car anymore, packed in with my belongings, and I step out into the chilly wind that doesn't yet feel like spring.

What the hell am I going to do? I have a couple thousand dollars saved, but that's going to go really fast while I look for a new job. All the things I own in the world are stuffed into the trunk or back seat. Glancing through the window at the boxes and the duffel bag packed with all my clothes, I sway forward and cross my arms on the roof, laying my head down on top. My cheek presses against the metal, and the cold of winter bites into my skin.

I need to get out of Thunder Bay before the city crushes me under its weight, but I'm never going back to my dad's place, even if that means I have to sleep in my car. *So what then?*

Danny's invitation whispers to me again, pulling at my shoulders and my hips and my feet. It would take a couple days to drive there, but it wouldn't be that bad. And I've never been out West before.

Inhaling a deep gulp of freezing wind, I pull out my phone again and dial the number that I never saved in my phone.

Chapter Three

Danny

For the second time this evening, I set down my phone on the kitchen counter. *Curtis Wyatt.* I let his name roll around in my head. *He's really coming.*

After our first phone call, I was pissed, and I managed to make it through two-thirds of a beer before he called back.

Lifting my eyes from the patchwork colors in the butcher-block countertop, I stare out across the open layout of my home without actually seeing any of it. *What has Curtis been up to?* Every few months I do some Facebook stalking, but other than that, I haven't seen or heard from him in years.

He was upset when I moved to Toronto for university, which I understood. We'd both planned to stay around home and attend Lakehead in Thunder Bay.

He stuck with the plan. I didn't.

I understood his anger, but it was still a surprise when he stopped taking my calls that first semester. I figured we would hash it out when I went back home for winter holidays, but when I showed up at his door over Christmas break, he just looked at me for a long minute before shaking his head and shutting the door. He never asked why I broke my promise to go to Lakehead with him. Not that I would have told him the truth – at least not then – but I still expected him to ask. I would have gladly taken a punch over him just ignoring me.

My eyes have drifted farther now, beyond the rough-sawn post and beam framing of my kitchen and living room, through the plate glass windows that face into the trees behind my home, and finally over the sloping path as it stretches downward to the aquamarine water of Sooke Basin.

I suppose it's technically raining now, even though I don't really consider this type of weather to be rain anymore. It's more like heavy misting. The kind that gets blown onto fresh produce at the grocery store.

I'm not sure whether I should be annoyed that Curtis didn't reach out until he was in desperate need of help, but it doesn't bother me. Regardless of what emotions I *should* be experiencing, the only feeling I have is a warm bubbling of anticipation in my chest. After all this time, I'm going to see Curtis again.

"What are you grinning about? And who was that?" My neighbor Lauren's voice calls from the couch beside the fireplace. It's where I left her when I got up to take the second call from Curtis.

"An old friend," I say, padding across the ancient hardwood to take a seat beside her. "He's coming to visit."

"Oh really? I didn't know you had any friends."

"There's no need for that," I say quickly. "And besides, you're my friend."

"Your *only* friend, and I don't even count because we're technically neighbors." She smirks as she brushes several long brown hairs out of her eyes and tucks them behind an ear.

I shift my gaze away from her to the darkened bricks of the fireplace. I was meaning to start a fire tonight, but I kept getting interrupted. First Curtis called, then Lauren came over early, then Curtis called again…

Is Lauren really my only friend?

Her voice softens. "You'll find a guy, Danny," Lauren says, resting her hand on my wrist. "One that will stick around."

A frown sneaks onto my face. I don't want to think about my last relationship, but even if Lauren didn't keep bringing it up, it would still be impossible to keep it off my mind. Adam was a guy I met at a bar, and that should have been the first warning sign. That he worked in construction was the second one. I used to do that too, so I should have known better.

I couldn't believe he wasn't straight, but apparently it was too much to expect for him not to be an asshole either.

It ended over two months ago, and I don't regret that. What bothers me more than anything is that in another year, I'll be twenty-nine. And maybe it's a silly idea, but part of me wants a family someday. Each failed relationship is a reminder that chances are passing me by. The worst part is that my four-month stint with Adam wasn't worth half the time I've spent agonizing over it afterward.

"I know, I know," I say, risking a look at her and those understanding eyes. Why does she have to be so supportive? Would it be so hard for her to at least once tell me to man up and quit moping?

She sighs as she leans back into the couch, her knee brushing against mine. "You're doing it again."

"Doing what?"

"That thing where you wish I was tougher on you or whatever."

I shrug. "Maybe you should be."

"Sure, if that's the way you want it." When she addresses me again, the softness is gone from her tone. "Get up off your ass and stop feeling sorry for yourself. Adam was a dick, and it's time to get over him."

I glare at her. Maybe I wasn't quite ready for that. "You're mean," I grumble, abandoning the couch.

"You still love me, though."

Retreating back to the kitchen, I cross my arms. "Something like that."

"So who is this friend of yours?"

"A guy from high school. We used to be close. Best friends, actually."

"Hmm," Lauren muses.

"What's that supposed to mean?"

"Oh, nothing," she says hastily before moving on. "You're going to clean before he arrives, right? Your kitchen has been a disaster ever since..."

A pang of guilt tightens its fingers around my chest. I've been neglecting a lot of things lately. "Yeah, I've got it. You want to help?"

Lauren gives me a frightened look. "Actually I need to check on my cat. He's been... ill lately. Rain check?"

"Sure," I say, easily seeing through her lie.

She smiles apologetically before slipping on her shoes and stealing out the door.

I shake my head and smile as I begin filling the dishwasher. I like living down the road from her, even though her corporate job and organized life sometimes make me feel like a failure. Well, not a *failure*, but like my life could be a lot more on track than it is. I run my own business and I'm really proud of my house, but besides those things, I feel like the rest of my life is more carelessly stacked than the pile of dirty dishes on the counter.

When I've packed the dishwasher to the brim, I pop a detergent brick into the little hatch and set the cycle for *heavy*. Unfortunately the kitchen is still a disaster, so I start running hot water in the sink.

Lauren's dilemmas these days are primarily related to the renovation going on in her living room. Lighting, flooring, furniture, and I don't even dare bring up the paint colors anymore… but I have bigger concerns. Like whether it's been long enough since Adam dumped me that I can start going back to bars. I know it's not a good place to find guys, but it makes it so easy. Maybe that's part of my problem.

My hand swishes absently in the water to draw out the suds, and once more my gaze gets lost out the window, lost in the mist that drifts down over the island so often in the spring that it's almost a part of the landscape.

"*Fuck*," I hiss, withdrawing my hand from the soapy water. Blood pearls at the tip of my finger where it bumped into one of the knives at the bottom of the sink. Lauren bought me a new set as a gift a month ago, complete with a wooden block and everything. She did warn me that they were sharp, but damn.

As I lick the blood off my finger, my eyes travel across the room to the spot on the couch where we were sitting a half hour ago. The darkness outside is starting to slip into the house, and suddenly I feel terribly alone.

Wiping a soapy hand on my jeans, I pull out my phone and stare at my recent call list. The two calls with Curtis were short, but knowing that he's coming makes me feel better than I have in a long time.

The next morning, my alarm cuts cruelly into the morning stillness. Reaching a hand through the darkness, I slap the snooze button and roll over. I actually like mornings, but five-thirty a.m. still feels too early. I could get up later – I am self-employed after all – but it helps me feel more productive to start the day slightly sooner than I'd like to.

Another ten minutes of stolen rest slip past, and finally I force myself to push the covers off. I sit up at the edge of my bed, and an involuntary smile sneaks onto my face as I remember that Curtis is coming.

It's that thought that carries me through the next few minutes as I stumble over a lump of dirty clothes and make my way to the kitchen. It took over two hours last night, but the counters now gleam spotlessly. After starting a pot of water on the stove, I head to the bathroom to get ready for the day.

Stripping down, I step into the shower and turn the handle hard over to hot. As I wait next to the stream while the water heats up, I gaze through the clear glass of the shower wall and into the mirror above the sink. Blue eyes stare back at me, and I have to admit that the guy isn't that bad looking. I might have gained five pounds since I got flaky about swimming recently, but for the most part, my lifelong dedication to the pool has been unaffected by the last two months.

Stepping under the searing stream of water, I let it drum over my shoulders as I wonder when Curtis will get here. He did say he was coming, but I haven't heard anything from him yet. He doesn't even know where I live, other than that it's somewhere on the island. I suppose that's enough information until he gets a lot closer.

After my shower, I return to the kitchen wearing only a fresh pair of underwear. Bracing myself on the counter, I pull in a breath of morning air as I pour boiling water into my coffee press. Besides my less-than-frequent sexual encounters with other men, my coffee press is probably the gayest thing about me.

My phone vibrates on the counter and the screen lights up with a message from Curtis. *What's your address?*

Turning first to get a mug from the cupboard, I smile to myself as I tap out the information, followed by: *when will you be here?*

The reply comes quickly. *Tomorrow sometime.*

Saturday, then. I hesitate for just a second before sending back what I've typed out. *See you then, Curtis.* For some reason it feels important to use his name. I want him to know that I never forgot him. It seems stupid but it's not, even though I can't really explain why.

Chapter Four

Danny

Bringing my face close to the surface, I gaze down the smooth length of raw wood, admiring the wide and straight grain. I can guess it will have a variety of colors because of the varying shades of gray in it, but until it's finished, it's hard to say exactly how it will look.

Resting my cheek on the board, I draw in a breath and close my eyes. I love the smell. Most woods have a unique scent, and over the last few years, I've developed an appreciation of them. Brazilian walnut is a new one for me, and it smells... wild.

I've spent the morning planing down and cutting to length all the boards I'll need for the project. Why Henry Wellington wanted this particular species of wood for his dining room table, I have no idea. He and his wife probably got the idea while at a dinner party with one of their equally rich friends who had their floors done in Brazilian walnut.

I'm not quite as impressed with the wood as he seemed to be. In fact, I tried to talk Mr. Wellington out of using this species, not only because I'd never worked with it before, but also because it's dense as hell. It's one of the hardest woods in the world, it sinks in water, and supposedly it's been classified with the same fire rating as steel. I'm not sure I believe that last anecdote, but it seems to get batted around often enough.

When my push to use a more standard wood proved unsuccessful,

I decided to price him out of the table. Citing the extra hassle of working with the wood, I quoted him twelve thousand dollars.

The bastard commissioned it anyway. I didn't like the idea, but twelve grand – actually ten after expenses – is damn good for a week's work.

So I work. Even though I feel like I'm forcing concrete through my machines.

The hours in my shop fly past, probably because I'm so preoccupied with Curtis's impending arrival. Unfortunately, custom furniture building isn't a good profession for wandering minds, and eventually I pay for it with an error.

Lifting the tape measure so the end lets loose, I hold it firm while the metal tape gets slurped back up in a flurry. "Shit," I growl. I cut the goddamn board too short.

The rookie mistake is particularly frustrating because it means I have to buy more wood. I didn't order any extra because I'm never going to use this stuff again. I refuse.

It's hot in here, and I'm tired, and knowing that Curtis is coming is making it almost impossible to concentrate. "I'm done," I say to no one as I set the tape measure harder than necessary on the wasted board. I don't like putting off projects, but I like making mistakes even less, so it's just going to have to wait a few days.

From the most recent Facebook stalking I've been doing, it seems like Curtis hasn't changed all that much – physically at least. He hasn't gotten out of shape or lost his hair or anything, and I'm hoping whatever he's been up to the last few years hasn't sent him off the deep end.

Curtis Wyatt was a kid that seemed relaxed in every situation, even when we were in elementary school. On the inside he was usually a wreck, though, but no one else knew about that.

The problems he had at home didn't really change as we got older, except maybe to get a little worse. His home life sucked, and I feel like the reason we became so close was that he just needed someone to lean on. I didn't mind being that for him because from the moment we met – with him flat on his back and me trying to remember how to do CPR – I had a good feeling about Curtis.

Glancing up from my empty plate, I allow my eyes to wander across the surface of my *own* dining table. It's flat-sawn black walnut with maple accents, finished with Danish oil and a satin lacquer. I drag my fingers across the top, feeling the places where the wood has shifted with time and admiring the streaks of lighter color where the young sapwood meets the darker heartwood.

Some woodworkers consider it a flaw to include sapwood in furniture, but I think it has character. It's the same reason I didn't use quarter-sawn wood with its straighter grain, even though it's supposed to be more premium. I love character.

My eyes dance across the tabletop, chasing the lines as they curl and meander like smoke rising into a still summer night. I could search out a hundred details in this table that I adore, but I don't need to because I know them all by heart.

Building this table took weeks, and it was a tedious process, because it was my first real project, back before I ever considered woodworking for a living. Back before I had a shop. Back before I really knew what I was doing.

It's not a perfect table, but it is perfect to me. While flaws don't make something better, they do make it real.

My attention wanders, moving onward into the brightly lit, open space of the living room. I leave lights on in my house even though the thought of wasting resources normally makes me cringe. I do it because the house just feels too damn lonely otherwise.

Pushing myself up from the table, I begin the task of cleaning the house in preparation of Curtis's arrival. Thankfully the kitchen is still mostly spotless, so that leaves the guest bedroom and main bathroom, as well as way too many piles of old mail and other random papers.

When I inherited this home from my grandfather, it was worth barely more than the land it sat on. No one else in the family wanted it because it was in shambles. Decades of neglect as he succumbed to age had left a once beautiful home in an abysmal state of disrepair, and none of his relatives wanted to rehabilitate it.

Where my cousins saw only a money pit, I saw potential. It's true that almost everything needed to be replaced or remodeled, from the failing roof and windows to the painfully outdated kitchen and bathrooms. But from the moment I stepped into this house, I knew it was something special.

Over a hundred years old, it was built at a time when houses were made right. The massive posts and beams that form the bones of my grandfather's home are solid – *more* than solid because they could easily support twice the weight that they do.

It was those beams that convinced me to bring this home back from the brink of demolition, but it wasn't until after I traded in most of my share of the inheritance for the house and dove into the work that I realized what a gem I'd found. Underneath shag carpet and a subsequent layer of asbestos tile, I found the original flooring – solid hardwood that had waited patiently for a century for me to find it.

Shooing away the memory of the house before I dumped thousands of hours of my life into it, I cross my arms and survey the living room. Apart from the exposed beams, the dark oak of the trim and floors is my favorite part of the home. Unfortunately, at the moment they're hiding under dirt and smudges, so I might as well start cleaning there.

I've been too preoccupied to concentrate on anything all day, but it's not until afternoon is well underway when a knock on the door seizes my attention. My heart thuds in my chest as I stand up from the couch and cross the room to my front door. Taking a deep breath, I close my fingers around the knob and turn.

The man standing in front of me has shadows clinging to the areas beneath his eyes, and he seems even more weathered than the worn duffel bag slung over his shoulder. He looks at me, and I look at him. In that second, everything I ever felt for Curtis comes rushing back. He's fifteen again, and we're being pelted with the first drops of a thunderstorm, and I'm desperately waiting to hear his answer to a question.

"Hey, Danny," he breathes, his voice quiet.

After a tentative pause, I say, "You look like hell."

"Um, thanks," he says with a soft sarcasm as his dark brown eyes settle on me. In the area between the defined jawline and strong cheekbones, he might be blushing a little, but it's hard to tell. Still, with the exception of his tired state, he's just like I remember.

I decide to try again. "Come here," I say, grabbing his shoulder and pulling him into a hug. Under my grip, he sighs, and his shoulders sink.

Holding him this close, I can tell he's chewing gum, because the muscles in his jaw tighten and relax every other moment. I let go and take a step back, if as much because he doesn't smell that great as that it's time to break the hug.

"You going to invite me in?" he asks. Exhaustion clings to his words just as it does to his appearance.

"Right, sorry." I step aside to make way for him.

Curtis moves into the entryway, which is really just a part of the living room. As he passes, my gaze slides over him, taking in the black leather jacket and dark jeans he's wearing. His hair is still the same – dark, almost black, and cut short on the sides. When we were in high school, I always thought it was cool how it contrasted with the lighter brown of his eyes.

"This is a *really* nice place," he says, his voice bordering on astonishment. I watch as he glances from the heavy timber framing to the oak floors, then to the fireplace and finally to the expansive windows of the kitchen. "How'd you manage to buy this?"

The envy in his tone brings heat to my face. "It's kind of a long story, but the short version is that I got it cheap and put a lot of work into it."

"Seriously?" His eyes dart around the room once more before settling on the kitchen windows and their view of the dark blue water of Sooke Basin. "I bet this place is worth like half a million."

"Um," I begin, my voice hitting an awkward note, "not quite." Being right on the water, it's actually closer to a *million and a half*, but I'm not about to tell Curtis that. The look on his face is already making me uncomfortable.

Pushing toward a different subject, I ask, "Can I get you something to drink? Water, juice, beer?"

"Water," he answers immediately. Shrugging off his coat, he drapes it over the bench beside the door and heads toward the kitchen.

"Where are your cups?" he asks.

Amusement pricks at the edges of my lips as I retrieve a glass and fill it from the sink.

"Thanks." He guzzles the water and his Adam's apple pumps up and down. I watch him, noticing too many subtle details that I used to love about him. The stubborn way his hair bends sideways in the front, the flecks of light birthmarks that dot his neck, the strength in his shoulders.

Uninvited, a vague pull stirs inside me. It's a feeling that's still too familiar, despite the years since I saw Curtis last. Peripherally aware of the frown forming on my face, I force my eyes from him and push the thought out of my mind.

Curtis sets the glass down hard on the maple countertop, and I flinch at the sound. Not appearing to notice, he says, "I feel like I'm about to pass out. I slept in my car for a bit last night but basically I've just driven the whole time. You mind if I crash for a couple hours?"

I glance at the clock on the wall. It's barely past three in the afternoon. "Uh, sure," I say, trying to keep the disappointment from sneaking into my voice. I've spent years without talking to Curtis, so I suppose I can wait another few hours. "Do you think you could, um, shower first?"

He raises an eyebrow at me. "What are you trying to say?"

"I just changed the sheets before you got here, and you kind of… smell," I admit.

"Always the perfectionist, Danny." He shakes his head with a half smile. "Sure, I'll shower if you want. You have a towel for me?"

Ten minutes later the drone of water running in the bathroom seems to fill my ears completely. I know it's messed up, but I can't get the thought of him showering out of my head. We were best friends in high school, and we showered together after gym all the time. But I wasn't out back then. Hell, I didn't even know for sure that I was interested in guys. Not at the beginning, anyway. There were some signs, I guess, but it wasn't until I really fell for Curtis that I figured it out.

Not that I ever told him how I felt.

Not that I ever will.

First I hear the water shut off, and then the door opens, but I stand resolute in the kitchen. I already showed him where his room was, and he doesn't need my help to get himself into bed. Gritting my teeth at my careless mental phrasing, I close my eyes in resignation. This isn't starting the way I'd imagined. After so long apart, it should have been easy to be around him. Those stirrings were supposed to have withered away with the passing years until they faded completely into memories. It hasn't even been an hour yet, and already I'm starting to remember the way I never wanted to feel again.

I glance up, letting my gaze roam across the house. The sun is shining through the large windows overlooking Sooke Basin, and golden light streams into the room, catching a thousand bits of dust on their daily migration. Staring into the gleaming particles drifting through the air, I decide to get out of the house for a while. I need to clear my head, and if Curtis is going to sleep for the next few hours, I might as well be somewhere else. And if he wakes up, he'll be able to take care of himself until I get back.

*   *   *   *   *

In front of me, the water is calm, almost thoughtful. Standing at the edge, I inhale, relishing in the uniquely bitter scent of chlorine. I love when the pool is empty. Swimming is inherently a solo affair, but it's a treat being the only one here.

Running a thumb absently along the top of my black swim briefs, I glance through the plate glass to the rest of the gym and the guys working out. There isn't a machine or lift in there that I don't feel comfortable with, but lifting isn't the reason I come to the gym.

Without hesitating any longer, I dive forward. From the tips of my fingers to the rest of my body, the cool liquid rushes in, pressing against every line and curve of muscle in my one hundred seventy pounds. In less than a second, I've been swallowed completely.

When I surface, the concrete edge of the pool is far behind me. Stealing a breath, I turn my face back into the water and propel myself onward. At the end of the lane, I ready myself to reverse directions. It's a maneuver I've performed countless times, but somehow I misjudge the distance and end up whacking my shoulder against the side of the pool.

Back down the lane, I feel heat in my face despite the coolness of the water.

All the way to the end, flip turn, then back again. Over and over, until my arms burn and my chest is trying to crush my lungs. Until the unwelcome reaction to seeing Curtis again is a forgotten pinprick compared to the physical toll of tearing through the water.

When I finally drag myself out of the pool, there are swimmers in two other lanes. Chest heaving and heart thundering, I give my head a shake to throw off the drops of chlorine draining down my face.

It's been a while since I've come to swim, and even longer since I pushed myself so hard, but I needed it. Glancing at the gym beyond the glass, I almost consider lifting too, but my legs are already shaky and Curtis is at home. Looking away from the guys there, I head into the locker room to change.

As soon as I get home, I make myself a protein shake, flop down on the couch, and turn on the TV. Leaving the volume low so I don't wake Curtis, I find myself concentrating more on the clinking sound of the metal blender ball in my protein bottle than the trashy reality show.

For the first time since leaving to the gym, I let my thoughts wander back to earlier in the day… and to Curtis. He's straight. I used to wish so hard that he wasn't, that he could give me the things that I desperately wanted, but wishing never changes anything.

When we were younger, it was his personality that I fell for. I don't know if I didn't notice his looks back then because we just hung out so much, or if it was for some other reason, but damn. After seeing him again today, there's no debating that he's… well, hot. Not only does he have that all-American boy thing going for him, but he's built too. He's a hair shorter than me, and maybe not quite as lean, but in a way that makes him sort of just right all around.

Almost involuntarily, I glance at my crotch. *Nope, not with Curtis in the next room.* I take another pull from my protein shake to ward away the arousal creeping up on me.

The creak of hardwood flooring from behind pulls my head toward the sound. Curtis is standing in the doorway, wearing a white t-shirt and basketball shorts and generally looking more rested. "Hey," he says, his voice hoarse.

"You get some sleep there, buddy?"

A lazy smile lifts up the corners of his mouth. "A couple hours, yeah. What time is it?" he asks through a yawn.

"Quarter to seven. You hungry?"

Curtis nods vigorously. "I didn't really eat much on my way here."

"You like burgers still? There's a bar up the road that we can walk to."

He looks at me like I'm nuts. "Is that even a question? Of course I still like burgers."

"Then put some jeans on and we can go."

It takes Curtis a few minutes to get ready, so I've already changed out of my gym clothes and am waiting by the door when he joins me. "Is it cold outside?" he asks, noticing my windbreaker.

"Not too bad, but with the humidity, you feel it more. You need to borrow a jacket?"

His gaze finds its way to me, pausing there for a moment. "I'm okay."

The beers in front of us arrived a minute ago, but neither of us has taken a drink yet. Resting my fingers on the base of my glass, I rotate it in a slow circle. The thrill of getting to spend time together once again

– just the two of us – is tempered by his confession on our walk here that he's starting to miss his now ex-girlfriend.

No, not a confession.

But it felt like it.

I can sense his eyes on me for a while before I finally look up. When I do, he takes a bright green wad of gum out of his mouth and presses it against the cardboard coaster before picking up his glass. "Cheers?" He says it like a question.

I lift my glass in response and we clink them together, a sip worth of beer sloshing over the top of mine. I watch the liquid carry bubbles down the edge of the glass as I lift it to my lips. The golden goodness combined with the undertow of hops is almost enough to banish the surly elements of my mixed mood.

"So what happened with your job?" I ask, afraid to bring it up but knowing it's a conversation that we're going to have eventually. The beers might help, but they won't kick in for a few minutes yet.

Curtis stares at me from across the table before giving in to a long sigh.

Taking an anxious second sip of my beer, I venture, "That bad, huh?"

"It wasn't like the end of the world or anything. I'm going to be fine," he says, staring me down. When I don't say anything, he goes on. "I worked for a title company, doing real estate stuff. Closings mostly. I was never that great at it, but when Celia and I started having problems…"

"Your work suffered?"

"More like a nose dive," he corrects me. "I got distracted and started messing stuff up." He sighs again and stares at his beer. "There was this purchase… a short sale," he glances at me, "like when the bank lets someone sell their house for less than they owe–"

"I know."

"Oh. Um," he flushes, then continues. "The whole thing fell through because I fucked up. The owners didn't have any more time to sell, so they went into foreclosure. And the buyers… well, I don't know what they did, but the whole deal had been a couple months in the making. They had to start over looking for a house, I guess."

As his words come to an end, I try to catch his gaze but he won't look at me. I hate that Curtis is hurting right now, but even more than that, I hate that I can't do anything about it. I want to pull him to his feet and crush him with a hug until all the tough stuff he's gone through over the years has been squeezed out of him.

When he finally does look up, his expression is soft. It's the one that I never saw on his face except when it was just me and him. Curtis had other friends in school, but he never opened up to any of them the way he did with me.

Faced with his intent stare, I glance to my beer, dragging my thumb down the side of the glass.

"Something wrong?" Curtis asks. His dark eyes examine me over the top of his beer as he takes a drink.

A light feeling flutters in my chest as he looks at me, but instead of making me feel good, I'm just getting pissed off. I don't want to feel this way about Curtis. I didn't want to when we were younger, and I sure as hell don't want it now. He was my best friend in high school. Why can't I just be satisfied with that?

I wonder if I could get away with standing up right now and leaving. I could pretend to get a text, tell him a friend is having an emergency, and let him walk back to the house alone.

The twenty-dollar bill in my pocket would cover our tab. It would get me out of here.

The tips of my fingers feel hot as they itch with temptation. But the inquisitive face across from me is pinning me down, making it impossible to move. Because for as much as I want to get out of here, any idiot could tell that Curtis is enjoying himself – despite what we've been discussing – and that he's glad he's here with me.

"Danny?" he asks, the first cracks of concern showing in his expression.

"Just spacing out. Sorry, it was a long week," I say, having to force the words out before he becomes even more suspicious. He's already half done with his beer, which makes me feel guilty. If I don't hurry up, he's either going to have to wait without a beer or be one ahead of me. Putting him in either of those positions is a clear violation of man-etiquette, so I down a third of my glass at once, putting me back in step with him.

"Damn, dude," he says. "You learn to drink like that in college?"

Redness burns in my cheeks. "Just catching up with you."

A smile spreads across Curtis's face. "Must have been college."

It takes all my effort not to scowl at him, because the memories of those years rising in my mind feel particularly sour at this moment. If it weren't for Curtis, they might never have happened at all.

Watching my reaction, he lowers his voice, "Sorry."

The waitress drops off our burgers and fries, and I watch as Curtis digs in with vigor before realizing how hungry I am myself.

Between bites he asks, "What about you, where do you work?"

I try to chew faster, but my first bite was a big one. Holding up a finger, I make him wait until I force myself to swallow. "I build custom furniture. Tables, bed frames, trunks... stuff like that."

"So you're like a *carpenter*?"

"What's wrong with that?" I ask, defensiveness filtering into my voice.

"Nothing," he says quickly. "It's just..."

"Just?" I prompt.

This time he digs into his own burger, stealing moments to think while he chews. When he finally swallows, he explains, "It's just the last thing I ever would have imagined you doing. Guys who build stuff are just..." he gestures vaguely with the burger in his hand, "not like you."

"What do you mean by that?" I demand. I'm not convinced that he means it in a bad way, and I don't even disagree with him necessarily. But I'm not going to let him get away with that without a challenge.

"Jeeze, Danny, chill out. What I mean is that you've got money, and you're clean cut, good looking, and too damn smart for your own good," he snaps.

The speed and harshness of his reply surprises me. The speed because it means he doesn't question the validity of what he's said, and the harshness because... he doesn't seem happy that it's true.

I take a long drink of my beer before responding. "Those aren't the only important things in life," I say carefully.

"When we graduated, you were on a swimming scholarship and everything was looking up for you." He pauses, considering his next words. "I expected you to end up working for an investment bank or something, but you still seem to have done pretty damn well for yourself. I guess it worked out for you that you left Thunder Bay." His statement is loaded with a silent accusation.

I have an explanation for why I left, but this doesn't feel like the right time, so I bite down on my words.

For several minutes we eat in silence, until only a fourth of my burger remains. His voice is quiet when he asks, "How did you go from attending Toronto to being out here building furniture?"

Events from that year race back to me, from the moment I made the decision to leave school to when I built my woodshop. Some of the memories are good, others are painful. "Pure bad luck."

"What's that look for?"

My lips tighten into a line, forcing back the rueful grin that was meant only for myself. Most people just move on after I tell them my one-liner quip, but he was watching me intently enough to notice. And he still is.

Oh, what the hell… it won't hurt to just tell him the truth, right? This is Curtis, after all. Glancing away from those chocolate eyes, I admit, "I didn't like college. I had to get out of there, so I took a semester off and…" The words left unspoken simmer on my tongue. *And I never looked back.*

"Sorry," he says, and when I look up, he's still watching me.

Instead of responding, I stuff the last piece of burger into my mouth.

"I have to piss. Be right back," he says, standing up and brushing crumbs off his jeans. Despite his recent spate of misfortune, Curtis looks like he actually takes care of himself. I let my gaze move over him as he walks past. He's athletic, and he's got more muscle than he did in high school. He even shaved after he showered earlier too.

The thing about Curtis is that his home life growing up was shit, and when that happens, it's damn hard to get out of it. He managed it though, more or less.

In my case, the bad that happened to me in college was ultimately my own fault, the result of my own decisions. Once I got the hell out of Toronto, things started to look up.

When Curtis sits back down, I shoot an intentional glance at his empty beer before asking, "You ready to head home?"

He nods. "If that's okay. I'm kind of tired."

After leaving enough cash on the table to cover the bill, I let him go ahead of me as we make our way outside. Walking side by side, we move out of the circle of light cast by the solitary streetlamp and into the cool, wet air of the night.

Eventually Curtis says, "You didn't have to pay for me."

"I wanted to." I could kick myself for not coming up with a better response than that, but it seems to satisfy him.

Beside me, his footsteps are barely audible on the road as we walk. Normally I'm not a big fan of being out at night – not only because there are semi-frequent cougar and bear sightings here, but also because I live so far from Victoria that dark really *is* dark. But I've been on this road hundreds of times, and I could walk it blind. Which is sort of the way I am right now. Chock it up to bad genetic luck, I guess, but I can't see for squat at night.

"Why did you leave?" His question is abrupt, catching me off-guard because it still managed to find its way to me in the darkness.

My voice is guarded as I respond. "Why did I leave Thunder Bay to go to school? Or why did I leave Toronto and move to the island?"

"Take your pick."

For a minute, we just walk. The rhythm of our footsteps counts time to the passing seconds as my eyes continue trying helplessly to adjust to the darkness. Between the sounds and the lack of visibility, an old memory stirs within me, and for a moment I'm back in middle school, walking through the woods at night with Curtis at my side. The night is humid like tonight, but it's the height of summer and a lot hotter. My shirt feels sticky against my back, and sweat is slick across my palms.

Then my mind abruptly rejects that version of reality and plants me back firmly in the present. Pulling in a full breath of the damp Pacific air, I say, "I left Thunder Bay, because..." I pause, considering what I should actually tell him.

I didn't leave because I was a closeted gay teen living in a small, judgmental town, even though that would have been a good enough reason. The truth is, I left because I'd fallen in love with Curtis, and it was agonizing being around him and being completely unable to admit what I really needed from him.

"It just wasn't a good fit for me. I wanted to be in the city."

"It was good enough for you when we were growing up," Curtis retorts. His voice isn't sharp, exactly, but I'd be foolish to believe that there isn't deep emotion buried beneath this topic. For both of us.

"Things changed," I say quietly. "I didn't leave because of you, you have to know that." Technically a lie, but the way he thinks I mean it *is* true. I didn't leave to be far from him. I left because I couldn't be close to him.

"Yeah, I know," he says, his breath tight. "But you didn't *stay* because of me, either."

This isn't the right time or place for this conversation. Not the first night that Curtis is here. And maybe not ever, but definitely not tonight. "I just had to get out of there, okay? I'm sorry I bailed on our plans. You were my best friend and I didn't want to leave you. It sucked, and I missed you a lot, but I had to go."

"Yeah, sure," he says as we approach the porch light of my house, and I know that the distinction isn't lost on either of us that I had to use the past tense when referring to him as my best friend.

Fighting to keep my exhaling breath from turning into a sigh, I slide my key into the lock and open the door for him. He walks past me, and his eyes catch on mine. Curtis deserves a real explanation for why I broke my promise and left Thunder Bay, but I'm not ready to give him one.

"I'm going to bed," he says as he kicks off his shoes.

I want for us to talk more, but I don't know what I'd say. And he clearly needs more rest after driving across half the continent in two days. "I'll be up for a bit longer, let me know if you need anything."

"Will do." He hesitates, but after a moment he turns soundlessly away and disappears into his room.

Throwing myself onto the couch beside the lifeless fireplace, I let my gaze venture upward into the timber-framed ceiling. It was a nightmare to do the rehab on this place. Aside from the post and beam framing, everything needed refinishing. Endless hours of stripping the worn finish off the original trim, scraping gunk off, and finally putting down new finish. But it's beautiful now, and I suspect that it looks something like it originally did when it was built.

My eyes come to a rest once more on the giant wooden beams. At thirty by thirty centimeters, each one is easily several hundred pounds, and the ones that run the entire length of the house are even heavier. A hundred years ago there was no shortage of original-growth heavy timber, but whoever built this place went above and beyond because the structural supports are overkill.

Even though I'm not particularly thrilled that logging has played such a significant part in the history of Vancouver Island, I can't help but appreciate my home. Sometimes I think it would be cool to meet the original owner. To pick his brain about why he laid out the house like he did. More than anything, I'd want to thank him for building it right. Even after years of abuse and neglect, its bones endured. And I'd like to think that its soul did too.

I have to smile to myself because it's only been a few years since I moved to the island, but I'm already starting to feel like I belong here.

I doubt that every one of my neighbors would agree with that sentiment, but Lauren would put up a fight for me.

I glance over the back of the couch and notice that the light from underneath the door of the guest bedroom has gone dark. Leaning my head back on the padded edge of the couch, I let my thoughts cast back to those first few years when Curtis and I really became close.

At the beginning, I think we were both a little wary of each other, but after the first few months, that feeling pretty much disappeared. My friendship with Curtis wasn't one that was *meant to be*. I think it was just one that became special on its own because we poured so much of ourselves into it. And because we trusted each other without reservation. Back then, anyway.

Seventh Grade

Curtis tosses the flashlight onto his sleeping bag and ducks into the tent. "What took you so long?" I hiss. I'm scared. Because there *are* bears and other animals out in these woods. Mr. Michaels warned us about the dangers of camping before we came out here. Most of our class just thought it was a joke, but it's different when you're alone in the dark. Every sound is suspect.

"Had to piss," Curtis says as he zips the tent shut. "You get scared or something?"

"No," I state firmly.

His lips part into a playful grin. "I thought you didn't get scared, Danny?"

He's just messing with me, because he knows that I don't like it when I'm not in control of what's going on around me. I roll my eyes at him but then admit, "There were noises and stuff."

Curtis gives me his trademark shrug. "Probably just other guys in their tents." He slides into his sleeping bag and clicks off the flashlight.

A minute of silence passes.

"Good night," I say from my own sleeping bag.

I hear slight movement from his direction, but he doesn't answer me. Closing my eyes, I pull the nylon fabric closer to my chin. Today was fun, and I'm thankful that Curtis was able to come. His dad said that he couldn't like a dozen times, but after I told my parents that he wasn't allowed to go on the school trip, my dad called up *his* dad. I don't know what they talked about, and I don't really care, because we're both here now.

More rustling is coming from the other side of the tent, so I roll onto my side and ask, "What are you doing?"

Immediately the sound stops, and silence again settles on us until Curtis asks, "You ever jerked off before?"

"Um…" My face feels hot. I heard guys joking about it once in the locker room at the beginning of the year, but having done it myself isn't something I'm ready to admit to anyone. Not even Curtis.

"It's cool if you do," he says quietly. "I've done it. It feels pretty damn good."

I hear the smile in his voice, and I figure what the hell. This will just be one more secret that we share. "I have too," I admit. "But why did you ask?"

He tries to muffle a laugh, but he doesn't do a very good job. "I was sort of, uh… doing it just now."

Oh. I don't respond because I'm too busy thinking. Thinking about the new knowledge that my best friend jerks off. Thinking about him admitting that he was doing it just a minute ago. Thinking about the warm feeling slinking through my belly. It's an odd sensation, but I kind of like it.

It's also causing a reaction between my legs. At first I panic, my heart thudding and my cheeks reddening in the darkness. But Curtis just admitted to jerking off right next to me. So why should I be embarrassed?

"You going to say anything?" he asks softly.

"Sorry. I was just thinking."

This time Curtis is the one who doesn't reply. Finally I venture, "You mind if I do it now too?"

"Nope. You mind if I keep going?"

That feeling in my belly and my penis… it's excited by the thought that Curtis is doing the same thing next to me. I don't know if that's normal, but then again, the guys in the locker room joke about a *lot* of stuff. I always thought that's what it was, though. Joking.

My voice is tight. "I don't mind."

The muted hush of Curtis's hand moving in his sleeping bag is joined by the more present sound of my own hand on myself. It feels good. Damned good. Even better than when I'm by myself.

My reservations curbed by the hot waves rolling off my dick, I say, "I wish we didn't have to do this in the dark."

A long pause fills the tent, until finally Curtis speaks again. "Nah. It's better like this."

I ignore his response and what it means, because I'm already about to come. From the way Curtis is breathing, it sounds like he isn't far off either. On some level I'm aware that I'm about to make a mess in my sleeping bag and that I haven't taken any precautions to deal with that, but I don't care. It feels too damn good.

Clenching my teeth, I keep pumping away with my hand until I push myself over the edge and come on my stomach. A moment later, the action from Curtis settles down too.

"Shit," he says. "I didn't really think this through."

Sticky wetness is slippery on my hand and my stomach and against the lining of the sleeping bag. "Same here. What now?"

"Uh…" he says, and I can hear movement, followed by the sound of his hand groping around in the corner of the tent. There's more shuffling, and then he tosses a piece of clothing at me. "Use this."

I know it's something of his, because his scent is thick in it. But he gave it to me to use, so he must not care. My clean hand closes around the fabric, and I shove it into my sleeping bag and start to tidy up. "This is your t-shirt, isn't it?"

"Yep," he responds with a chuckle. "I accidentally grabbed yours first and used it on myself. Sorry."

"Gross." But actually it doesn't bother me. It's weird, and it's something we probably won't ever talk about again, but I feel like what just happened makes us closer somehow.

It's then that I remember my rash suggestion that Curtis promptly shot down. I shouldn't have said it, and it was for the best that he said no.

It would have been weird to… *see* each other. Best friends aren't supposed to do that.

At least that's what I'm trying to convince myself of.

I push the thought away before my erection comes back. Rolling onto my side so I don't squash anything important, I tug the pillow closer to my shoulder and wait for the heavy sense of relaxation to carry me to sleep.

Chapter Five

Curtis

Sunlight is pouring through the windows when I wake up the next morning, but it still takes me several seconds to remember where I am. I know it's crazy that I drove this far just to have a place to stay, but… from the moment that Danny made the offer, I couldn't get it out of my head. I had to see him.

All the years we spent apart, I felt like something was missing. Not just that I didn't have the best friend that I used to, but something more. As if Danny had taken a piece of me with him when we parted ways.

But what now?

I need to ask how long I can stay. His house is pretty damn nice – including this bed – and I wouldn't mind being here a while. Assuming that everything works out between Danny and me, that is.

I have a lot of questions for him. Questions that have waited a decade to be answered.

We made a deal when we were in high school, and he broke it. At the last minute and without an explanation. And then he moved away to live his own life.

I'm still mad at him, and I'm not afraid to bring it up. Whether or not Danny will finally spill his story after all these years… I have no idea, but I'm still going to ask.

Rolling onto my back, I yawn at the ceiling, noticing for the first time the fine craftsmanship in how the heavy timber beams give way to the soft white of the ceiling. My last apartment – which was actually my girlfriend's – wasn't that great. Stuff was always breaking, and the hallways stunk, and the neighbors were lousy.

Forcing myself out of bed, I pull on a pair of basketball shorts and shuffle into the kitchen. Facing away from me, Danny is standing beside the sink wearing just a pair of sweatpants as he pours himself a cup of coffee. I would make fun of him for having a French press, but it smells too good in here and I don't want to cheat myself out of a cup.

"Coffee?" he asks over his shoulder.

"Yeah," I manage, my voice rough from sleep.

Turning around, he sets a cup in front of me. The aroma vies for my attention, but it loses to Danny. My eyes skate over him, first to the waistband of his sweatpants and then to his abs and finally to the toned lines of his muscled chest. *Damn, Danny.* He was skinny in high school, but now... well, he's not like *jacked*, but he has some mighty fine definition.

"What?" he asks, glancing down at himself and brushing a self-conscious hand across his chest.

"Nothing," I say quickly, diverting my gaze and lifting the mug to my lips. The last thing I want is for Danny to think that things have gotten weird between us. I should probably just fess up that I'm impressed with the way he's put on muscle since high school, but I don't feel comfortable saying that.

Especially after last night, when I kept staring at him during dinner.

I didn't mean to, but I couldn't really help it. He looks different now, and it feels good to just look, to adjust to the man that Danny has become. His jaw is squarer and more defined, his mop of blond hair at age eighteen is now cut short and styled, and those eyes I used to be so jealous of – they're still the same elusive blue they always were, but somehow they seem, I don't know... more mature now.

In front of me, steam rises lazily from the surface of the coffee as I encircle the mug with my hands and let the heat sink into my fingers.

"You interested in getting out into the woods today?" Danny asks.

His voice drags me away from the mug. "Like hiking?"

"The trails are amazing here. It's a lot different than back home." His eyes flick up to mine. "You interested?"

The hopefulness in his tone almost makes me smile. "Sure. Let me shower first, though?"

* * * * *

My fingers squeeze the handle at the top of the passenger's side window as Danny steers his truck around a sharp corner. I clench my teeth together as my stomach gurgles. The eggs and bacon he had ready when I got out of the shower tasted fantastic, but I'm regretting them now. I don't know if Danny learned to drive like this only recently, or if there are just too many damn curves in the road, but if we don't get to our destination soon, he'll have to stop so I can throw up.

It takes all my willpower to focus on the road in front of us as Danny goes on about the logging efforts on the island. "It's really a shame," he says, gesturing out the window. "This is all second growth." He pauses and glances at me, "which means they clear cut it all – years ago – and now it's grown back, but the forests just aren't the same."

"Uh huh." I make myself take slow, controlled breaths.

Danny keeps force-feeding me information on the island, and he keeps taking the turns just as fast. I'm about thirty seconds away from telling him to stop the truck when he turns off the main road into the dense woods that have surrounded us for a while now.

"Here we are," he announces as he brings us to a stop in an empty parking lot.

Bailing out of the truck, I double over, hands on my knees, and wait. Steady breaths, in and out. I try closing my eyes, but that just makes it worse.

"Hey, you okay?" Danny's voice is right beside me.

"Just give me a minute."

Quieter now, he says, "Car sick, right? Don't feel bad, it's common here."

Finally I'm able to get a burp out, which helps a lot. Straightening, I look to where Danny is leaning against the side of the truck. I don't know if I was expecting him to make fun of me or not, but I can't detect anything in his expression except mild concern.

"How can car sickness be more common in one place than another?"

"It's the winding roads." He gestures back to the road with an apologetic grin. "Seriously," he adds when I give him a look. "I've seen parents stopped on the road near my house, letting their kids out to puke. It's kind of funny."

I burp again, then inhale deeply. "You're horrible."

"I know," he says, still grinning. "Feeling better now?" When I nod, Danny slaps me on the shoulder.

"Come on," he says, motioning for me to follow him.

As Danny leads us from the truck, I'm able to appreciate our surroundings for the first time since arriving on the island. When I drove in yesterday, I was sleep-crazed and just looking for road signs. Last night it was dark, and this morning on the way here, I was trying not to lose my breakfast.

The distance between the parking lot and the conifers isn't much, but it's like passing into another world. Massive and covered in moss, the trees rise from the earth like lush emerald pillars. Ferns and undergrowth dot the ground, while a dense, wet fog rolls down from the clouds overhead.

The water in the air feels so thick that I can't tell if it's just humid or if mist is actually coming down. And all around us, the scent of forest and green press in so close that the trees might as well be brushing up against us.

Thunder Bay was still frozen under snow when I left, and there was no green. I'd never been out West before this trip – hell, I'd hardly left Ontario. I only got my passport for a school trip I never ended up going on because in the end, my dad decided it was too expensive.

Beside me, the sound of Danny's footsteps pulls me back to the present. "Is this place even real?" I ask, still craning my neck upward to follow the trunks of the trees.

"Doesn't seem like it's possible for all this to be hidden out here on the coast, does it?" His laugh is simple and carefree, like he doesn't mind who or what hears him. The sound echoes into the trees, reminding me of when we were younger, and for the briefest second, my heart aches for the friendship we used to have. For a time when there were no secrets between Danny and me.

Ahead of us, the forest abruptly ends, giving way to an open patch that must be hundreds of meters wide. Hardly any trees are left standing, and the ground is littered with massive toppled trunks. A shiver creeps down my back, and I ask, "What the hell happened here?"

"Weird, isn't it?" He sounds amused.

"Were they cut down? Why would a logging company just leave all the trees here?"

Danny shakes his head as we continue on the path through the devastation. "It wouldn't have been loggers because this whole area is protected. It happened just after I moved here. It was some sort of weird storm. A micro vortex or something… I don't remember exactly what it was called." He glances back at me. "Coming?"

Dragging my attention away from the trunks lying in all different directions, I do a little jog to catch up with him as he continues. "Sort of like a tornado, but we don't actually get those on the island. Anyway, it ripped down into the woods right here and knocked over everything. BC Parks had the whole area roped off until they cleaned it up a bit."

"Weird."

Once more I have to jog to catch up with Danny as he passes out of the clearing and back into the thick green forest. The trail carries us steadily downward, hinting in certain spots at the rocky shoulders of the island, hidden just beneath the soft earth.

"When I first moved here, I couldn't believe how cool the forests were," Danny says, jumping down from a small ledge in the path.

As much as I'm enjoying this hike, his last statement prodded a question back into my mind from last night that he never really answered. So I try again. "Why did you leave?" I ask.

I can feel his gaze on me, but I keep my eyes aimed ahead. I'm not going to let him get away with the classic Danny bullshit – the verbal duck and weave that he always uses whenever he wants to get out of actually answering a question.

"I was a mess in college," he begins. "I kept looking in the wrong places for… things I wanted. My life felt more and more screwed up, until I couldn't handle it anymore. I knew I needed to get out of that place, so when an opportunity came up to move out here, I took it."

Danny getting into trouble? I don't know if I buy that.

He gives me a look like he's afraid to say more. Playfully tapping his shoulder with my fist, I admit, "You always had your shit together, so I kind of like the thought of you messing something up."

He tries to smile, but it just looks like he's eaten something sour. "Yeah, I guess."

I feel bad for whatever he dealt with, but I went through hell and back when I was growing up, and that didn't make me abandon my friends.

"So why did you leave Thunder Bay in the first place?" I demand. "If you'd stuck around, you wouldn't have gotten into any of that other shit, because I wouldn't have let you." I wish I could keep the bitterness from my voice, but I can't help but feel regret for the years of college and afterward that we could have spent together if Danny hadn't moved away.

Beside me, Danny stops walking, forcing me to do the same. "Why do you keep pushing this? Can't you just let it go? I left, all right? I'm sorry, but that's what happened."

"Fuck no, I won't let it go," I snap. "I want to know why. We used to be best friends. We knew *everything* about each other. Our plans, our dreams, the songs we liked… hell, even the stuff that friends don't usually know, like your worst birthday and your favorite food and which pair of boxers you liked the best, *I knew that shit about you,*" I growl. The harshness in my voice surprises me, but it makes me realize how important it is to get this out.

"And then," I say, my voice abruptly filling with emptiness. "You were gone. You just left. Out of nowhere and with barely an explanation. You. Left."

Danny cocks his head to the side, curiosity misting into his features like the fog through the canopy overhead. "What was my worst birthday?"

It's almost funny that he's testing me on this, but the anger inside prevents me from seeing any humor in it. "Your thirteenth. I'll never forget because it was September 11th, 2001. Everyone forgot your birthday because of that terrorist attack." As an afterthought, I add, "I didn't forget, but you were still really broken up that everyone else did. You cried, man."

His eyes scroll to the side, getting lost somewhere in the distant trees before eventually coming back to me. His voice is soft when he asks, "You remember that?"

"Of course I do."

He nibbles the corner of his lip, then begins, "What about my–"

"Chicken parm. And the silky ones with yellow stripes," I interrupt him. "Don't even know why you asked, those are both easy."

Danny frowns, but he seems at a loss. "I don't have those boxers anymore."

"So are you going to tell me why you left? I get that it was your choice, but don't I deserve an explanation, at least? Like, a real one?"

There, that's it. If he doesn't answer me now, I'll drop it. I'll be mad as sin, but I won't ask him again.

Scanning the area, he gestures to a fallen log a ways off the path.

"Can we sit?"

My pulse quickens as I nod and follow him. I've been waiting about a decade to hear this. Sitting down beside him on the moss-covered log, I prompt, "Well?"

He sighs and runs a hand through his hair, messing up the way he had it styled. "I left Thunder Bay because it was... too small. Too small for me to feel comfortable."

"We grew up there," I counter. "How could you feel anything but comfortable?"

"Damn it, Curtis," he says. "I'm trying to get this out. Can you just back off and let me say it?"

I give him a hard look, and then I shrug. "The floor is yours."

He stares at me, and the wet air grows thick between us. Holding a tense breath, I ask, "Danny?"

He glances down at the mossy log, at my hand resting on it, and then he says, "I'm gay."

Finding out about something like that out of the blue is hard. Pretending that I didn't figure it out years ago is harder. "Huh?"

"You heard me," he says, holding his voice steady.

"But, we..." I begin, trying to sound convincing. "You messed around with girls. I *know* you did." More words coil up in my throat, but I can already sense Danny bristling beside me.

"So?"

"I just mean, gay guys don't usually do that."

"It doesn't matter whether I was with girls or not," he says, leveling his eyes on me. "Did it ever occur to you that maybe I pretended to be straight in high school because I felt like I had to, and not because I wanted to?"

Swallowing heavily to make it look like I'm nervous, I apologize again. "Sorry, I wasn't thinking. And yeah, okay. If you say that's the way you are, I'm not going to argue with you, man."

I won't argue because I've known it's true since we were teens. But knowing and being comfortable with it are different things.

The thought nudges to life a dormant memory from deep in our past. The first night I put it all together. A night that I had almost forgotten completely.

"You want to keep going?"

"What?" I stare at him dumbly.

"On the trail?" he clarifies, sounding annoyed.

"Oh, right. Yeah, let's keep going."

Over the next fifteen minutes, the path pulls us steadily downward over rocks and short ledges, making it easy to forego conversation in favor of finding the best footholds on the wet earth and rock. Above us, the towering trees follow us down toward the coast, just as they have the whole way – except for that huge area torn out by the storm.

Finally, with one last turn, the path deposits us on the beach. Hands stuffed in his pockets, Danny hops casually onto a log and surveys the waves rolling up onto the sand. The trunk he's standing on is massive, just like the trees behind us, but it has the scoured and bleached look of driftwood. It's not the only one either – numerous logs lie along the line between the sand and the forest.

"Where did these come from?" I wonder aloud, venturing tentatively from log to log as I follow him.

"Probably escaped from logging booms years ago," Danny calls over his shoulder.

"I thought those were just used in rivers."

"Ocean too," he assures me as he jumps down onto the rocky sand.

Side by side, we move down the beach past barnacled rocks and pools exposed by the retreating tide. All the while we're followed by the scent of salt teasing the air. It's a new smell to me, but I like it.

Overhead, the sky is still overcast and gray, but it doesn't bother me. Somehow it feels right for the day – a slow, contemplative gray. It should be easy to discuss simple stuff with Danny right now, but it's just... not. Because every time he says something, I wonder if there's something else he really wants to say.

It doesn't matter that I knew about him all this time. What matters is that I don't believe he told me the real reason he moved away.

Maybe I'm just grasping for answers to why I feel so conflicted about what he said. It's possible he didn't know for sure in high school, so maybe he didn't feel comfortable coming out to me. But still, it just makes me feel weird.

I'm not stupid enough to think that Danny's revelation has any retroactive bearing on our friendship when we were teens, but it does make me wonder. It makes me wonder how long he knew that he was interested in guys. Did he know back when we showered after gym class or when we changed in front of each other before going swimming? Or when we jerked off together on that camping trip?

"What are you thinking about?" Danny asks. His hands are shoved in his pockets again.

"Take a guess."

"I figured as much." His tone is painted with a color that reminds me of the overcast day.

"I'm glad you told me," I venture. "I just need time to… process."

Danny pulls in a deep breath of the salty air. "That's fair."

Six hours later, I'm reclining on one of the couches beside the empty fireplace, stuffed from the salmon chowder that Danny made for dinner. I have no idea when he became such a good cook, but damn.

From the other side of the sprawling living room, I watch Danny cross the space and take a lounging seat on the opposite couch.

Suppressing a shiver, I gesture to the fireplace. "Does that thing work?"

"Of course."

Danny gets back to his feet and opens a wood box at the end of the couch. He works with a practiced efficiency, and in just a few minutes, he's back on the couch again and gazing at the crackling fire in front of us.

I don't know if it's quiet here all the time, or if the windows and walls are actually able to block out every sound from outside, but we're surrounded by a velvet silence. Interrupted only by the heated snaps of the fire, the stillness watches over us as darkness begins to filter through the windows.

Eventually Danny turns his eyes from the fire. "How long are you planning to stay?"

I nibble on my lip, unsure what to say. "A week or so? If that's fine with you."

"Whatever you want. You could stay longer if you'd like," he says, his voice poised on the edge of sounding hopeful. "While you figure stuff out."

"Thanks."

The fire pops and kicks a burning ember onto the surrounding tile. I expect Danny to jump up and kick it back into the fire, but he doesn't move.

As the ember's orange glow fades into black, I wonder what it would be like to stay here for longer. It's only my first full day here, but I've enjoyed it. And even Danny's belated confession doesn't seem that big a deal anymore.

"You work tomorrow?"

Danny nods. "I'm in the middle of a job, so I can't really take much time off. I start early, so you're going to be on your own for breakfast. And whatever you want to do during the day. I've got a bunch of movies if you want to hang around here, or I have a map of hiking trails if you want to get out of the house."

"What about work? I could help out too," I suggest.

He flashes me a lopsided grin. "You want to earn your keep?"

"Something like that. You have anything that needs doing?"

The playful look spreads from his grin to his eyes, and I can tell he has something in mind.

"What?"

"As it turns out, I *do* have a project, but I don't think you're going to like it," he says evasively.

Sitting up straighter against the couch, I cross my arms. "Spill it."

Danny stands and beckons me to follow him as he walks to a sliding door off the kitchen and steps barefoot onto the deck outside. It's dark, but enough light is cast by the house that I can see the tilled earth of a garden bed sloping down the backyard.

"You grow your own stuff?"

"In the summer, yeah. That's actually what this is about." Danny comes to a stop at the very end of the deck. "See what I staked off?" He points to a rectangular area that has been roped off with red ribbon. It's not huge, but he could fit his pickup truck inside it.

"What is it?"

"Nothing right now. The thing is that even though we get a lot of rain in the winter and spring, it dries up really fast during the summer, and I don't have enough water to keep the garden irrigated."

It's hard to imagine that the forest we were at earlier today could ever get dry. It was just so... lush. Danny seems to be following my line of thought, because he says, "Where we went hiking has a different climate than here."

"Huh? That was like a half hour away."

"Right, but on the island that makes a difference. Today we were at China Beach near Port Renfrew, which gets more than twice the rain because it's outside of the rain shadow of the Olympic Mountains."

I stare at him. "You lost me."

He chuckles, but it doesn't feel like he's laughing *at* me. More like he's just amused. "Humid Pacific air hits the Olympic range in Washington, cools, then dumps all its rain. By the time it gets here, it doesn't have nearly as much rain left to drop. That's a rain shadow."

It's like science class all over again, where Danny always knew way more random facts than the rest of us. Rubbing the back of my neck, I ask, "So what does this have to do with your backyard?"

"Right," he says. "Because we don't get enough rain in the summer, I want to dig a cistern to catch water. I had a surveyor come out, and in that spot we can dig down almost three meters before hitting rock," he gestures to the roped off area again. "I've been meaning to hire a guy with a backhoe, but it costs something ridiculous to get one out here because the road is too narrow," Danny finishes.

"You're serious?" I ask as he watches me expectantly. "You want me to dig a giant hole in your backyard?"

He gives me a sheepish look. "You're the one who asked what you could do to help out."

Chapter Six

Curtis

Danny is long gone from the house when I get up the next morning, even though the clock on the microwave reports that it's not even eight o'clock yet. It takes me a few minutes to figure out how his coffee press works, but eventually I get it sorted out, and I have to admit that it's a lot better than what comes out of a normal coffee maker.

With caffeine pumping through my blood, I find the ambition to hunt down some breakfast for myself. His refrigerator is a nice stainless steel one – the kind that has the freezer on the bottom so you don't have to duck into it – and it's filled with healthy stuff like eggs and milk and fresh vegetables, which isn't really a surprise considering how fit Danny is. The bastard even has abs. Not that I'm doing too bad myself, but I don't make it to the gym as often as I used to.

After making and subsequently finishing a three-egg omelet with spinach and cheddar, I get changed and survey the yard from the sliding glass door off the kitchen. It doesn't look too cold out, but my brain is convinced it shouldn't get warm for another couple months.

Toting a second cup of coffee, I step barefoot out onto the deck. It's a bit chilly, and I zip my hoodie up the rest of the way before stepping onto the boardwalk path that leads down the sloping backyard.

Easily visible now, the numerous rows of Danny's garden cover nearly half of the open area on his property. Despite the milder weather here, nothing is growing yet. Passing the garden, I survey the rectangle that Danny roped off. It doesn't *look* that big, but digging always ends up being a harder job than it seems.

Fingers tightening absently on my coffee cup, my attention lingers on the wet grass until the cool air rolling up from the shore breathes against my face.

The breeze whispers a promise of ocean salt, and it draws me further down the path toward the rocky line where the water laps up on the land. Padding barefoot down the wooden steps, I follow the boarded path as it continues out onto the water. Graying wood creaks under my feet, but I don't stop until I'm standing at the very end of the dock.

My eyes venture into the distance, and I immediately realize that Danny doesn't actually live on the ocean. It's a bay or something.

In direct disobedience to the light breeze, the surface of the water is so still that it might as well be glass. Smooth and glossy, it catches the sun's rays without reservation, selectively painting its surface with the gold light of morning.

Setting down my coffee, I lower myself onto the edge of the dock and let my feet slip into the water. It's *cold*, and for a moment I consider dashing back into the house. But this morning is too perfect.

So instead of fleeing, I pull in a breath, savoring the coolness in my lungs and the salt water licking my feet. On the opposite side of the bay – not more than a few kilometers away – dark pines are packed together, neither afraid to flirt with the water's edge nor to scale the steeply rising terrain.

Before we went to bed last night, Danny gave me a few pamphlets on local trails, but I'm not particularly keen on wandering around by myself. I know this is still Canada, but it feels so different from home. And besides, hiking is always going to be more fun when Danny is along.

I want desperately for us to be close like we used to be, but I don't know if that's possible. After how we left things at the end of high school, it already feels like a lot for Danny to let me stay with him.

Has time really erased our friendship? Has it washed away a thousand moments of closeness and made them count for nothing? I hope that's not true, but I just don't know.

I want desperately for us to be close like we used to be, but I don't know if that's possible. After how we left things at the end of high school, it already feels like a lot for Danny to let me stay with him.

Has time really erased our friendship? Has it washed away a thousand moments of closeness and made them count for nothing? I hope that's not true, but I just don't know.

Swishing my feet back and forth in the water, I delay finishing my coffee for as long as I can. But when there's nothing left in my mug but sooty black dregs, I don't hesitate to get up. Not only is the cold starting to get to me, but I'm determined to make myself useful.

So after changing clothes, I fetch a shovel from Danny's garage and return to the ribbon barrier in the backyard. I suspect my muscles are going to regret this, but I'm sort of looking forward to hours of exhausting physical labor. Keeping my body occupied will allow my mind to work through things. And between losing my job, getting dumped, and Danny coming out to me, I can definitely use the time to think. Poking the tip of the shovel into the grass, I hold the handle upright and jump down, forcing the spade deep into the earth.

By midafternoon, the sky is still clear and the sun is beating down with a vengeance. It might not be hot, exactly, but it sure feels like it. Sweat is dripping down my forehead and my back and other places too. It makes me glad I didn't shower this morning, but it also means that I *really* don't smell good now.

I ditched my shirt hours ago, and the skin on my shoulders feels hotter than it should. I'm probably getting a sunburn, but I don't care because I've accomplished a lot today. I've dug the entire area down almost a third of a meter. Of course it will get a lot harder as I go deeper, but I still think that's pretty impressive for one day.

"Looking good." Danny's voice comes from somewhere behind me.

Stabbing my shovel into the moist dirt to hold it in place, I turn to look up at him. His hand is held above his eyebrows, keeping the sun at bay. He seems to be surveying the work, but his gaze also stops on me more than once. With a twinge in my stomach, my eyes jump to my forgotten t-shirt lying in the grass at the edge of the hole. Was his *looking good* comment meant for the progress… or for me?

"Thanks," I say, shielding my own eyes to get a better look at him. "What time is it?"

"Just past two. You want a break?"

"I'm okay for a while longer," I say. "I could use some water, though."

"Sure. I'll be back in a few minutes."

Involuntarily noticing the way his shoulders fill out his shirt so well, I watch him retreat across the yard and disappear into the house. Being around Danny again feels weird, and no matter which way I spin it, I can't figure out why that is. It's like when our whole grade went through a Rubik's cube craze. Danny and I both got one, but no matter how hard I tried, I could never get even one side to be the same color. Danny had his solved by the second day.

The memory stirs up a years' old annoyance with him, and I'm still frowning at my shovel when he hops down into the hole, shovel in hand. He holds out a red water bottle toward me, and again I can feel his eyes stopping on my chest. And my arms. *Damn it, Danny.*

I take the water from him and tip the container back, taking several long gulps. When I'm done, I toss it up onto the grass. "You're going to dig after you already worked since early this morning?" I ask him. Every now and then, I would hear the buzz of a saw coming from his shop, so I know he was keeping busy.

Danny smirks as he forces his shovel into the dirt. "I can't let you have all the fun, can I?"

The following days shuffle past, slowly at first, as I settle into a routine. I wake up after Danny is gone, drink my coffee on the dock, spend most of the morning digging, take a break for lunch, then dig some more. Every afternoon after working in his shop, Danny joins me and helps dig until dinnertime. I almost hate to admit it, but I actually enjoy the manual labor. There's something satisfying about working an entire day and having little to show for it except sweat and exhaustion.

It doesn't bother me as much anymore when he strips off his shirt and jumps into the deepening hole in the ground beside me. The space is tight, and it's not easy to work so closely next to someone else, but I'm starting to actually look forward to when he joins me in the afternoon. Sometimes we talk, and sometimes we just work in silence.

At the end of the week, Danny has to lower himself into the hole because it's gotten so deep. "We're going to have to start hauling buckets out of here pretty soon," I tell him.

"Shit, yeah. I hadn't really thought of that," he admits.

"Really?" I tap him lightly on the back with my shovel, smearing dirt across his bare skin. "I thought you always had everything planned out?"

Danny pushes my shovel away. "Just because I'm about to get dirty doesn't mean you have to speed up the process," he says.

"Jeeze, no need to get snippy." I grin at him when he glares.

For a while after that, we work without talking, needing to be extra careful as we heave the shovelfuls of dirt out of the hole. It's so deep now that the grade of the yard is level with our shoulders – well, my shoulders. Danny is a little taller, and we have another couple inches to go before we get to his.

For fear of giving him the wrong idea, I've been cautious not to look too closely at him. His shoulders are broad, and his arms and chest are toned with muscle. Whenever he hefts a shovel of dirt out of the hole, his arms and back tense together, and I can see the tight ropes of muscle that make him appear so solid. And if I'm really honest with myself, I sort of like seeing how he's become more mature over the years.

"What are you looking at?" Danny asks, a coy smile playing around his lips.

Instantly flushing, I drop my eyes. "Nothing, man." I try to put extra emphasis on the *man*, so he'll know that me watching him has nothing to do with any sort of gay stuff. Danny is a good guy, and I like being here, but if he starts getting the wrong idea, then things will get awkward.

"Sure," Danny says. He tries to laugh it off, but the sound is strained.

I refuse to look at him after that, because I want to make sure I'm being perfectly clear with him.

Time ticks past and the sun dips lower in the sky, and even though it's still warm, I reach up and grab my shirt from the lawn. As I'm tugging it over my head, Danny asks, "So what's the story with your ex?"

Adjusting my shirt so the bottom rests properly around my hips, I shrug as though I'm not really sure. Which is a complete lie, of course.

He doesn't resume digging, so I guess he's not going to let it go. I suppose I should be thankful for having gone this long without Danny asking about her, but that doesn't mean I'm any more interested in talking about it.

He's still staring at me, waiting for a response. Sighing, I lean my shovel against the side of the hole. "It wasn't going well with Celia for a while," I concede. "By the end, she was going off on almost every single thing I did. I felt like I was always walking on eggshells around her."

Bracing himself on his shovel, Danny looks apologetic. "Sorry to hear that."

"It was really fucking uncomfortable is what it was." In an undertone, I add, "And the sex was never that great." Almost immediately, I regret saying that, because I don't want to start telling Danny about my sex life. About how bad it was. Celia and I just weren't a good fit, but we kept trying to make it work.

She kept trying. I sort of gave up.

Danny is quiet for a long moment, and then he says, "That sucks. I'm really sorry."

"Whatever. It's done. Nothing I can do about it now," I say, watching him. He looks like he's amused by something, which pisses me off. "What's so funny?"

"Sorry," he says quickly. "I was just remembering the time you broke up with that girl in school by taping a note on her locker."

The flare of anger from a moment ago fades as I step into the past with a smile. "She was so mad."

"Didn't she do something to your truck or something?"

I nod, trying not to laugh. "She threw dog shit on the windshield."

Danny is laughing with me now. "I remember now. That was your dad's second truck, right?"

In an instant, this foray into our shared memories crosses into darkness. *Second truck.* My fingers tighten around my shovel, and tension ripples over my skin.

Danny pales. "Oh shit. I didn't mean to bring that up."

"It's fine," I say, my voice flat. But really it's not. "I think I'm done for the day."

"Okay. I'll clean up out here." He speaks softly, like he's handling something fragile.

I'm barely out of the shower when I decide I need to get away from here. At least for a few hours. Because not even the water of the shower – scrubbing every bit of dirt from my skin – could wash away the sourness of what Danny inadvertently brought up earlier.

"I'm going for a drive," I announce.

Danny looks up at me from his stance in front of the stove. "Dinner will be ready soon, and I make a mean broiled salmon. You sure you want to leave now?"

The concern in his expression at the possibility that I'm going to miss dinner makes me feel guilty, but I really need to get out of the house. "Yeah."

Strained comprehension joins the concern, and his features bunch together as they fill up with unspoken thoughts. Finally he says, "You can take my truck if you want."

"Thanks. I'd like that." I know he loves the thing to death, so in a way, it's like I'm taking a piece of Danny with me. That seems important, but I'm not sure why. Maybe so I don't feel so completely alone, even though I will be.

Leaning to the side, he stuffs a hand into his pocket and sets his keys on the counter. "All yours." In his voice I can hear tenuous notes of worry, but I think he understands what I'm doing. Maybe not exactly, but in his own way.

Without giving him any further explanation, I take the keys off the counter and walk out the door, feeling Danny's gaze on me the entire way.

Hoisting myself into the driver's seat of the truck, I turn the key until the engine rumbles awake with the sound of brawny strength. I pull out of the driveway and head down the road toward the highway, noting how smooth the ride is. The curves in the road pass as the kilometers disappear beneath the hood of Danny's black Chevy 1500. This is nothing like my dad's truck. Either of them.

The thought brings me back to the reason that I wanted to get out of the house in the first place.

The sunlight dims as evening pushes toward night, until eventually I reach the edge of Victoria. Navigating with my phone and the help of road signs, I pull around the back of Victoria General Hospital and into a parking spot between the helipad and the emergency room entrance.

My fingers are sweaty on the key as I kill the engine. I want to yell, to tell myself that I'm being stupid and that there's no reason for me to be here. But that wouldn't be true.

I roll down the crank window to let in fresh air. It helps me breathe as the seconds roll into minutes, which count slowly up to hours, and all the while I watch. I watch as the ambulances pull up and unload patients on stretchers into the ER. Mostly it's a lot of waiting, but it's worth it. I don't know if I could explain it to anyone – maybe not even Danny – but I need to be here.

I couldn't help that woman the day I wrecked my dad's truck, and ultimately the paramedics weren't able to either. Maybe if they'd gotten there faster.

I know it's a pointless hypothetical, because I was only sixteen at the time, but… I wonder if I'd had the training, if I could have saved her. It's stupid, but I can't help but wonder. And I can't help but wish.

Another ambulance rolls up, quelling its sirens and blazing lights as the rear doors open and a pair of paramedics wheel a man on a stretcher out of the vehicle.

Did they save his life today?

My phone vibrates in the cup holder. I'm about to silence it when I recognize Danny's number across the screen. I really need to put him as a contact in my phone.

"Hey," I answer.

"How are you?"

"Doing all right. Sorry I missed dinner."

"It's okay," he says, sounding like he wants to say more. A second passes, then he asks, "You're in Victoria?"

"Yeah. I'll head home soon."

"Take as much time as you need."

For several moments I'm not sure what to say. "Okay," I finally say into the phone. "Thanks."

"Anytime. Drive safe." Then he hangs up.

Night settles around me as I drive back to Danny's place, but it doesn't help to assuage the restlessness inside. The dotted yellow line down the center of the road leads me dutifully onward, but only the smallest sliver of my attention is consumed by the driving. Road signs sail past and oncoming headlights blaze through the darkness, but all I can think of is that terrible day.

It feels like barely any time has passed when I let myself through Danny's unlocked front door. With the exception of a solitary light in the kitchen, the house is layered in darkness. Kicking off my shoes and socks and crossing the hardwood that stretches from the living room into the kitchen, I peer inside the fridge. On the center shelf beside a bundle of asparagus is a Tupperware container with a yellow sticky note on it. *Curtis.*

Danny set aside leftovers for me?

Suddenly the back of my throat is tight, and I don't even feel hungry anymore. Shutting the refrigerator, I lean back against the counter. My eyes travel across the empty space in the house, surveying everything that Danny has made for himself. Jealousy pours into me swiftly but unevenly, like cream into coffee. It swirls, eventually diffusing into an unpleasant heat through my chest and face.

It's like he has everything.

Even though I know he doesn't.

I close my eyes, wishing that this day would be done. I should just go to bed, even though I'll probably wake up hungry in a few hours.

But I know that rest won't come to me right now anyway, so I go outside.

The sliding door to the deck closes with a loud thunk behind me, and I silently chastise myself for not being more careful. With just enough of the moon visible to light the way, I follow the steps toward the water.

The night isn't actually that chilly, but the rawness of the humidity is enough to make me shiver anyway. It cuts through the white cotton of my t-shirt, digging through the fibers until it presses against my skin.

At the end of the dock, I fold my legs underneath me and stare out over the water. My bare feet are already cold, and I don't dare dip them into the water. Crossing my arms tight against my chest as a breeze picks up, I draw in a breath of fresh air and wish that I could turn back the years. I want for Danny and me to be young again, to be best friends like we once were.

The creak on the wood behind me goes unnoticed until a voice glides through the darkness. "Nice night," Danny says.

"How'd you know I was here?" I turn to look at him as he sits down beside me. He's only wearing basketball shorts and a long sleeved shirt.

His eyes stare out across the water, and he doesn't turn to face me as he answers. "I heard the door to the porch."

I knew I should have shut it more carefully.

"Don't worry about it," Danny says quietly, as if sensing my thoughts. "Sometimes when I can't sleep, I come out here to think."

"You couldn't sleep tonight?"

"Not really." Danny glances at me, and in the night his eyes glisten like black glass buried inside his shadowed features. It strikes me as a secret and quiet tragedy, because I love the color of his eyes. That mix of blue that no one else has. The blue that's a color all its own.

I don't know what to say, so I stay quiet until he speaks again. "I left some food for you in the fridge."

Kicking the words off my tongue one by one, I say, "You don't have to do stuff like that." Being around Danny again is harder than I expected, and not at all for the reasons I anticipated. As though caught in his gravity, I feel like I'm falling toward him. And it only gets harder to be around him when it's so obvious how much he cares.

"You're my guest. I'm just trying to make your stay more comfortable." His tone is defensive on the outside, but I can sense vulnerability underneath.

"I wish you wouldn't," I whisper. I'm afraid he's going to ask why, and if he does, I won't have an answer that I can give him. At least not an honest one.

Danny hesitates, and I steal the moment from him.

"I miss the times we had together when we were younger," I admit.

More hesitation, followed by the creak of the dock under his subtly shifting weight. "Because everything was simpler back then?"

"Because we had more fun." It feels like a childish thing to say, but I don't care.

Danny snorts out a huff of amusement, and I can feel the smile in his words when he replies. "What you actually mean is that we used to do stupid shit. It wasn't fun, it was foolish."

"Isn't that the same thing?"

"Sure, sometimes." His gaze finds its way to me once more. "Nothing is stopping you from still doing things like that."

"Yeah. I guess," I say, keeping my eyes fixed on the place far in the distance where the water washes into the night sky.

Standing up beside me, Danny moves back from the edge of the dock, and I assume he's going inside. Then I hear the brush of fabric over skin, a deep breath, the thudding of feet over wood. And a second later Danny's pale, naked form sprints past me. With his last footfall, he pushes hard off the dock and propels himself into empty space.

He sails forward with a reckless shout, legs kicking against nothing but the chill in the air and the taste of white moonlight. He falls toward the water, tucking his bare butt underneath him as he pulls his legs into his chest.

Danny hits the water with an enormous splash, and droplets fly outward. His voice is abruptly silenced the moment he goes under, but the sound seems to echo across the basin, as though the water and the rocks and the trees want his song to endure just a little longer.

When he breaks the surface, he shakes his head and stares back at me. Beneath the dark water, I can see the pale outline of his arms swaying back and forth, holding him afloat.

"You're insane," I call across the distance between us. "It's got to be freezing in there."

"Maybe a little," he says through chattering teeth. "But it's worth it. Come on."

Does he seriously think I'm going to jump in after him? "No way."

But I stand up, and against all reason, I actually consider the idea.

"It's not that bad," Danny says, quietly this time. "Come on."

His voice tugs on something in my chest, and temptation swells inside me. I know it's absolutely freezing, but that's not the thing holding me back. I'm not afraid to drop my shorts in front of Danny, either – even in light of his recent confession – because we've seen each other naked too many times to count.

Danny drifts closer, and even though his eyes are barely discernable in the dark, I can tell how much he wants me to jump too. It's then that I realize what's preventing me from joining him in the water. It's because what he's trying to do is impossible.

We'll never be who we were, because time cannot be turned back and it cannot be undone. A younger me would have kicked off my shorts and underwear and gone tearing off the end of the dock after him, buck naked and balls slapping against my thighs until the moment that the water swept up around me.

But we'll never be able to get that back, even as much as Danny might try to convince me. He's in the water trying to make a point while I'm on the dock overthinking an action that wouldn't have earned the briefest shred of consideration ten years ago.

I lean into the dock post as regret takes hold. "Sorry, Danny. You're flying solo tonight."

He sighs, and the water swirls around him as he starts back toward the dock. "You going to help me out, at least?" He reaches up, holding a hand out toward me.

Cold, wet fingers close around mine, and I hoist him upward. Water pours from his body as he steps onto the wooden planks of the dock. At first a deluge, the draining water becomes nothing more than isolated drops. He stands there naked, silently dripping.

In defiance of my curiosity, I try hard to avert my eyes as he walks to where he left his clothes. It's true that I've seen Danny like this a hundred times, maybe more even, but it's been years since then. Nothing about him should have changed in that time, but he filled out in his shoulders and arms so much that maybe he also…

Annoyed, I swallow away the rest of the thought before it can form. What the hell am I thinking?

"Something wrong?" Danny asks, looking up and expecting to meet my gaze, which for the moment is still focused on the t-shirt he's now holding in front of his crotch.

"Huh?"

"You're, um, staring," he breathes, his eyes locking onto mine.

Shit. "I'm just tired, jackass. Don't get any ideas." I glare at him, but really I'm only angry with myself.

"Right. Sorry," Danny says quickly, but just enough doubt lingers in his tone that I don't think he really means it.

I force my attention away from the water dripping down his body, away from his nipples hard with cold, away from the lines of his stomach as they glide downward in a familiar v-shape. "I'm going to bed," I say roughly as I push past him and walk away down the dock.

His words chase after me, but I'm moving swiftly up the path toward the house now, and only the first few sounds are able to catch my ears. "Damn Curtis, I didn't mean–"

I slam the sliding door behind me, and it bangs shut, but I don't hear the noise. The only sound in my head is the rush as Danny's body sprinted past me into the night. That, and the drops of water falling off him as he stood on the dock afterward.

Gritting my teeth, I kick off my shoes and head straight to my room. Danny is probably still on the dock getting dressed, but I hurry anyway, because being near him is the last thing I want right now. Closing the door to my room behind me, I lean back against the solid wood and sink to the floor.

Eighth Grade

A self-help show blares on the TV across from Danny and me, but it's barely more than an unwelcome distraction, because what I really want to do is just… talk. Danny has been gone for weeks on a family vacation, and I've missed him. A lot.

Leaning forward, I stuff my hand into the bag of chips between us and take as many as I can. I'm halfway back to my lap with the plunder when Danny grabs me hard around the wrist. "What is that?"

Clinging desperately to the clumsy handful of chips, I follow his gaze to the back of my hand, and the reddish circle there. *Fuck*. Since school is out, no one else has noticed it, but of course Danny would. He knows me too well. He knows that when he left on vacation, there wasn't a fading pink scar on the back of my hand.

As if to force an answer out of me, he shakes my wrist, and the chips fall from my slackened fingers onto the couch. "Well?" he demands.

"I, uh… was messing around with some fireworks and one hit me."

His eyes jump to the scar on my hand, then back to me. He doesn't respond, and he doesn't let go. The teens in the show are screaming at their parents while a studio audience looks on. It's supposed to be entertaining to watch other people's messed up lives.

Danny mutes the show. "I don't believe you." His grip on my wrist tightens until it almost hurts.

I'm stronger than him, but I'm not going to wrestle out of this one. I sigh, dropping my eyes to the floor. "My dad caught me smoking," I admit.

Danny frowns. "Okay. So what happened to your hand?" He says it like he already knows, and maybe he does.

But even if that's true, I'm going to say it anyway. "He grabbed the cigarette and put it out," I grimace, remembering the searing heat and the reek as my skin burned.

The fingers around my wrist loosen now, and Danny's expression turns despondent. "He can't do that to you."

"Oh yeah? And are you going to stop him?" My words are harsh, and I feel bad being mean to Danny, because it's not his fault.

"You shouldn't have to live with someone who does that to you," he says softly.

"I don't *have* anyone else," I snap. "They would put me in like… a *home*, or something."

"Wouldn't that be better than what you have now?"

My chest grows tight with fear. If Danny says something and I get taken away, I'll never see him again. "Look, you can't tell anyone, okay?"

He doesn't answer me.

"Seriously, Danny. You can't tell *anyone*."

"I won't, but…"

"But what?"

He sighs, and in that moment he sounds way older than he really is. "But only if you promise to always be honest with me. I can't be wondering every time you get a bruise or a cut or God knows what… if it's because of your dad or just you being clumsy again."

I glare because I know he's messing with me. "I'm not clumsy."

He grins. "Sure." Then his smile falls, and he repeats his binding condition. "Promise?"

I can't agree to it. Danny is my best friend, but I can't give him what he wants. I just can't.

"*Promise?*"

"Yeah, okay," I say, hating that he's making me do this. "I promise."

Chapter Seven

Danny

It's late in the evening, two days since Curtis and I talked on the dock. He acts like I'm trying to trick him into being gay or something, but he's the guy with the wandering eyes. The ones that keep finding their way to places they shouldn't be.

I don't understand it. Maybe I should stop trying to.

It's been hours since we came inside from our digging escapade in the backyard, but Curtis only started showering a few minutes ago. The sound of the water drifts from the bathroom, gradually filling my thoughts until the front door sails open and bangs into the wall.

I jump and stare wide-eyed toward the noise.

"Do you have any idea what it's like to work with two dozen other women?" Lauren huffs as she closes the door and crosses the room before throwing her purse onto my walnut table. It lands heavily and slides across the smooth surface before coming to a stop near the center.

"Nope. Do you have any idea what it's like to refinish that table?" I ask, muting the TV and pointing a look at her.

"It sucks," she says, ignoring my comment. "It sucks more than you could ever imagine. You're lucky to only work with men."

I raise an eyebrow. "You mean myself?"

Lauren scowls and drops onto the couch beside me, accidentally whacking her elbow into my chest on the way down.

"That hurt," I say, pretending to be offended.

"Did not, you big baby. Anyway, we've covered my day. How have you been?"

Completely out of my control, a smile sneaks onto my face. "I, um..."

"Oh my God," she interrupts me. "You met a guy, don't you?"

My eyes narrow. "Why do you think that?"

"You're easy to read," she says. A moment passes, and she prods me with a single word. "Well?"

"Doesn't matter. He's straight."

Grabbing a pillow, she hugs it to her chest and crosses her legs. "Tell me everything," she demands.

"There isn't much to say," I admit, feeling guilty that I'm even talking about this.

Lauren's phone chimes in her purse on the table, and she hops up to go check it. "Seriously, though," she says as she taps the screen on her phone. "When did you meet this mystery guy?"

"Um, in elementary school. He's the friend staying with me."

Her attention snaps back to me, resting for only a second before her gaze swivels toward the guest bathroom and the sound of the shower. "You're kidding, right?" Lauren's typical good humor is gone, and in its place an icy sobriety has found a home. Hands on her hips, she's staring me down from across the table.

I wince under her accusatory glare. "You really want me to say it again?"

Her eyes narrow so much that her pupils almost disappear behind her eyelashes. "Yeah, actually I do. Because you clearly didn't hear the absurdity of it when you said it the first time." She looks at me expectantly. When I don't respond, she prattles on, "No? Okay, let me rehash this for you."

Raising fingers as she goes, she counts off my sins. "You convinced him you were straight, coerced him to travel across the country to visit you, and now you're trying to convert him."

"I did not *coerce* him, and I'm not trying to convert him, either," I say through clenched teeth. "He called *me* up and wanted a place to crash. And I didn't trick him into thinking I was straight or anything. He was just already under that impression from when it was... more true, and if it makes you happy to know, I told him on the second day." More for myself than Lauren, I add, "If I was really scheming like you say, I wouldn't have even told him. He might never have guessed on his own."

She laughs. "Not unless he saw what you keep in your sock drawer."

Redness hits my cheeks. "When were you looking in my sock drawer?"

"I stopped over once and you weren't here. I was about to leave when I saw a basket of laundry fresh out of the dryer, just sitting there getting wrinkly. I know how guys forget silly things like that. I was being nice and went to fold and put it away," she says, her tone carrying more amusement than irritation now. "But let me tell you, some things just cannot be unseen."

"Oh, Jesus." I roll my eyes. "Just because you have a key doesn't mean you can come in my house whenever you want." I'm pissed that she went snooping through my shit, but I like having her as a neighbor too much to make a fuss about it.

Her steely gaze relenting for the first time since my confession of being into Curtis, Lauren pokes her head into the refrigerator and reappears with a bottled chia seed drink. "How long does this guy usually shower for, anyway?" She raises an eyebrow at me.

"I'm sure he'll be out in a minute," I say, abandoning my defensive position on the couch in favor of sitting at the table. "You want to meet him?"

"I could use a guy in my life," she muses. Taking a sip of her chia slurry, she chews intently as though trying to crush the seeds. "Assuming that he's straight and not a raging homosexual like yourself... sure, I'll meet him."

"Go to hell," I say mildly, inspecting a bit of dirt under my thumbnail. When I glance back at her, she's still nibbling on chia seeds.

Curtis emerges from the bathroom a moment later, wearing only a towel around his waist. "We have company?" he asks, glancing surreptitiously at his exposed chest and the trail of fine hairs leading from his belly button down under the towel. I feel guilty, but it's just too easy to follow his gaze myself.

"This is Lauren. She lives down the road," I introduce her. "But be careful, because sometimes she lets herself in the house and starts snooping around."

Lauren sighs, holding me with her eyes for several seconds. "I don't do that." Shifting her focus to Curtis, she smiles at him in a way that makes me cringe. "So what's your story?"

"Um," he begins, slipping a thumb in the top of his towel like he's a fucking cowboy or something. "I know Danny from school."

"So he said," she says gently, returning to the couch. "You should join us."

"Sure," Curtis says, nodding. "But, uh, I'm going to put some clothes on first." He grins self-consciously and then disappears into his room.

I know it's stupid to worry that they'll become friends – or even more than that – but a filament of jealousy twists around my chest anyway, tightening until its metallic teeth begin to cut into my flesh.

When his door is safely shut, I turn my annoyance to Lauren. "If you want, I could step out for a minute while you guys flirt."

"That's not fair," she insists. "You said yourself he's straight. What's wrong with flirting?"

I don't have an answer for that, but it doesn't make me any less pissed off. "Fine. Do whatever you want," I concede.

Curtis joins us – clothed this time – and over the next hour, Lauren goes on to pepper him with questions. He's not usually a big talker, but he seems to enjoy the attention. Still, a rather vocal part of me would love to kick her out so I can spend the time with Curtis myself, but something stops me.

Maybe her comment about my sock drawer.

Maybe just that she's right about Curtis, that no matter how much I want it to be different, he's straight.

"I'm going to head home," Lauren finally says after having exhausted every conceivable question about someone's background and interests. "Unless you want to go for a walk on the Galloping Goose?" She directs this question, like all the others, to Curtis.

Anger begins to fester inside me, because she's not only suggesting taking Curtis away for the rest of the night, but she also knows that I don't like hiking in the dark.

"Not sure what that is, but I'm game for whatever." Curtis glances at me where I'm leaning against the counter looking surly. "Danny, you want to go?"

"No thanks," I say, my voice tight. "I think I might go to bed early tonight."

"Oh… okay." Curtis sounds concerned, and I know he can tell that I'm irritated. But if he wants to go, he should. Mostly I'm just mad at

Lauren, even though I don't have a good reason to be.

"Actually, I think I'll pass," Curtis says.

Is he not going because of me? I shouldn't be happy about that, but I can't help it.

"Home it is, then," Lauren adds unnecessarily. I like her, but it's no contest between her and Curtis. It shouldn't have to be a competition, but if she's inviting him to hang out, doing an activity she *knows* I don't like, then it sure feels like one.

"Have a good night," I call as Lauren lets herself out, but the words are empty.

When the sound of the shutting door has faded into nothingness, Curtis turns and gives me a long look. "What was that about?"

"What?" I ask, keeping my voice light.

"Don't bullshit me, Danny. I know you better than that."

My eyebrows bunch together and my lips tighten to an unmovable line. Even after all the time apart, I'm still terrible at trying to deceive him. "I just think it's weird that she invited us on a night hike when she knows that I hate them."

"So she wanted to get me on my own?" Curiosity steps into his words, and I resist the urge to let my frown deepen. "Hmm," he muses. "She *is* kind of cute."

"For a girl, I guess."

He shakes his head with amusement. "Shut up."

Pausing, he drags himself away from his own thoughts and brings his gaze to me as he barks a laugh. "Oh shit, that's it. You're *jealous*, aren't you?" He grins as he stares me down, and the accusatory overtones I'm expecting are conspicuously absent. "Danny," he points at me, "is jealous that I," he points at himself, "might get with a girl."

"I am not," I lie.

He's still grinning, clearly amused. "My own buddy Danny," he teases, popping my arm with a punch.

"Screw you. I am *not* jealous," I snap, throwing a fist back and getting him in the shoulder – harder than when he hit me but still far from inflicting actual pain.

An instant before Curtis moves, I recognize the mischievous glint in his expression. It's enough to know what's coming, but not enough to do anything about it.

Curtis slings his arm around my neck, holding me tight in the crook of his elbow as he drags me to the rug at our feet. Yielding under his grip more from lingering surprise than anything else, I let him take me to the floor before finally pushing back.

Muscles tensing as I grapple with Curtis, I fight for the upper hand. For a whole minute, we're locked together without either of us taking a lead. Our breaths are coming heavy, but I refuse to let him beat me.

"You still wrestle like shit," he says through a grin as he maneuvers on top of me.

Grunting through gritted teeth, I heave with all my strength, pushing him over and onto his back. He might be right that my form is crap, and I'm sure he still has weight on me, but I'm a lot stronger than I was in high school. Forcing him against the floor, I jam an arm into his collarbone.

"Fuck, you're heavy," he groans.

He struggles underneath me, but regardless of form, I have him pinned. For the first time since he tackled me, his grin falters. "Crap," he says.

"It's not high school anymore," I shoot back, cracking a smile but not letting him up. "I work out now."

"Damn, I guess so." He sighs. Tapping my arm, he demands, "Okay, okay, let me up."

"Only if you take back what you said," I insist. It's silly to ask for that, but I'm kind of enjoying pinning him down. Not enjoying it *too* much, but enough for a bubbly playfulness to have worn down my inhibitions. Enough to force him to recant a statement that was completely true.

His eyes narrow. "You know you're a dick sometimes, right?"

Giving him a sly look, I say, "I don't even know what that is."

"Yeah right," Curtis scoffs. "So are you going to let me up now?"

"I'm not jealous of you messing around with some girl. Take it back, or we can stay here all night." *Actually, that wouldn't be such a bad thing.*

"Fine," he grumbles. "I take it back. You're not jealous. Now let me up."

Reluctantly I do as he asks, wishing that he'd held out a bit longer. Curtis hoists himself to his feet and brushes the wrinkles out of his shirt. If Curtis really thinks that I'm jealous, I doubt that the prolonged pinning swayed him in anything but the wrong direction, but the victory is still a moral one.

We used to roughhouse a lot when we were kids, but the only

times I ever "won" was when it wasn't a fair fight. Either I got the jump on him, or he was hung over, or he let me win. It was always *some* handicap, so this is the first time that I've beaten him straight up. That has to count for something, I think.

"It's too bad you don't like hiking at night." Curtis is staring out the window, looking up at the sky. "It's so clear out."

Conveniently forgetting my earlier assertion that I wanted to go to bed, I join him at the window. "We could sit out on the dock. It's cool out, but not too bad."

"Sure."

After finding a sweater for myself and another for Curtis, we venture out into the backyard, toward the shore of Sooke Basin. Walking out to the edge of the dock, I lie down across the wooden slats and intertwine my fingers behind my head.

"What are you doing?"

"Like you said," I explain, "it's a clear night. We should take advantage of it."

"Huh?"

"Look up," I instruct.

Curtis does as I say, followed by a long pause before he acknowledges what he's seeing. "Wow," he breathes, dragging his gaze away to glance down at me. "It's beautiful."

"It's harder to catch a clear sky here than back home, but the stars are never washed out by city lights, so I still think it's worth it."

"What's worth it?" he asks, lying down beside me.

"Living here, instead of in Thunder Bay."

Curtis is quiet for a moment, and my fears that he's analyzing me are realized when he speaks. "It sounds like you're trying to convince yourself that it's better here."

"What's wrong with feeling good about where I live?"

"Nothing," Curtis responds immediately. "I'm just not sure that you do."

I can feel his eyes on me instead of the thousand points of light above us. "That's ridiculous. The island is beautiful, the climate is mild, and I have a great home. Why would I have moved out here if I didn't love it?"

He turns back to face the sky. "Maybe I'm wrong."

But he's not. It's true that I *do* like it out here, and I love my home. But it wasn't my choice to move here. Not truly. I left because of Curtis. There were always other reasons, small ones on the side. But at the heart of all of them was Curtis.

He has the good sense to drop the subject, but I don't believe he's actually letting it go. He's too perceptive to come to a conclusion like that by accident. And he trusts his instincts too much to think he's wrong. That was one of the most frustrating parts about growing up together – Curtis always had an impeccable sense of what was going on with the people around him. It's a wonder that he didn't figure out the moment he arrived that I was into guys. Some things are just too far off his radar, I guess.

In an abrupt change of subject, Curtis asks, "How many more days of work do you have for me?"

I stare at the side of his face, but he doesn't turn toward me. "I don't know. Not too much more, I guess. But like I said before, you're welcome to stay as long as you want."

"I'm not a freeloader."

I sigh, but I shouldn't have expected anything less. Curtis has always been stubborn about pulling his weight. "You can throw me some money for rent if you really want, but seriously, it's not a big deal."

"I could pay you a few hundred… but I don't really have much to spare for rent," he says sullenly.

"So shut up about it until you can afford to chip in," I tease.

Curtis is quiet for what feels like too long. Eventually he admits, "I've been looking for a job."

My pulse picks up, tapping with excitement. "Jobs in Thunder Bay? Or here?"

"Both."

I let that sink in, wondering whether he's actually considering sticking around for longer. I'd like it if he did, but I've never been able to push Curtis into anything. Since the day we met, he's always insisted on making up his own damn mind. And once he makes a decision on something, it's impossible to change how he feels.

"Do you remember when we were lying in your backyard before that one storm?" he asks.

I have to smile, because as vague as Curtis is being, I know exactly what he's talking about. "Um yeah, actually. It was clear overhead, but we could see the thunderheads plodding across the sky."

Almost before I've finished speaking, he asks, "Do you remember how much lightning there was?"

"Of course."

The breeze picks up over the basin and whisks cold fingers over us, daring us to head inside. But the night is too perfect for that. The waves on the water roll against the dock pilings on their way to shore, and the stars overhead gaze down at us with eyes of silver white. It's the exact opposite of the night of the thunderstorm.

Pushing myself up to my elbows, I look over at him. At the outline of his shoulders in the sweater, at the way his chest rises and falls with his breaths. My lips part, and the salt air skims across them.

It's then that Curtis speaks, even though it's barely more than a whisper. "Back then, I thought I had everything figured out. But now… it's like I missed my shot to be something, and now that it's gone… I won't fall in love, I won't have an impressive career, and I won't accomplish anything great. I'll just have an average relationship and an average job and an average house and a below-average car."

Out of necessity, I cut in before he can go any further. "You've got to think more positive than that. We're not even thirty yet."

"Easy for you to say. You're set here. You've got everything you want." The bitterness on his lips is dark like the night air, but it's directed more at himself than me.

I'm afraid to ask the question that's running through my mind, but suddenly I feel like it's terribly important to know the answer. "Do you remember anything else about that night?"

He hesitates. Longer than a few seconds. Long enough that I don't know if I believe him when he says, "Not really besides the storm. Why?"

"No reason," I reply quickly. "Just curious if there was anything else that made it memorable."

"Hmm."

I don't know if he's being honest or not, but it's better if he doesn't remember, because I don't want him recalling any more details about the night that I almost kissed him. I didn't make a move that night, but I was about to. In retrospect, the thought scares the hell out of me because I was perilously close to crossing a boundary that would have changed our friendship forever.

But after all this time?

I wish I had.

Chapter Eight

Danny

On Friday, Lauren comes over and the three of us watch a movie together. It's some action flick that I'm not interested in, and I'm pretty sure that Lauren isn't into it either. Which means the only reason we're watching it is because Curtis wants to.

When it finally finishes, I yawn conspicuously and aim a look at each of them. "I'm tired."

"Oh, actually that's good," Lauren says quickly. "I was going to ask Curtis again if he wanted to hike on the Goose." She gives me an apologetic glance that feels more for show than anything else.

Curtis nods vigorously. "That would be awesome."

Between working together in the backyard and spending the evenings together, Curtis and I have basically hung out all week, so it's not like Lauren is stealing him or anything. Still, I can't help feeling annoyed as they get up from the couch and move toward the door.

Craning my neck over the back of the couch, I watch them put on their shoes and jackets before crossing through the doorway and into the night. Curtis gives me a little wave before they disappear, and then I'm alone.

A reluctant glance at the microwave clock confirms that it's already past ten, which means I really should go to bed. Back in college, I could bounce back from a late night as easily as taking an hour nap the next day. But like my tolerance for alcohol, my sleep schedule doesn't have the same resiliency as it used to.

Across from me, the refrigerator compressor awakens, settling after a few seconds into a contented purr. My vision floats off to the side, fading into fuzziness as my thoughts move toward Curtis and the time we've spent together this week.

Involuntarily, my memories seem to chart their own course, focusing on the tiniest individual moments. The brief seconds when he was leaning over my shoulder as I showed him the trail map for our hike on his second day here... or one afternoon when his eyes kept settling on me as we excavated the cistern hole... or the time he farted after thinking I'd left the room. I smile at that, remembering how red he got when I laughed.

But for all those little moments, I can't help but be drawn back to the *first* one. When he appeared in the doorway after years of not seeing him and stopped the words in my throat. Those strong features offset by soft eyes, topped off with messy hair cut short on the sides. And his shoulders, his biceps, his...

Fuck, I growl as frustration ripples through me. I've indulged this line of thinking for too long, and now my dick is hard. There are only two ways to get rid of this feeling, and I'm not sure either of them is a good option right now. A familiar urge rises within me, nudging my hand awake and beckoning me toward the bedroom.

Reaching down into my underwear to adjust myself, I press my lips into a tight line. Jerking off to Curtis isn't going to help anything. Which only leaves the other option.

The chlorine is thick in the air as I dive into the pool.

As though expecting me, the water moves aside as I become a part of it. But instead of propelling myself forward, I lurk under the surface, completely motionless. What I love most about being in water... what I love most about swimming, is that liquid can only accept, never reject. And it's forced to accept me now, silently brooding beneath its surface.

I hold my breath in my lungs, and the water holds me in its hands. Seconds slip past as bubbles rise past my face, but I don't make any move toward the surface. I feel safe here, insulated from the world outside.

Finally when my chest starts to sting more from stale air than the longing for someone I can't have, I kick upward and come up sputtering. Treading to keep myself afloat, I wipe the water off my face and check to make sure I'm still alone. It's past eleven, and the gym and pool are both deserted, which is good, because I need this time.

Ninth Grade

Splinters of lightning splash across the darkened sky, but it isn't until nearly half a minute later that the distant thunder ripples through the air. It's the height of summer, and this week has been so hot and sticky that it's just gross. I've spent the last few days living in tank tops while the sweat drips down from everywhere. Tonight the humidity is going to break.

Curtis and I are lying in his backyard, in one of the few areas where the grass grows as thick as it should. The rest of the yard is a mix of unkempt weeds and dirt patches. It sucks being at his place, but the view of the sky isn't blocked by trees like at my house.

Beside me, Curtis sits up, reaching to adjust his tank top beneath him on the grass. The humidity encouraged us to peel them off a while ago, but the grass is still pokey in our backs. At least it is in mine.

My gaze travels over his bare chest, trying to make out the details that the shadows are concealing from me. Not that it really matters, because Curtis and I have been friends for so long that I know exactly how he looks. But still I stare.

I wish I didn't feel this way. Being around Curtis used to be so easy and fun.

It's still fun, but it sure isn't easy anymore.

Having to police my eyes around him has gotten tough, especially since they're so interested in things they never used to be. Obvious stuff like his abs and his crotch. And less obvious stuff like his eyes and his shoulders and the place his hair stops on the back of his neck.

Even my own thoughts have become difficult to deal with. A month ago he called me out for getting hard while we were watching a movie. We're both teenage guys, so it's not like that's never happened to us before. It might have been okay, but the movie was an action flick, so it was difficult to explain my way out of it. Now he probably thinks I get turned on by exploding cars.

"There's a new Spider-Man movie coming out next spring," Curtis says. "We should go see it when it releases."

I glance over at him, but he's staring up at the sky. "Sure."

He's silent after that, which isn't a surprise. Curtis always gets a little spacey when thinking about Spider-Man.

Overhead, the lightning is relentless. Time after time, brilliant white cracks spread across the sky. Dozens of bolts snake between the clouds but only sometimes down to the ground. The wind picks up and thunder tramples over us, but still no rain comes.

"What do you like about him so much?" I ask, giving voice to the question I've silently asked myself a hundred times since we met.

"Huh?"

"Spider-Man," I clarify. "What's so great about him?"

Curtis is quiet for a long while, but I know he's still thinking, because he never makes me repeat a question.

The flip side of that is that sometimes I have to wait for the answer. Eventually he says, "I like that he was a nobody who became a superhero."

"Aren't they all like that?"

Curtis rustles beside me, and I assume he's shaking his head. "Not at all. Take Superman. He was always destined to become a hero. There was never anything he could do about it, because he had powers right from the beginning."

"And…" I begin slowly. "Spider-Man wasn't special until he got bitten?"

"Exactly." He hesitates, then adds quietly, "It makes me feel like there's hope to get out of here and become something."

"You're something now," I say as a roll of thunder overrides my words. I repeat myself before going on, "Everyone at school loves you, and half the girls would sleep with you if you wanted."

"I guess." He says it like he doesn't believe me. "I would rather do something important than be popular, though."

I think superheroes are silly, but I would never tell Curtis that. He would probably take it okay if I confessed my complete disinterest in them, but I don't want him to think he's driving his best friend to boredom when he talks about Spider-Man all the time. With anyone else, I would tell them to shut up, but I don't mind listening because it's Curtis.

The realization hits me that I regularly subject myself to Curtis's one-sided discussions about imaginary superheroes, in which I have absolutely zero interest. And I do it just because… it's him.

My eyes skim over him once more, lingering longer than they

should. In that moment, a familiar and uncomfortable sensation manifests itself at the back of my mouth. I don't want to feel this way. *But I do.*

I glance at his hand, lying palm down in the grass between us. That feeling in my throat whispers to me, lending me courage when I shouldn't have it, awakening a desire to push my fingers through his.

I don't *think* that Curtis leans that way, but who knows. He talks about girls a lot, but he's never actually said that he isn't interested in guys.

He's close. I could lean over and kiss him. I could touch him like I desperately want to.

"Curtis," I say, unmoving.

He turns onto his side, ignoring the flashes above and the first fat drops of water pelting down. "Yeah?"

A wet ball of rain lands in my eye, and my vision turns blurry for a fraction of a second until I blink, bringing clarity back to his curious expression.

Anxiety paralyzes me. What if he pushes me away? What if he hates me for it? What if he never speaks to me again?

My muscles stand at the ready, waiting for the order to reach out and touch him. But I don't.

"Do you, uh," I begin, having to pause, because I'm not sure what I'm trying to say. "Do you ever wonder if we're better friends than… other best friends are with each other?"

"Huh?" His tone is so filled with puzzlement that I almost smile.

I wish I could just *say* what I want to, but I can't. High school is a place where you have to be careful, sometimes even with your closest friend. So I try again. "Like, do we have a closer friendship than most other guys' friendships?" I practically bite my tongue, because I'm still not really making sense.

"Um, yeah, I guess so." Curtis sounds confused as raindrops fall around us, splatting against our skin. "Look, can we finish this conversation inside?"

Just like the rain coming down harder now, it feels like water is rising up inside my chest too, trying to drown me from the inside. I shouldn't keep going, but I need to give this a real chance. Because after this night, I swear to God I'm never going to bring it up again. "Do you think there's a reason for that?"

His expression darkens and then he shrugs as he sits up. "Just luck of the draw, I suppose."

I don't respond because the weight in my chest is trying to pull me under. Eventually he says, "I'm glad we're friends, if that's what you mean. But dude, I'm going inside." He gets up and sprints into the house as the storm really lets loose.

Now alone, I close my eyes as the water runs down my face and over my chest. "Yeah," I say to the rain, fighting to release my grip on the desire for me and Curtis to be anything more than friends. "That's what I meant."

Chapter Nine

Danny

The next day begins late for me, and it's just before noon when I crawl out of bed and drag myself to the kitchen. Curtis's shoes weren't by the door when I got back from the gym, but they're there now. When the hell did he get home last night?

Forcing my tired brain to start working, I put on a pot of hot water and begin the wait until coffee can work its miracle.

Cup in hand, I set about catching up on the things I've been putting off since he arrived – paying bills, responding to an email from my parents, and finally starting a book that Lauren lent to me. It keeps my attention well enough, and the afternoon hours pass as I wait for Curtis to get up.

The overcast sky of navy blue is already descending around the house, hinting at an early evening, when I hear the door of the guest bedroom open and shut. A minute later, the sound of running water begins in the shower. Gratefully abandoning my book on the coffee table, I wander into the kitchen to make dinner.

The aroma of burgers is thick in the air when Curtis finally walks in. His hair is wet and pointing away from his head, and he looks refreshed. Of course those are all secondary observations, because the shirt he should be wearing is still in his hand.

My eyes move down from his wide shoulders, pausing at his chest and the dark circles of his nipples. Down further to the outline of his abdominal muscles and the thin trail of hair that starts above his navel and ends somewhere below the top of his jeans. With the exception of that alluring line of hair, his stomach is smooth. It's certainly not the first time I've seen him shirtless since he arrived, but that doesn't mean it's any easier to look away.

"Danny?"

"Uh, hey," I say quickly. It's good that he said something, because otherwise I would have just kept staring. Turning back to the stove to hide the reaction pushing against the inside of my jeans, I ask, "Hungry?"

"Starving." He tugs his shirt over his head and sits down at the kitchen table, watching as I return to the stove. Now that he's not flashing that chest of his, it's only a minute before my dick gives up trying to bust out of my pants.

From behind me, he says, "This table is sweet as hell."

I turn, smiling when I see that he has his hands spread apart on its surface as he gazes at the grain. "Thanks. It was the first thing I built."

"It's beautiful," he says, and I can hear the awe in his voice. "I wish I had a desk like this."

Serving up a plate for each of us, I carry them over to the table and take a place across from him. "Why a desk?"

He shrugs. "When I lived at home, I never had like… a *place*, to work on homework and stuff. College wasn't much better."

He looks away, and I abandon the topic. "Did you have a good time with Lauren last night?"

Just having taken a bite of his burger, Curtis just nods vigorously. Chewing like it's his job, he finally swallows. "Lauren and I walked on that trail quite a ways, and then we went back to her place and had a glass of wine."

She invited him over? "I didn't know you liked wine."

"It's okay." Gesturing with his burger in hand, he adds, "And this is really good for being made on the stove."

I raise an eyebrow. "So you like my meat."

"Gross, dude," he laughs.

I shrug innocently.

"What do you want to do tonight?" he asks between bites. "The day is more than half over and we still haven't even left the house."

Yeah, because Curtis stayed out even later than I did, and then he slept all day. "If you're interested, I was thinking we could go for a round in the sauna."

His eyes grow wide. "You have a sauna?"

"Sure do. It's just inside the trees, down toward the basin."

He grins with excitement. "That would be awesome. I was kind of hoping we could get into the woods a bit too."

I try not to frown. "I guess there's still time to go for a hike, but it's getting dark soon."

"Sorry I slept late," he says with a dejected look. "I didn't realize I was at Lauren's so long last night."

"It's fine. I'm just looking forward to doing something together that isn't digging a hole in the backyard."

His gaze lands on me, unmoving for too many seconds. "Me too," he says. He pushes his plate forward a couple inches and leans back in his chair with satisfaction. I press my lips hard together and force away the thought that I'd enjoy satisfying him in other ways too.

For Christ's sake, he's a friend, not a hook up.

Pulling a stick of gum from his pocket and popping it into his mouth, Curtis prompts, "Let's go."

In defiance of the recent nice weather, the temperature has dropped to nearly freezing, and the humid air feels raw on my face as we step outside.

"Which way?" Curtis asks, his breath casting white vapor into the air.

I steal a glance up at the sky growing steadily clearer, estimating that it will be dark in just a couple hours. "We'll head up the hill. There's a cool trail I want to show you."

Without further prodding, Curtis sets off into the evening with me following behind. Confident as he moves forward, Curtis doesn't even hesitate as I point toward a spot off the road.

"Where are we going?" he asks as we plunge into the woods.

It's darker than I anticipated under the cover of the trees, so it takes me a moment to find the start of the trail. "This way," I say, pushing through the undergrowth until I reach the beginning of a large concrete pipe, where dirt has been mounded up at the end so hikers can get onto it. About a meter wide and covered in thick moss, the cylindrical concrete pipe leads away into the forest like a giant snake.

"Whoa. What *is* this?"

"It's called the flowline trail. A hundred years or so ago it used to be a major aqueduct supplying water to Victoria. Now it's just a cool place to hike."

I let Curtis go first again, because there's no way he can get off track as long as we follow the trail. The only risk is actually falling off the pipe – it's big enough that it would be tricky to get back on if one of us fell off, and the walkable area on the top isn't all that wide. As we head deeper into the woods, I consider that this might not have been the best choice for an evening hike.

After about ten minutes, Curtis calls over his shoulder, "How far does this thing go?"

"Far. It was originally over forty kilometers, but some parts have been destroyed or buried."

"That's too bad," he says, his voice projecting ahead.

This is one of my favorite trails on the island, and it's definitely the most unique. There isn't any climbing involved, but it requires you to be careful with your feet, so it still has a challenging aspect to it.

The cool evening brushes up against us as we follow the narrow concrete trail onward. Trees wander past, and at one point the pipe is lifted onto a trestle as it crosses over a small river. But still we continue on.

"Want to turn around?" I call up to Curtis. "If we keep going, we're going to end up walking back in the dark." I try not to sound worried, but the truth is that I *really* don't like being in the woods at night.

"Just a little farther. I can see better at night than you can, remember?"

I frown, but I don't argue as we keep on walking. Shortly after, the pipe carries us out of the forest and onto the open rocky bones of the island.

Curtis is silent as he comes to a stop and sits down on the pipe. Anxious as I am to start back, I don't mind, because this is one of the best views from this trail. During the day you can even see across the Strait of Juan de Fuca to the Olympic Mountains. Sitting down beside him, I drape my legs over the curve of the pipe just as he has.

Eventually my thoughts move on, focusing once more on the view in front of us. Something about the silence in places like this helps me relax in a way that I never could back in Ontario. There are no cars or roads here, and even the ever-present hum of civilization is all but gone. The only company we have here are the close scent of humid earth, the stars gleaming down, and the chilly breeze passing through the fir trees.

In front of us, the land stretches out, sloping downward toward the ocean strait. A hundred shades of green mingle with the steady gray of the stony terrain. Vancouver Island has a heart of rock, but across its back and shoulders it carries a temperate coniferous rainforest. I've fallen in love with both of those parts, and I don't know if I would ever want to live anywhere else. Unless it was to be with Curtis, that is.

The thought smolders in my mind, refusing to burn out even as I'm adamantly wishing it weren't true.

Despite the freshness of the silence, it's not unwelcome when Curtis speaks. "So what's the deal with you and Lauren?"

Breath catching in my throat, I pick my words cautiously, "What do you mean?"

"You know..." his voice trails.

It seems like he's struggling, but I'm not going to make this easy for him. If he wants to know something, he has to damn well ask.

Curtis tries again. "I know you said you're into dudes now, but did you two used to be together or something? Or are you like friends with benefits?"

"Why would you think that? Did she say something?"

The snapping sound of his gum cuts across the space that divides us. "Even disregarding your last question, which makes it *really* sound like something was up between you guys... it seems like you two are oddly close. Lauren is pretty hot, and you're..."

Curbing my aggressive side is usually easy around Curtis, but this time it gets away from me. "I'm what, exactly?"

"You're not a, um," he hesitates. "Not a bad looking guy."

Turning my face away from him so he can't see how hard a time I'm having fighting off a smile, I wait a few seconds so I don't sound like a giddy schoolgirl when I respond. "Thanks. But no, she and I never had sex or anything." I wonder what he'll make of that.

"Huh, interesting."

Hoping to veer the conversation away from myself, I ask, "Why did it not work out between you and Celia? The last time we talked about it you didn't really explain much."

When he speaks, he sounds uncomfortable. "Not much to say. We moved in together after just a couple months, and it went all right at first. But she always wanted something more than I could give, I guess."

Feeling brazen from his earlier comment on my appearance, I suggest, "Because she was a girl?"

Curtis punches my shoulder harder than necessary, and I groan involuntarily as my deltoid absorbs the impact. "You and I have been friends a long time," he warns. "But watch yourself."

Sourness touches the back of my tongue, making me not want to say anything more. I don't mind getting rough, but his tone felt harsh.

"If not Lauren," Curtis begins again, "then you have some other girl?"

"I *told* you, I'm not into that," I say, not bothering to stop my irritation from coming through. If he keeps up with this, I might hit him right back, and I wouldn't go for his shoulder.

Glancing over at him and the curiosity in his eyes, I feel instantly guilty. *If* I ever hit him, it could never be in the face. Maybe his stomach. Yeah, I could punch him there.

"I was just thinking that it would be easy for a guy like you to find a girl." He pauses, adding quickly, "So like, you wouldn't have to be with guys if you didn't want."

I turn to really look at him, giving him my best *shut the fuck up right now* face. "Are you done?"

Even in the failing light, I can see him redden before he looks away. He's quiet for several moments until he asks, "You ready to head back? I'm getting a little cold."

I raise an eyebrow. "The indomitable, night-vision Curtis is *cold*?"

A shy smile fights with the corners of his mouth. "I've always been a bit of a cold baby. You know that."

I'm not sure what it is about his smiles – whether it's the subtle ones like he's got a secret to tell, or the wide ones that show up when he's excited – but they're contagious. If he ever caught a smile plague, humanity would be in trouble.

Between his confession of being vulnerable to the cold – which of course I do remember – and that unassuming expression of his, it's hard to keep my voice steady, but somehow I manage it. "Sure, we can head back."

As we follow the flowline back into the trees, it becomes immediately clear that it's a lot harder to see now. Even the silver starlight overhead barely filters down through the bushy pines, and as the trees grow even closer, I'm forced to follow Curtis more by hearing than sight. When the distance between us begins to increase, he doesn't make any comment about it, but he does ease up on the pace.

I'm about to ask Curtis to slow down even more when I misjudge a curve in the pipe. Shoes slipping beneath me, they grapple with the moss on the curved edge as my eyes grasp futilely for light that isn't there. My arms flail, but I'm losing ground, and in a second I'm going to fall off into the woods.

Hands clamp around the sides of my chest, squeezing hard against my ribs as they work to steady me.

"*Fuck,*" I curse, still trying to regain my balance while correcting my precarious footing. Curtis's hands don't move, not even when I'm standing safely on the middle of the pipe again. His fingers are warm through my jacket and t-shirt, and he's so close that I can taste his mint gum on the air.

My pulse is so loud in my ears that I swear he can hear it too. "Um, thanks."

Only then does Curtis relax his grip. He moves back and the mint disappears. Then he pats me twice on the side of my chest where he was just holding me. "Careful where you step, buddy."

"I can't see *anything,*" I say, finding my voice. "It's so goddamn dark out here."

I'm met by a moment of silence, and even though I can't see, I swear that he's got that same smile on his face. Except instead of the joke at my expense that I'm expecting, I hear his voice, closer and quieter than a moment before.

"Here."

The next thing I feel is a hand slipping into mine. It's warm like his touch earlier, but without my jacket between us. Then he gently pulls me forward.

My head swirls, battling against a numbness that's not from tonight's unseasonable cold. *He's holding my hand. My. Fucking. Hand.*

As he leads me on, he doesn't loosen his grip, and I actually start to enjoy myself. Instead of worrying about slipping off the pipe or looking like a fool who's afraid of the dark, I'm able to concentrate on the faint signals from my other senses. Like the pine scent licking the air, or the sound of our shoes moving over moss and concrete.

When we finally emerge from the trees and step off the pipe, Curtis lets go of me almost immediately. I swallow quickly to bury my disappointment, but I shouldn't have expected anything less. He's too much of a guy to have done anything else, and the only reason he took my hand in the first place was because I nearly walked off the edge of the stupid trail.

Coming to a stop beside him, I stare at the road in front of us.

"You can see fine now, right?" he asks. His tone strays between two distinctly different notes, neither of which I can quite identify.

"Yeah."

"Okay," he breathes, and the sound drips with disappointment. *Huh?*

Walking side by side, we start toward home under crystal starlight. The distance between us feels so much greater than when we were on the pipe, and not just because our hands are no longer touching. Our feet pass over the ground, and our breaths move in unison, but neither of us speaks.

When we get to my driveway, Curtis points at the small structure at the far edge of the yard. "The sauna?"

After the anxiety of trekking through the woods in the dark, I forgot all about it. But if his enthusiasm earlier is any indication, he's still game to get in there tonight.

"I can start it before we go in the house, if you're still interested," I try to suggest casually.

"That would be great," he says, eagerness pressing against his voice.

After detouring to turn on the sauna heater, we bundle back into the house, prickling with cold.

While I hang up our coats, Curtis takes two beers from the fridge and walks them over to the dining room table. Snapping the top off with a bottle opener on his keychain, he hands it to me as I sit down across from him.

I clink the neck of the bottle against his, keeping my eyes on him as we take our first drink. Carbonation tingles over my tongue, and I take another swig to keep the taste in my mouth.

"That was a trek," Curtis admits. "I really thought we were going to fall off that pipe and have a hell of a time getting back on."

I almost spit up a mouthful of beer at that, but I manage to contain my surprise to a sputtering cough while Curtis laughs. "Are you *serious*?" I demand. "The only reason I agreed to stay out that long is because you were so confident that you could find your way back."

"Yeah, but hey, we made it home fine." Then he pulls out the smile again. *Damn it, Curtis.* Does he know how unfair it is to keep using that on me? Especially so many times in one day.

My attention drifts downward. To the base of my beer bottle and the way it's pulling moisture from the air. To the creamy golden strokes of black walnut woodgrain in the table I love so much. To the palm of my hand and the callouses underneath my knuckles.

These hands have done so much during my time on the island. They've refinished this home from top to bottom, and they've crafted beautiful furniture. But for everything I've accomplished, I feel empty. Lifting my beer again, I tip it back until that's empty too.

Brown eyes touch mine, and the question is genuine. "What are you thinking about?"

"Doesn't matter," I say.

"Come on," Curtis presses. "Don't be like that."

Silence is the only answer he gets, but he continues to watch me for a long moment before standing up to get us another pair of beers. He opens the top for me again, and sets the bottle beside the first.

"Drink up," he says.

I give him a look as I rotate the bottle in place on the table. "You trying to get me drunk or what?"

"You don't need my help for that," he laughs. "But if that's what it takes to get you to open up... then yes." He flashes a grin that makes me giddy and nervous all at once. *What the hell is up with him tonight?*

As we finish our second round, I really do start to get buzzed, and as much as I'm not excited to go back outside, the bristling heat of the sauna sounds pretty good right now. "The, uh... sauna is probably ready," I tell him.

Curtis disappears to his room, and when he comes back out, he's only wearing a towel tied around his waist. His chest is just as perfect as it was this afternoon after his shower, except now instead of jeans, he's only wearing a goddamn towel. If the idea weren't absolutely crazy, I'd think he was purposely trying to make me so horny it hurts.

"You're sure it's hot enough?" Curtis asks as he walks past me to take a third pair of beers from the fridge and set them on the counter.

"Uh, yeah. Pretty sure," I manage, forcing my eyes away from the spot in front of his crotch where the towel has to stretch over his dick.

It takes all my will power to walk out of the kitchen. Is he doing this on purpose?

In my room, I strip down and wrap a towel around my waist. I'm already half hard, and it's only by concentrating on how much I hate filing taxes that I'm able to get myself under control. It probably also helped that I cinched my towel down really tight.

Stepping out of my room, I wait at the door while Curtis picks up our beers. When he's ready, I hold the door open for him as he towel-walks past me. We tiptoe through the frigid wet grass to the sauna.

"Hurry up," he complains, waiting at the sauna door. "It's getting chilly up under my towel."

"Whatever," I say with a grin as I join him and we step into a wave of heat. Alongside the scent of cedar, dry heat is packed into the room, and together they rub up against us and fill our lungs.

Under the single dim light, Curtis takes his beer and leans back on the cedar-slatted bench.

Leaning over to pick up my own beer, I halt abruptly as he tugs on the corner of his towel, lifts himself an inch off the bench, and pulls it off.

My fingers close around the brown glass bottle because there isn't anything else to hold onto. Between the heat and the tingling of alcohol I've already consumed, I feel like I'm being lured toward a place where inhibitions don't exist. Except that's not right at all, because it's just me and Curtis here. And if I'm not careful, I might fuck up the only friendship that has ever really mattered to me.

I take a swig of my beer, but it goes down rough. I'm trying to keep my eyes off him by focusing on whatever else I can – the swirling knots in the cedar ceiling, the cold bottle in my hand, the coils of the heater glowing sultry red.

"Come on, Danny," Curtis says casually, eyeing my towel. "We're both guys. Who cares?"

"I'm fine like this," I say, but my words sound even more dry and forced than the heat in here. Even so, I risk a single cautious glance. He's lying on his back, face pointed toward the ceiling with his eyes closed. I can't help but wonder if he's doing that just to make it easier on me to be around him while he's so… naked.

Emboldened, I take a small breath and let my eyes move downward. Since he's lying on his back, his abs have disappeared for the moment, replaced instead by a soft, flat belly that moves up and down with his breaths. Catching sight of that familiar line of dark hair, I follow it down over his navel, then lower to a dark patch of pubic hair trimmed short. And in the middle, draped across his leg, is his dick, fast asleep.

I take a nervous drink of my beer and tug on the corner of my towel to pull it tighter around my waist. I don't trust myself to lie down, and I can't even consider taking the towel off, so I just sip my beer and avert my eyes, letting the heat wash over me.

The temperature rises, and sweat pushes through my pores, collecting on my forehead and my neck and everywhere else too. Stealing another glance at him, I see that he's perspiring even more than me. I know I shouldn't stare, but it's impossible to drag my eyes away. So I just look, reveling in how fine a man he has become. His stomach still rises gently with his breaths, and he looks completely relaxed. Drops of sweat mingle together on his skin – along his hairline, on the inside of his elbows, just below his navel.

When I finally turn away, the admiration is tainted by regret. We were best friends once – a friendship that was torn apart because I loved being around him too much. And it's happening all over again.

It feels like fate is personally tormenting me. I didn't move out across the country to be a successful craftsman with a beautiful home on the ocean. I didn't give a shit about that stuff then, and I don't really care that much now. I moved here because I couldn't be with anyone without thinking about Curtis.

Longing for him didn't hurt at first. In a way it almost felt good, because I knew the feeling was real, and I didn't wonder anymore what people were talking about when they said the word *love*, and I wasn't afraid anymore that I might never feel it.

But then it began to grate against me. It hurt every minute I couldn't have him, because no matter what I did, every moment was a reminder that I wasn't with him. And for everyone in my life who told me that I would eventually get over him, or that I should just start dating… I never doubted that they were wrong, not even for a second.

They didn't know Curtis the way I did. *No one* knew Curtis the way I did.

But it didn't matter, because even though I was best friends with a guy who was fun, kind, and handsome as hell, he was fucking straight.

So I moved here, to find someone who was Curtis, but wasn't. To find someone who I could love the way I loved him. And this time, just maybe, it would be someone who actually loved me back.

I can feel the frustration beginning deep in my chest, rising through me into a sigh so raw it makes me want to scream aloud how broken the world is. Instead, I lean back against the sauna wall.

Curtis is staring me down, watching the thoughts on my face. "Seriously dude, what's wrong?" he asks. He sits up, and an outline of perspiration on the cedar marks his previous position. His towel is still folded beside him, but I can't bring myself to look at anything but those eyes.

Even that ardent look of his can't make me confess the way I feel about him. I promised myself that I would never bring it up again, and I won't break that vow. I uprooted my life because of that promise, and sometimes I feel like it's the only thing that has protected me all these years. Curtis couldn't understand what I needed from him then, and nothing has changed since.

"You're upset about something." He crosses his arms and holds them tight to his chest. "When we were younger, you'd always get that face whenever you'd messed something up."

"Wow." I don't have any emotion to spin on the word except surprise.

He blinks like he's gotten something in his eye, then wipes a hand across his sweaty forehead. "Danny, spit it out."

"It's just the beer and the heat," I say tightly. That's partly true – three beers and half an hour in a sauna have my head swimming.

"Bullshit," he snaps. "What the hell is going on with you?"

Inside me, a switch seems to flip, and immediately I stand. "I can't do this right now. I just can't." Throwing the door open, I walk out.

Towel hugging my hips, I step over poky wet grass as steam rises off my skin. Contrary to what I expect, the cold feels good – at once both sobering and refreshing. It almost makes it possible to push the last hour out of my mind.

The door to the house is nearly within reach when Curtis slows down out of a sprint and stops me with a hand on my chest. His other hand is clenched tight around the tips of his towel but he's barely keeping it up.

Flinching at his touch, I take a step back from him. "Will you just let this go?" I shout at him. "Just leave me the fuck alone, okay? That's all I want right now."

"Are you kidding me, Danny?" His hands work to tie his towel properly, and his expression is mixed up with confusion. "You don't need to be dropping f-bombs. I'm just trying to be a friend to you. Like I always have."

"That's the problem," I say, nearly choking on the sharpness in my voice.

His face is blank, but his words are nervous. "I'm not following you."

"Doesn't matter. I don't want to talk about it."

His exhaling breath is one of desperation. "I don't get you, Danny. It's like you're so upset about something, but I can't figure out what on earth it is. Half the time I don't know if you even want me here."

I try to move past him, but he shifts to the side and blocks my way. Strands of anger twist together and my fists tense, rising to a half-cocked position.

"Jesus, Danny." He steps forward to get in my face. "Is that what you want?" he challenges, his voice gruff like the chill in the air. "You want to hit me?"

Something about the way Curtis has been acting makes my skin prickle. It feels different than any other time I've been around him.

"Yeah, maybe I want to hit you." If saying that is what it takes to get him out of my way, then fine.

He steps back, and for a second I think he's going to back down and let me past. His voice is low when he speaks. "Do it, then."

My eyes narrow, and ten years of regret make me consider something I would never have otherwise. I know none of it was his fault, but that never made it any easier.

Still, I'm not going to *hit* him. Sheesh.

He shoves me back a step. "*Do it,* you pussy."

I pop him in the jaw before the last word is even off his tongue, and the satisfyingly thick sound of an impact on flesh joins us for the briefest moment.

We just stare at each other while a sinking feeling fills me. Barely visible under the porch light, blood collects on his lip. I can't believe I actually hit him.

I feel terrible.

And I feel good.

His jaw is set, but his expression is so vulnerable that I can't bear to look at him any longer. I push past him, and this time he lets me go.

The knob is heavy under my fingers, and for as hard as I hit Curtis a second ago, it feels like I barely have the strength to open the door.

I haven't even taken two steps inside when he stops me once more, this time with a hand on my shoulder. My heart pauses for the span of a single breath, and I'm sure he's going to take revenge on me for hitting him. But when he turns me around, nothing happens.

Blood trickles down from his lip into the stubble on his chin, and his eyes search mine.

"Goddamn it, Curtis," I growl. "Can't you take a hint?" I try to push him back, but he catches me around the wrist and pulls me toward him. His grip is firm as he tugs me closer, pulling me into a hug so close that his bare chest presses against mine.

I can feel his heartbeat and the heat of his skin, and it doesn't matter to me anymore if I break this friendship. Pulling back from his embrace, I stare him down. Before he can react, I plant my lips on his, and in that second, I taste him. His warmth, the softness of his lips, the rough of his stubble, the wetness of his tongue, and the trace of mint gum tempered by the taste of blood on his lips. That flavor of slick iron is the last thing shared across our lips as he snaps out of the moment and forces me away roughly.

"What the fuck, dude?" he snarls.

His glare burns over my face, and for a moment, every atom between us stands still.

Stepping forward, I hold down his arms and push him against the opposite wall of the entryway. My eyes find his as I hesitate, seeking confirmation that I'm not making a huge mistake.

In his expression I can see anger, absolutely. And indignation. And... desire.

This time when I kiss him, he doesn't fight and he doesn't push back. Except with maybe his tongue. My advance is returned with vigor, and the warmth at knowing that it's Curtis I'm kissing mixes with a more potent heat inside me. The earlier suspicion of mint comes on stronger as he gives in to the kiss, tasting me more deeply.

No longer having to hold him down, my hands begin to move freely over his body. Across his chest and up to his neck, pressing firm against the sides of his jaw. And just as my tongue becomes accustomed to him, I break our kiss.

Curtis is straight, always has been. And for all those times that I desperately wished for something to happen between us as teenagers, it never did. So why now?

Leaning in, I let my head tip forward. Our chests press together once more, and I can feel his panting breaths hot on my shoulder. So many times we've been this close to one another, but never, ever like this.

Close in my ear, he whispers, "I, um..." His voice is so heavy it's a wonder he can use it at all. It doesn't make sense what's happening right now, but I don't know if it needs to. Moving back just enough so that I can look into his eyes – those eyes, chocolate rich and mahogany smooth – I hold a finger up to his lips. For the thousand conversations we've had over the years, words seem useless right now.

Peripherally aware that our towels have somehow managed to stay on all this time despite the fight we've both been putting up, I reach out and slip my hand under the edge of the fluffy fabric beside his hip. Not to open it, but to make him follow me. I know he will, because I saw it in those eyes of his. The eyes I thought I knew so well. The eyes I want to lose myself in.

A singular silence follows us across the kitchen and down the hall, warding away the creaking of the hundred-year-old hardwood beneath our feet and the wind against the sides of the house. Through the hall swathed in darkness, I lead Curtis to my room, not releasing the edge of his towel until I climb onto my bed.

One second passes.

My heart drums with anxiety. If he chooses to leave now, I won't try to stop him.

Two seconds pass.

Then weight shifts on the bed, and he lies down on his side, facing me. Reaching out, I let my hand tread lightly over his arm, then down to his waist where the towel is still hanging on for dear life. Curtis doesn't make a sound as I gently tug the corner open and release him from it.

Fingers cautious, I move my hand toward the area I've uncovered and wrap my hand around his cock. He inhales sharply, seeming to shiver, but he doesn't pull back. "Danny... you, um..."

Releasing my grasp on him, I ask, "Yeah?"

He looks to the ceiling and rolls away onto his back. "I'm not gay." His voice is quiet, somber.

"I know." I have no idea what to think right now, but if that's what he needs to hear, I'm not going to deny him that. I'm not going to deny him anything else he wants, either. But what *does* he want?

My cock is on the verge of a serious case of blue balls, but I'm not going to push him. If this is all that happens between us, I won't regret a single second of it.

When he speaks again, it sounds like he has to force the words out. "You... don't have to stop."

He doesn't need to tell me twice. Moving closer, I plant my knees on either side of his waist and dip down to kiss him again. This time he's ready for it, and he melts into me with a distinct eagerness.

I love how he tastes, and I want to keep kissing him, but his cock is so hard that it's pressing up against my balls and driving me wild. I make my way down his neck and over his chest. Coming up on his pecs, I start on the right, tracing a line with my tongue around the dark circle surrounding his nipple before taking it between my lips and sucking. He groans, and his hips shift restlessly.

Unable to restrain myself, I continue lower, kissing down the side of his stomach before circling over to his navel. Flicking my tongue briefly inside, I smile to myself as he wriggles under me.

"God, Curtis, you're so fucking sexy," I breathe.

He tenses, and fear spasms through me. *He's going to bolt.*

But he doesn't move, and he doesn't say anything. So I keep going.

As I move lower, the hairs of his treasure trail graze against my chin, promising more to come. Veering away from his cock, I take his balls in my mouth, one at a time. Licking, sucking, even nipping his skin ever so lightly.

Any doubt whether I'm turning him on is banished the moment that his outstretched fingers slide through my hair, closing into a fist and pulling my head up to his cock. *Yes, sir.*

Taking him into my mouth, I savor his heat and girth. As I let him deeper into my mouth, I catch the heady scent of his pubes and give up trying to keep my hands off myself.

Kneeling over him, I keep working with my mouth, massaging his balls with one hand while using the other to touch myself. Pulling down on his balls so the skin around his dick tightens up, I swirl my tongue around the end, loving the slightly salty taste just under the head.

It's a subtle shift, but as I keep going, his dick seems to get a little hotter in my mouth and his fingers loosen up in my hair. His breaths get tighter, faster, and I let him as far into my mouth as I can, pressing him against the soft palate at the back at the same time that my tongue stretches forward, only just reaching his balls.

Curtis makes a sound like a frustrated moan, and with the hand in my hair, he taps a warning on the side of my head, twice in quick succession. Certain of what's about to happen and knowing I'm going to love it, I refuse to slow down. Keeping up as vigorously as I can – both on him and myself – I push us further toward the edge.

Curtis loses control just a moment before I do, his hips tipping upward as he exhales like he's never felt anything so good. Backing off just enough so that I don't gag, I keep sucking him off as he comes, filling my mouth as I lose my own load on the comforter.

The fingers in my hair are softly massaging now as I swallow, bringing an end to… something I can't wrap my head around. Not just because it was hot as hell, and not even because the thing I wanted most was for him to enjoy himself – even though that feeling isn't one that I'm used to. I'm not a selfish lover, and I know that there's give and take when you're with someone else, but this was just so… *different.*

I know it's because it was *Curtis.* The guy that I went through puberty and seven years of school with… the one that I felt closer to than any other friend.

Scooting up to lie beside him, I rest my head on the pillow and stare up into the shadows as my breathing gradually slows. Curtis still says nothing, and worry steals into my mind. Worry that he might feel regret or remorse for what we did, even though I can't imagine how anyone could ever think that. It was just so damn good.

It feels corny as shit to think that, but it's also completely true. What just happened with the man breathing quietly beside me… it makes me want to forget every other person I've ever been with, every guilty hook up, every boyfriend, and every person I ever found attractive. Because none of that even comes close to how I felt just now.

Curtis sits up, and even in the dark I can feel his eyes on me. "I'm going to brush my teeth," he says.

As hard as I strain, I can't detect any meaning in his words other than what he actually said. Standing and taking his towel from the bed, he leaves me.

Using my own towel, I clean up what I left on the comforter before I get up for a fresh pair of underwear from my dresser. Not willing to give up hope completely, I lie on top of the comforter and wait, despite the chill creeping over me.

When Curtis appears in the doorway again, he's only wearing a pair of blue basketball shorts. Apparently he didn't see any reason to bother with a shirt, not after what we just did.

Silhouetted in the light of the hallway, it strikes me again how attractive he is. It doesn't matter that I just saw him completely naked, that I just had him in my mouth, because he's every bit as handsome in basketball shorts as he is wearing anything else.

"I'm going to…" Curtis plods through his words. "Go to bed now." Gesturing with a thumb over his shoulder, he turns to go.

"Wait," I breathe, and he stops, looking back at me. "You can… stay, if you want."

His reply strikes from the silence, the tips of his words icy with venom. "I'm not one of your college fuck buddies, Danny."

I want to tell him he's got it all wrong, and I want to tell him that what just happened between us has a meaning… that it wasn't just a random blowjob.

Not saying any of that feels like the hardest thing I've ever done. "Um, goodnight then," I finally manage.

He nods and turns away for real this time, leaving me alone in the dark. Sunset was hours ago, and shadows have long since wedged themselves into the corners and the open spaces of my room. With Curtis gone, the darkness squirms toward me, carrying with it a determined silence that has no fear of being broken, because the chance for words has already come and gone tonight.

It's a long while before I finally get up to take a piss. Braced on the vanity, I stare into the mirror, first at the blue of my eyes and then at the sun's highlights in my hair. What does he see when he looks at me?

On the vanity, my toothbrush has been waiting patiently, but part of me doesn't want to wash the taste of Curtis out of my mouth.

What if I never get to experience him like that again?

I start brushing anyway.

The good thing about having a master bathroom is that I don't have to stand in the place where Curtis stood a half hour ago, wondering what thoughts were thundering through his mind as he cleaned himself up. The bad part is that I don't have any excuse for walking past his room.

Abandoning caution, I tiptoe into the hallway anyway and pause at his closed door, wishing that tonight had gone differently. Leaning against the wall, I let my gaze get lost in space. Curtis might have pushed back at first, but after that he enjoyed himself, no question about it.

But why? After all those years that we were best friends, if he were into guys or at least questioning, confused, curious – whatever people call it now – then why didn't something happen before now? Why didn't he ever say anything?

I linger just a few more moments before flipping off the hallway light and retreating to my bed.

Beneath the sheets, I take a deep breath, hoping that filling my chest with air will leave no room for the heaviness there.

I refuse to feel bad about what happened. It was fantastic, and I wouldn't trade tonight for anything. Curtis might regret it, but that doesn't mean I have to.

Still, I can't help but worry that he's in the next room, wide awake, telling himself it was all a mistake, probably even blaming me for it... He can believe whatever he wants, but I know he was right there with me. If he's telling himself that he didn't love every minute of it, he's straight up lying. I was there, I know.

And as far as the college fuck buddies go... I never invited any of those to stay the night.

Chapter Ten

Curtis

I wish I could convince the morning to hold off for a few more hours, but when I can't pretend any longer that the Pacific Northwest sun isn't blazing through my window, I sit up against the headboard. My hand rises to touch the bottom of my jaw where Danny clocked me last night. It's sore and probably turning into a splotchy bruise if it hasn't already.

I'm not sure what I was thinking, goading Danny into hitting me like that. I don't blame him, because I asked for it, and then some. The thing is, in that moment, I really *did* want him to do it. Ever since I got here, it felt like he was gradually pushing me farther away, shutting me out, and I didn't understand why.

I shouldn't have gotten Danny fired up that much, but when he hit me, at least I knew that he… still cared. I know that's messed up, but it was the only way I felt a connection with my dad through most of high school. It doesn't matter that I know it's all sorts of wrong to feel like that, because my brain is wired to think that's what being close to someone means. Like a dog licking up antifreeze that he can't get enough of, something inside me is drawn to the sickly sweet taste of being hurt by the people closest to me.

The worst part? I kind of feel like I deserve it too.

I am so fucked up.

But at least that makes sense to me. What happened afterward, when Danny went down on me… I don't even know where to begin with that. What the hell was he thinking? What was *I* thinking?

Throwing off the covers, I head into the kitchen.

When Danny finally gets up, I'm brooding over a cup of coffee, staring down at the table while my index finger traces the path around the inside of the mug's handle. I drop my hand as I hear him approach.

"Morning," he says.

I actually flinch at his voice, but then I force myself to relax. We just need to pretend that nothing ever happened between us.

"Um, morning," I say slowly, taking a tentative sip of my coffee. I wasn't sure what Danny would be like this morning. I hadn't completely discounted the possibility that he was going to sprint into the kitchen, dick out, and bum rush me or something.

"Did you make a whole pot?" he asks.

I nod, glancing up at him for less than a second before looking away again. "Help yourself."

Danny takes a seat across from me, and I start fidgeting with my mug again. He keeps looking at me while I drink in silence, but his eyes never rest on me for more than an instant. What's his deal?

Does he want to talk about what happened? Because that's the last fucking thing I want to do. It's already hard enough to not think about it without actually discussing it.

"I have some stuff to catch up on today," he begins. "I'm going to start preparing the garden, and I'll be in town for a while too. You cool with sticking around here?"

"Yeah, sounds good," I say, but my words are forced and hollow.

Standing up with his mug, he holds his hand out toward me.

"Uh…" I say, my eyes wide. *What does he want?*

He raises his eyebrows at me. "You finished your coffee, right?"

"Oh." It's hard to keep the relief out of my voice. "Yeah, sorry," I say and hand him my mug.

Tapping my foot against the base of the kitchen cupboards, I watch as Danny puts on his shoes and leaves the house. I'm glad that he's clearing out for the day.

My gaze roams across the kitchen and the sunlight splashing across the tile and onto the wood floor in the living room. Gritting my teeth, I try to ward away the rising anger within me at the shit that Danny pulled on me last night. It's the exact reason that straight guys are kind of uncomfortable about gay dudes… because no matter how well you know someone, you can never trust that they won't try to come on to you. *He tried to fucking kiss me… and I pushed him away.*

But no matter how hard I try, it's impossible to forget that when he tried a second time, I didn't fight back. And why didn't I?

A current of regret and shame sweeps through me, threatening to drag me into its undertow. I could have pushed him away again. I could have decked him in the face just like he hit me – not that I would have ever wanted to hit Danny, but I *could* have, and he would have backed off. But I didn't.

Jesus, Curtis… you came *in his mouth.*

Releasing a growl of frustration, I pace across the wide space between the living room and the kitchen, stepping through the patches of sun that the windows have welcomed in. Was that his plan all along when he invited me out here? To wait until I was comfortable, then get me buzzed and see if he could take advantage of me?

A memory surfaces from earlier that night when we were on the flowline trail, when I took his hand to lead him through the dark. I shouldn't have done that, but Danny has always been hopeless in the dark. Is that how he got the wrong idea about me?

If I'm honest with myself, I kind of enjoyed leading him like that on the trail, but it's not because I'm *into* him or anything. I just liked feeling that we were close like we used to be. But then Danny went and made everything so goddamn complicated.

With sudden clarity, I realize all over again that my best and oldest friend had my *dick* in his mouth. My face smolders with a cruel heat, and I know I can't stay here anymore. It's time to get the hell out of this place.

Rushing into my room, I furiously begin packing. For as much as I wanted this to work out, and for Danny and I to get back what we had… it obviously hasn't worked out. My chest aches as I shove the clothes into my duffel bag, but I just can't do this anymore. I force my reluctant hands to keep packing, and it only takes fifteen minutes until I'm ready.

I know Danny is going to be hurt when he comes back, but I don't really care about that right now. He crossed a line last night when he came on to me, and stuff happened that shouldn't have. So he better damn well understand that I'm going to cut my stay short. After all, I never said how long I would stick around, so it's not like I'm going back on my word.

After tossing my bag into the backseat of my car, I turn the key and wait for the starter to finally bring the engine to life. At the end of the driveway, I give Danny's house one last look in the rearview mirror. My fingers feel clammy on the steering wheel, and for a short few seconds I wonder if I'm making a mistake.

Swallowing away the sourness in my mouth, I let off the brake and pull onto the road.

I'm several dozen sloping corners from Danny's house and about halfway to Victoria when I see the flashing lights of an ambulance ahead. My fingers tighten on the wheel, and I pull off to the side of the road as quickly as I can. My chest feels tight, and I close my eyes and wait as the emergency vehicle screams past with a blast of wind and sirens.

Unbidden, another set of sirens from my past fills my ears, dragging me back ten years to the crash. Eyes shut tightly and breaths coming fast, the moment of the impact forces itself on me. The shattering glass and screeching metal, the heaviness in the air, and the sight of the woman sprawled out on the pavement.

I want to get away from it, but I can't. Locked in the moment, I relive the next minutes with a sadistic clarity.

Not until long after normal traffic has resumed on the road am I finally released from my memories, breathless and with my fingers clenched around the steering wheel.

"Fucking hell," I hiss. It's been years since I've had a panic attack like that.

After giving myself a few more minutes to steady my breathing, I pull back onto the road and continue into Victoria. Except instead of following the signs for the ferry, I turn at the blue H sign.

Coming to a stop across from the emergency room entrance to the Victoria General Hospital, I turn off the engine and wait.

I should have left the hospital and gone to the ferry. I should have gotten off this goddamn island while I had a full day of driving in front of me.

"What will it be?" the bartender asks.

It takes a few seconds for me to drag my eyes up from the polished wood of the bar. "Beer is fine. The cheapest you have on tap."

"That kind of day, huh?"

I grimace, because at that moment the guy reminds me of Danny. Not physically or anything – the bartender is like forty and looks nothing like him – but it was something that Danny would say. He's always trying to be supportive and understanding, which is honestly something I could really use right now. If he weren't the source of the problem, that is.

"Here you go." The man nods to me and slides a glass across the counter.

"Thanks."

The beer is barely better than malt-flavored water, but I don't care. It has alcohol in it and it's cheap, which is all I care about right now.

If I just have a beer or two, I'll still be sober enough to drive. I glance at the clock above the bar. It's not even four o'clock yet. If I leave soon, I could be back on the mainland in time to find a place to park for the night, or maybe even splurge on a cheap motel.

For the hundredth time today, I wish Danny had never made a move like that and messed everything up between us. I was really enjoying my time out here. The weather can be rainy and cloudy, but it's generally warm, and the island itself… well, it's breathtaking.

Pushing my empty glass away from me, I flag down the bartender with two fingers. "I'll have another." I'm a little surprised how fast the first one went, but it's light beer, so it goes down easy, even if it does taste like crap.

I take a long drink of my second beer to claim it as mine before setting it back on the bar and getting up to take a piss. The bathroom is kind of dingy, and the urinal could use a good cleaning, but in a way it feels kind of fitting. Alcohol nipping at my fingertips, I unzip my jeans and pull my dick out. Even though I really have to go, I have to wait several seconds until I actually start to pee.

Washing my hands afterward, I stare into the mirror above the sink. It's covered in water splotches that have long since dried, but the guy staring back at me through the glass is clear enough. Brown hair and brown eyes, good build. Danny told me once that he thought I had a great smile. I try it out experimentally. Maybe he's right, maybe not. It just seems normal to me.

But what does normal even mean anymore? I've never fooled around with a guy before. I didn't want to. So why the hell did I go along with it?

Forcing back the thought, I splash water up onto my face, as if that will provide some semblance of clarity. The thing that bothers me the most is that the guy in the mirror… he was freaked out at first at what was happening last night. But after the first few minutes, he just didn't give a shit anymore, because it felt good. Damned good.

It didn't feel wrong at the time, even though now I wish it would have. That feeling didn't come until later.

Returning to my seat at the bar, I take another drink of my beer, which is slightly warmer than when I left. Making a face, I set it back down. The only thing worse than cheap, light beer is when it's warm.

I'm still going to drink it, of course.

Thinking back on earlier, on the hours I spent staked out in front of the hospital, I wonder again if those guys saved any lives today. That's the kind of shit that's actually important, right? Not whether a guy gets his rocks off with his best friend.

Former best friend, I correct myself.

In the scheme of things, it's so trivial that it's not even worth thinking about. So why am I so hung up about it?

Lots of straight guys have an experience with another guy at some point in their lives. It typically happens in their teens and not their late twenties, but what the hell does it really matter? Danny and I messed around. He seemed to enjoy himself, and… so did I. What's so wrong with leaving it at that? I'm not going to do it again, of course. But Danny will respect that. He'll have to.

Closing my eyes, I try to find solace in this new explanation. It works. Kind of.

Pulling out my phone, I tab down through my contacts until I reach the number I saved a few days ago. Taking a quick drink from my beer to bring it down to half, I tap out a message and send it.

Hey Lauren, interested in a drink?

"There you are," Lauren says, sitting down next to me as I start my third beer.

"I wasn't sure if you'd show up."

She gives me a curious look while waving down the bartender. "Why wouldn't I? Aside from the fact that you're Danny's friend, and that he's been going on about you since the day you came out here, I also happened to have fun the other night." With a smirk, she adds, "Besides, you're cute."

While I process everything Lauren has just said, she orders a glass of wine.

I like that she said I was cute, but I ignore that in favor of the other thing. "Danny has… talked about me?"

"Oh please. All the time."

Huh? If she says that he's been lusting after me since high school, I swear to God I'm going to walk out of this bar and get the hell back to the mainland tonight. "What kind of stuff?" I ask, holding my voice guarded.

Lauren takes a sip of her wine, searching my expression. "Oh, you know…"

"No, I don't."

Rolling her eyes, she pushes her glass back and sets her elbows on the bar. "Stuff like how you used to be such close friends, and how he felt horrible that you never talked anymore, and that you were a really good guy… stuff like that. Happy now?"

"Yeah," I say, feeling a weight tumble off my shoulders. "You want to eat here too?"

Chapter Eleven

Curtis

After we finished dinner and a few more beers – for me, anyway – Lauren insisted on driving. I'll need to get a ride back to my car from Danny at some point, but I'd rather not think about that now.

I don't see any point in informing her that the bag I retrieved from my car contains all the stuff that I own in the world, or that she's interrupting me on my getaway from Danny and the island. Thankfully she doesn't ask about it, either.

Compared to the worn interior of my car, Lauren's leather-clad Lexus is an unusual taste of luxury for me. I suppose that Danny's place might be considered *luxury* too, but that's different. His house and the furniture in it are beautiful, but there's something simple and authentic about his stuff that... I don't know, brings it down to earth.

But this Lexus, it doesn't make any concessions about being classy and expensive. It's meant to make a statement, and that's what it does as Lauren drives us west out of Victoria, taking the slopes and corners of Sooke Road even faster than Danny does. Outside, the yellow and orange lights of civilization flash past, reminding me that she's taking me back to a place I'm not sure I actually want to be.

I'm glad that her driving isn't making me sick, but maybe I'm just getting used to the twists and turns in the roads out here. Not only do I not feel ill, I'm contentedly full and pretty buzzed, in addition to the warm feeling in my crotch. That last part is because Lauren's hand found its way there briefly a few minutes ago.

She hasn't really been behaving herself in general. She was checking me out all through dinner and kept finding excuses to touch my shoulder and even my leg a few times. I can't say that I mind the attention, and I suppose I was checking her out too, just like I was the other night. But I still wasn't expecting her to practically grab my dick once we got in the car.

As we take a sharp corner particularly fast, Lauren tightens her hands on the wheel. "Damn," I say. "You're pretty aggressive."

Glancing over, she gives me a wry look.

"Driving, I mean," I clarify.

"I don't like going slow."

"Yeah, I can see that."

Turning onto the road that both she and Danny live on, she asks, "Would you rather we go to my place or Danny's?"

"Um, how about we go to your house?"

Even under the faint glow cast by the instrument panel, I can tell that she's smiling. "Oh? I thought you'd prefer to be at Danny's. I'm sure he wouldn't mind if I stayed over tonight…" Her voice trails suggestively.

Actually, he might. I'm pretty sure Lauren wants to mess around, and since I just did that with Danny last night, I don't know if he would be too impressed. "We should just go to your place."

Pulling into her driveway, Lauren turns off the engine with the push of a red button on the dash. "Come on, stud," she says as she steps out of the car.

Following her into her house for the second time this week, I kick off my shoes and shut the door behind us. Without waiting any longer, she drags me toward her and into a kiss. Her lips are soft and smooth, the way a woman is supposed to feel. But as she kisses me deeper, trying to rouse my tongue with hers, I can't help but think that something is missing… that this would be better if the touch were rougher, with a hint of stubble on those lips.

It's not even half an hour later when Lauren drops me off at the end of Danny's driveway. Retrieving my duffel bag from the trunk, I heave it over my shoulder and begin the walk toward his house. Behind me, the headlights of Lauren's Lexus swing across the yard as she backs up and drives away.

The engine's purr fades into the night until I'm left once more in darkness. I take slow steps past Danny's workshop and toward the front door. Not a single light is visible through the windows, making the house blend into the backdrop of the night. Apprehension fills my chest as I approach the door. I really hope Danny hasn't gone to sleep already.

Through the tiny glass panes set into the oak door, I see dim splashes of orange light. I try the handle, but it's locked. Lifting my hand, I knock instead.

The echo on the wood feels like such a lonely sound.

I wait, and it's not until nearly a minute later that I see his shape moving behind the door. When Danny opens it, touches of redness surround his eyes.

"I thought you left," he says cautiously. Behind him, the fireplace glows with dying embers.

"I'm back. If the offer to stay is still good."

He steps aside and holds the door open for me. Passing him, I drop my bag onto the floor. I can feel his gaze following me, but I don't know what he wants.

"You going to say where you were?" he asks.

I should tell him it's none of his business, because it's not. But I don't want to hurt him. I already feel bad, because I think he might have been crying earlier. Something I know he'd never admit to.

Finding my voice, I begin slowly. "I drove around for the day. Then I ran into Lauren at the bar and we sort of went back to her place." It feels like I've just confessed to a crime, but I haven't done anything wrong. What does it matter if I hang out with his neighbor?

Danny just watches me as comprehension overtakes his expression. "I see." His tone is cold, and I can tell he's pissed. It's the side of Danny that I hate seeing. His hair-trigger temper, his tendency to be hurt by something before he fully understands it. The problem is that he's usually right, and when he's upset it's probably because I fucked up.

"I'm sorry," I say hastily, unsure where I'm going with this. "I just thought that..." My words get quieter with each passing syllable, until the sounds fade wholly into silence.

His words fall like stones into the quiet dark. "I'm going to bed. Goodnight, Curtis." His eyes linger on mine, and then he turns away.

"Wait," I call after him.

He stops, his shoulders squaring. "What?"

Mouth partly open as though my voice suddenly got stuck in my throat, I just look at him for a moment. Then I push through my hesitation. "Last night... was a one-time thing. It's cool that you're gay or whatever, but I'm not that way, so could you please just forget that anything happened?"

I hold my breath and wait for his response.

"You can do whatever you want, Curtis, and if that's really what you want..." He stares down at the floor, shaking his head slightly. "Then sure, I'll pretend it never happened."

For everything we've been through, I don't know why this one thing has to be so much different, but it is. I hate that Danny is so stuck on this, but there isn't an easy way to make it right.

"Look," I reason. "I know you're mad, but–"

"I'm not fucking mad," he hisses, his eyes glinting in the dark. Their intensity cuts into me, hurting more than if he tackled me to the floor. I swallow, and I can feel emotion rising in my throat.

The air is still between us until he says, "I'm going to bed."

I watch him retreat to his room as I fight the urge to stop him. Not because I want to fool around or anything, but because I can't bear to see him like this. For all the times that Danny was there for me, supporting me, right now he's the one in pain. Not only can I not help him, but it's also unquestionably *my fault*. My fault for letting it go as far as it did, even when I knew that...

I stop myself, wondering for the hundredth time today why I *didn't* stop him from kissing me, or from moving his hands over my chest, or from tracing his tongue down my stomach. My face flushes, mixing embarrassment with my desire to somehow comfort him.

Rooted in place, I stare at his closed door. The most screwed up part about all of this is that thinking back on last night, what I regret most is that I never touched him in the way he did for me. Not only was that kind of selfish, but I feel like I missed out on something. I had my one gay experience, and I barely even *touched* Danny.

Forcing my feet to move, I return to my own room and drop my duffel bag onto the floor. Throwing myself back on the bed, I try to calm my racing mind, but it's a hopeless task. Conflict brews in my stomach as my thoughts flit relentlessly through my head.

And the thing that's really backwards? It's that right now I wish Danny were here with me – not because I *want* him or anything, but because I always used to feel better when he was around. Something about him just being there with me… it helps calm me down. And I could really use that right now.

Tenth Grade

Tossing the groceries into the passenger's side of my dad's truck, I hop up behind the wheel and slam the door. Why can't he go shopping for himself? He barely even works. And despite what he says, I don't believe that cashing a check every month counts as work.

I'm also fairly certain that he only let me get my driver's license so I could pick up stuff for him, because other than driving to school, those are the only times I get to use the truck.

I turn the key, but I have to wait for the engine to turn over three times before it actually starts. *What a piece of shit.* I grind my teeth in frustration as I pull out of the parking spot, giving the truck some more gas so it will actually get going. The engine grumbles, echoing my frustration, but reluctantly it moves faster.

Coming to the end of the row of cars, I glance to the left and to the right, and then I force the pedal down and make the turn. I'm just moving past the next row, nearly to the end of the parking lot, when I catch a blur at the edge of my vision.

Something is moving fast. Way too fast.

Adrenaline jets into my veins, and the next half-second feels like much more than that because I somehow have time to understand that the object is a motorcycle. And that it's going to hit me.

I close my eyes, but it doesn't matter, because it's impossible to block out the impact. Metal and glass scream as they're bent and twisted, and I'm thrown sideways against my seatbelt as two hundred kilos of motorcycle slam into the truck. Like a peal of thunder, it's over in an instant, but my ears are left ringing.

I hear a shout, and a man runs past the front of my truck. My neck aches, but I lean over anyway to watch him kneel beside someone lying on the pavement on the opposite side of my truck. At that moment, I come to two realizations.

The first is that the person lying unmoving on the black surface of the parking lot is the rider of the motorcycle. The second is that it's a woman.

The minutes pass, slowly, cruelly. My frantic breathing doesn't abate, but it has nothing to do with the trickle of blood from my cuts or the soreness in my neck or my buzzing headache. What's taking the ambulance so long?

Flashing lights of police cars are everywhere, but I can't seem to concentrate on any of it. My mind is covered in a fog that refuses to lift, and the harder I try to break free, to wake up from this nightmare, the more it presses in on me. And still there's no ambulance.

People move past, vehicles move past, time moves past. Some things I process, while others don't make a whole lot of sense.

The first ambulance finally arrives and the woman is loaded into the back.

The second ambulance on the scene is for me.

The paramedics talk in soft tones, trying to make me feel safe as they help me out of the passenger side door and onto the stretcher, but it doesn't help.

They load me into the ambulance, the doors close, and my stomach tells me that we're moving. Overhead, I hear the siren's muffled scream, and it makes me want to scream too.

The paramedics are talking to me, but the fog makes it hard to give them answers that are more than a couple words. A flashlight shines into my glazed eyes, then away, then back again.

"Likely concussion," one of them says.

Inside I feel like I'm crumbling, because I can't process what's just happened. What's *happening*. I want to shout at them that a concussion is not the problem. It's fucking not, because a woman was lying out there on the pavement.

I don't say anything, and no one listens.

At the hospital, I'm shuffled through the emergency room, and a doctor confirms that I have a concussion. A cut on my arm and another on my chin both get stitched up.

They tell me I'm being kept overnight for observation.

My dad comes in, and he says words that I don't really listen to. Ones about him not knowing what the fuss is about, because I look just fine. Then others about how the truck is totaled and why couldn't I have been paying more attention. The only thing I do listen to is when he mentions that the woman is in critical condition. That she's a mom to a three-year-old boy.

My dad leaves, and I don't feel any more alone than when he was here.

Later on, a cop that's dressed too nice for a cop comes to ask questions. He asks how fast I was going, and where I was coming from in the parking lot, and whether I was wearing my seatbelt. Then he says that the blood tests the hospital did came back negative for alcohol or drugs. He says that it's unlikely there will be any charges against me because I had the right of way and the motorcyclist was speeding, according to witnesses.

None of that matters, though.

I saw her lying on the pavement. He didn't.

Even after the ER doctor decides that the concussion isn't severe enough that I shouldn't sleep, I don't. And I don't really try because I don't want to. What if my dreams are worse than the events that won't stop running through my head? Worse than the memories cut into my mind with ink so fresh that it's still wet to the touch.

The next morning, my dad comes back.

"The woman on the motorcycle," he says, his voice seeming to hold a semblance of emotion for the first time since I arrived in the hospital. "She didn't make it."

Those four words are like lead weights landing on me, dragging me down with them.

She didn't make it.

I sit up in the hospital bed, and my dad pulls me into a quick hug. I accept it because I'm too numb not to, but he isn't who I need.

When he takes me home later that morning, I force myself through the motions.

Shower.

Get dressed.

Tie the laces on my shoes.

And then I run. I run through the chilled November air. I run to the park, through it, and past it. Until my lungs and throat sting, and I'm standing at the door of a familiar blue house with crisp paint.

When his mom answers the door, I force my face to the side as if that will hide the tears streaking down. I keep my voice as clear as possible and ask, "Is Danny home?"

"He is. Is everything okay, honey?" Her voice is soft and sweet, but she isn't the one that I need right now, either.

Still holding my face away, I struggle to get the words out. "Can I see Danny? I really need to see him."

"Of course," she says, her words lined with wary concern. But regardless of what she's thinking or worried about, she holds the door open and lets me pass without further questions.

For as fast as I ran here, I can't manage anything more than slow, careful steps as I walk downstairs and push open the door to Danny's room. He's at his computer watching some video clip, which he pauses.

"Oh, hey dude, I didn't know you were coming over. Where have you–" He cuts himself off when he sees my face. "What's wrong?"

I take a step forward, trying to find my words. "I... um..." But I can't keep going because I'm choking up with tears. Embarrassment burns red in my face for only a moment before Danny closes the distance between us and surrounds me with his arms. He draws me close, and I abandon my restraint, letting myself melt into him. Burying my face in his shoulder, I'm able to cry for the first time since the crash.

He holds me, his hand on my neck, as a flood of sadness pours out of me. I feel like I'm finally shattering apart under the pressure, and thank God that Danny is there to catch the pieces.

When at last he lets me go, I sit down on the edge of his bed. I just look at him, and he looks back. Yet still he doesn't ask what happened, and I love him for that.

Curling up under the blanket, I pull his pillow into my arms and squeeze. His scent surrounds me, and it's so comforting, because for all the bad that has happened, there's nowhere else in the world that I'd rather be right now.

And then, in the way that Danny always manages to do, he makes it just a little bit better. He slides under the covers beside me. Not *right* beside me, but near enough that I know he's there.

I almost wish he would come closer, which doesn't quite make sense to me. Whatever the reason, I'm glad he's here. With his hand resting on my arm, I finally sink into sleep.

Chapter Twelve

Danny

Like so many times before, the surface of the pool stretches out before me. Ripples pace across it like lazy messengers, whispering that the water is waiting for me.

Taking a deep breath, I dive in, grateful for the water rushing over me. I pull myself forward out of the dive and begin my first lap down the lane.

I'm alone in the pool, maybe even the whole gym. Earlier in the evening, that feat would have required a few stars to align, but at a quarter to midnight on a Friday night, I didn't really expect to run into anyone.

I'm going to regret staying up so late – something that seems to be happening a lot more often lately – and I'm definitely going to be sore from how hard I'm pushing myself, but I need this. I need it really fucking bad.

It's been a week since Curtis and I messed around, and aside from the following night, we haven't discussed it at all. When I saw Lauren drop him off, I was pissed. Enraged, even. But that's not going to help anything. It's not like she knew that anything had gone down between us. And Curtis... well, he's apparently straight as ever, so who am I to begrudge him for hooking up with a girl?

I grind my teeth in frustration. If only I could make my heart understand the situation like my mind does.

To be fair, the week has gone better than I feared. But it still hasn't been that great. Curtis is acting like nothing has changed between us, and even though it bugs me to no end, I've been humoring him. The only thing to have changed is that he tries to minimize the time we're in the same room and keeps our conversations short if possible.

But at least he hasn't talked about leaving again. He finished digging out the cistern hole a few days ago, and a guy is coming out to install the tank later this week, so there isn't a whole lot for Curtis to do anymore. I haven't asked how he's planning on occupying the rest of his time, because like a lot of other things I want to ask, it's really none of my business.

For the next hour and a half, the chlorinated water retreats under my advance, restoring my emotional stability even as it saps my physical energy. I don't mind the trade off because I know it's a necessary one. And there's the added perk of staying in damn good shape. Not that Curtis cares about how I look, because – I make imaginary finger quotation marks in my mind – *he's not that way.*

Frustration burns through me like wildfire, torching everything inside in an instant. I stop abruptly in the middle of the lane, my chest heaving from the exertion as water drips down my face. I've been in the pool so long that the chlorine is starting to get to me.

I wish I could get him out of my head. I've had plenty of hookups since I came out in college, and even a few before then. Why does it have to be so different with Curtis?

I fooled around with a hot guy. He got off, I got off, and that was it. Why can't I be satisfied with that like I have plenty of other times?

The answer is obvious, of course.

Pushing onward through the water, my mind wanders back to the night I promised to forget. To that easy-going smile and the taste of mint gum, to the dark silk of his eyes and the smooth skin over hard muscles.

When I made my move that night, I figured there were two possible outcomes. Either he'd push me away, or he'd go for it. I didn't consider the follow through – namely that even though he *did* go for it, he would feel guilty as shit about it afterward.

It makes me hurt for him. I don't know exactly what his deal is, but regardless, I know that it's tough as hell to navigate through being unsure what you're into. But what can I do for him?

Coming to a stark realization, I stop once more in the middle of my lane, treading water as I pull in breaths thick with chlorinated air. It's not enough to just avoid bringing up the topic. If he's truly the best friend I've ever had, then I owe it to him to not push him again. Not like I did last week, anyway. Straight, gay, bi, or whatever he is, I'm not going to make a move like that again.

But damn if I wouldn't give anything to be with him that way again. Not that it matters, because I don't think it's ever going to happen. He made it clear that it's not his thing, and I'm not so naïve to believe that a single gay experience makes a guy gay. It would be great if it did, but it doesn't. It was a spur of the moment thing, he was horny, and he went along with it. That's it.

Through labored breaths, I bite down on the emotions rising in my throat.

Flailing myself with a midnight workout was supposed to help tame the conflict inside me, not set it loose again. With one last glance at the clock on the wall now pointing just past one a.m., I decide to call it quits for tonight. The pool will be here tomorrow.

Chapter Thirteen

Danny

"Curtis?" I call from the living room. I don't *think* he left the house, but I haven't seen him in a while.

"Just a second." His voice echoes across the house, and I follow the sound toward the hallway, expecting to find him in his room. Instead I catch myself on the door to the guest bathroom. Curtis is standing in front of the toilet, shaking his dick off.

Noticing me staring, he angles away as he zips up. "Um, do you mind?"

"Shit, sorry," I sputter, forcing my eyes to the ground as he reaches out to flush. "I didn't know you were peeing."

"Whatever," he says with an annoyed shrug as he washes his hands. "It's not like you haven't seen it before, I guess."

My eyes bulge and my face burns hot. *Did he really just say that*? Although maybe he was referring to us showering together back in high school or something.

Hovering around the corner from the bathroom, I wait until he comes out.

"What's up?" he asks, wiping his hands on his shorts.

"I was hoping to, uh," I swallow, fighting to forget that I just walked in on him pissing.

"Yeah?"

Reddening, I push forward with my original request. "I thought we could talk quick."

"Uh oh," he says, sounding like he's not entirely joking. "This is where you tell me you've changed your mind and that I have to leave?" His expression flickers with uncertainty, and I get the feeling that he's more afraid I'm going to bring up the forbidden topic than kick him out.

Does he actually think that I'd do either of those things? "Dude, that's not it at all. Can we talk in the kitchen?"

Curtis still looks uneasy, but he nods and follows me, taking a seat on the opposite side of the table.

"So… I got you something," I begin carefully, sliding an envelope toward him across the polished wooden surface.

Ignoring it, he watches me carefully before asking, "What for?"

"You think you're the only one who can a remember a birthday? It's tomorrow, right?"

He grins a sly smile. "You're shit at remembering dates. I'm surprised you even got the month right." His tone is amused, partly cautious, but his eyes flick downward to the envelope.

"Well," I admit, "I did double check it on your Facebook."

He raises his eyebrows and gives me a knowing look. "There it is. Anyway, you didn't have to get me anything, you know."

Sweat nestles inside the creases of my palms, and I try to sound nonchalant, like it doesn't matter what he thinks of what I got him. "You're supposed to get gifts on your birthday."

"I guess. I can't believe I'm turning twenty-nine. It feels so old."

"Well, I'm still twenty-eight," I tease. But not for *that* much longer. Six months and we'll be the same age.

"I always forget that you're younger." He takes a moment to just look at me. "Don't look so surprised," he says. His cheerfulness fades as he watches me. "We've been friends for eighteen years."

"That's a long time."

"Even though it doesn't feel like it," he says, his tone pensive.

For me, it's felt like far more than eighteen years, but that's something that I neither want to admit nor discuss. So I let his statement hover uncontested between us until the kitchen is wrapped once more in sweet silence.

"Are you going to open it?"

Abandoning his suspicion, he snatches the envelope off the table. "Of course I am." He tears into the paper and pulls out a five pack of mint gum. A sheepish smile spreading across his face, he looks up at me. "Is it that obvious that I'm addicted to this stuff?"

"Yeah, kind of. There's something else in there too."

"Oh?" Squeezing together the sides of the envelope so it opens up in the middle, he withdraws the folded paper inside. He glances at me as he opens up the sheet, and his eyes skim over it. "Occupational first aid?"

"It's a class," I explain.

"First aid?" Curiosity presses at the edges of his voice and his expression.

I'm still sweating and my heart is beating fast in my chest. Why am I so nervous that he won't like what I got him? "It's the prerequisite class before you can begin EMT training. I figured you've always been interested in that, so I thought you might, um, enjoy it."

I keep waiting for him to show some kind of reaction, but he just stares at me. "Anyway," I add, my voice falling a bit as I reach over to point at the bottom of the paper, "It's just two weeks, starting next Monday, so I figured you could get it done while you're he–"

"Look, Danny," he cuts me off, finally breaking out of his trance. "I can't accept this."

I feel my eyebrows pulling together as the acidic taste of disappointment hits the back of my tongue. "I know it's kind of a weird gift, and I know you've never actually *said* that you're interested in working in emergency services or anything, but I always sort of thought that…" I pause and take a breath so I can keep reasoning with him, but his expression makes me stop.

"I can't," he says, his voice hard. "Believe it or not, I do know how much this class costs, and I'm not going to just take your money like that."

It *was* over seven hundred dollars, but it would have been worth every bit to see Curtis finally getting to do something that's important to him.

"It's a gift," I whisper in futility, feeling wetness behind my eyes and hating how close it is to the surface.

Folding the paper back up, he turns it over in his hand before setting it on the table. "I'm sorry."

Frustration balls up in my chest, winding itself into a tighter knot the longer I sit here. "It's fine," I tell him, not bothering to conceal the lie. I stand slowly, purposefully, leaving him at the table as I step out onto the deck behind my house.

"Danny, come on," Curtis calls after me as I slam the sliding door shut.

My feet carry me over the wooden planks, down the path, and finally onto the dock. Crossing my legs beneath me, I lean my shoulder against the dock piling and close my eyes. I told myself when I left Thunder Bay that I would never cry over Curtis again, and I'm not about to break that promise now.

I take a breath, drawing the overcast day into my lungs, and it takes all the strength I have to hold it inside.

In rare form, the island seems to comprehend this moment, and it reaches out with tiny wet hands. Blown in on the wind, the rain kisses the dock and my skin alike.

One by one, drops slide down my face and onto the planks beneath me, painting dark splotches onto the wood. But I haven't broken my promise, because those drops are the rain and only the rain.

Even the ones that are hot and a little salty.

That's just because of the sea air, I think.

Chapter Fourteen

Danny

"I was thinking we could go hiking again today," I begin, trying not to look too hopeful.

Curtis glances up at me from the steaming cup of coffee in front of him. "You sure that's a good idea?"

My fork stops halfway to my mouth, and a thick square of pancake glistening with syrup stands in the air. We haven't really talked since yesterday, which is making me feel pretty lousy because today is actually his birthday. "Um, okay?"

"I could still use a little, uh, space," he says.

The clock on the wall grinds to a temporary halt as I stare, expecting him at any moment to admit to his joke, crack a smile, and tell me, *Dude, you should have seen your face!*

He doesn't.

The clock's second hand resumes, and a glob of syrup slips from my forkful of pancake onto the plate. Like watching a firework that was lit but still hasn't gone off, I keep staring at him. His eyes slide away from mine, and a hollow feeling burrows down my throat and into the place behind my ribs.

"If that's what you want," I say, and I hate every word. But what the hell else can I say?

His expression softens, venturing toward remorse but stopping shy. "You're a good friend, Danny." He's about to say more, but I don't want him to.

"I get it. You don't have to explain yourself." My voice is tight, but my chest is tighter. Taking a last swig of my own coffee, I abandon the half eaten pancake on my plate and get up from the table.

"Danny," he calls after me as I walk toward my room. "What are you doing?" He sounds upset, but this is what he wanted, right?

Bitterness prickles along my tongue, but it's not from the coffee. "Giving you space."

"Come on, you know that's not what I meant."

Except it *is* what he meant. He can't ask for space and then be surprised when he gets it.

I keep walking away and I don't turn around, not until after I've shut the door to my room harder than necessary.

Maybe I was right back then. Back in high school during the thunderstorm, when I had a chance to push the issue between us. Something could have happened that night, I could feel it. But if this is how things would have turned out between us afterward, it was probably for the best. At least we got a few more years of friendship. Not that most of those years counted for anything at all.

Was it destined to never work between us?

My last thought lingers as I sink down to the floor and rest my head against the door. Sometimes Curtis is just too damn much.

The saws in my workshop have been silent today. I haven't gotten another order since finishing that dining table from hell, which is fine with me. Especially since I'm so distracted that I'd probably mess up whatever I was working on.

Instead, I'm gluing scraps together into butcher-block cutting boards. The work isn't difficult, just time consuming. Which is perfect right now.

Most of my scrap is black walnut, cherry, or maple because those are my favorite woods to work with. Spreading a line of wood glue between each piece, I clamp them together and set each cutting board on my workbench to dry.

I could sell these, but usually I just give them away as gifts. Since they're made of scraps, they're often not quite perfect, but my neighbors still seem to like them. Maybe I should have given one of these to Curtis for his birthday instead... but what's he going to do with a cutting board? Christ, he doesn't even have his own place.

I toss another clamped cutting board onto the bench to dry and survey my scrap bins. There's probably enough wood there to make fifty boards, but that would take all day. Who knows, maybe that's what I need. Maybe that's what *Curtis* needs – for me to just be out of the way.

"You're moping," Lauren diagnoses me from the kitchen where she's making dinner for both of us.

I mute the TV and glance at her from over the back of the couch. Like nearly all the furniture in her house, it's upholstered with some kind of faux leather. "I am not. Moping involves being upset about something, which I am not." At this point I'm trying to convince myself more than her.

Without turning away from the pan of chicken curry that smells so good it makes me want to lick the air, she fires back, "Just because I don't know what's bothering you doesn't mean I can't tell that something *is.*" Now she does bring her gaze to bear. "Who is it?"

"Screw you," I snap. "Why do you assume it's a guy?"

She shrugs and adopts a sardonic smile. "I guess it could be a girl, but I just don't see it. Can you even get it up for a girl?"

I laugh, shaking my head at how much I enjoy having Lauren as a neighbor, despite how fast and loose she plays with the insults. "I managed it once..."

She rolls her eyes. "So it's definitely a guy. My money is on Curtis."

Now I actually glare at her. "I don't want to talk about it."

"Let me guess. You came on to him, but then he blew you off?"

My face reddens. *More like I blew* him, *and then he came in my mouth.* "Um, no. He's straight, we're just friends. End of story." *Also, he's avoiding me.*

Lauren scoops up two platefuls of rice and curry and carries them into the living room. I move my feet to the floor so she can sit down beside me on the couch.

She hands me a plate and says, "Sorry you're crushing on him."

"I am *not.*" I scowl and take my first bite. "Oh Jesus, that's good."

Smugness fills her expression, as if the quality of her food is somehow indicative of the accuracy of her assertion on what's bothering me.

"How did you learn to make this, anyway?"

"Indian roommate in college," Lauren admits through a mouthful. We eat in silence, which I'm grateful for. It's hard enough to keep my mind off Curtis when I see him seven days a week. Is it so much to ask to not talk about him when I'm not even home?

We've almost finished when Lauren adds, "I get it, though. He's really cute." She watches me for several seconds, but when I refuse to respond, she moves on. "What are your plans for Easter? You going to visit your family?"

"No, just going to stick around here this year."

"Mm," Lauren murmurs. "Well, I'm going to be gone all day tomorrow in Vancouver. So you'll have to find another place to hide from Curtis."

"I'm not *hiding* from him."

"Sure you are. This is, what, your third time here this week?"

Chapter Fifteen

Danny

"Hold up," Curtis says as I try to make a getaway from the kitchen after making myself a sandwich. I haven't cooked a meal for both of us since he asked me for *space*, whatever that means.

"Yeah?" I ask, eyeing him. What's he up to?

He seems to detect my suspicion at his deliberate attempt to start a conversation, and that makes him hesitate, if only for a moment. "You want to grab a beer tonight? It's been a while since we did anything. Besides bum around the house, that is."

It would be stupid if he tried to count that anyway, because we've been more or less avoiding each other since he *asked* for that.

My expression tightens, because the last thing I want to do right now is get beers with Curtis. Maybe it's immature to be acting upset with him, but I have my pick of reasons – he's been avoiding me for days on end, he probably slept with Lauren the day after we messed around, and he refused the birthday gift that I got for him.

For the first time, the thought crosses my mind that I should just tell him to get lost. But part of me knows that that truly would be the end of our friendship.

"Sorry, I can't," I say, sounding anything but apologetic. "I have plans tonight."

In response, he just stares with troubled features.

"Why are you looking at me like that?" I demand.

"Because" he snaps, "I think you're full of shit and that you're not actually busy."

Despite everything, I almost laugh when he glares at me, because the look is so uncharacteristic of him. But the humor is tempered by the realization that Curtis is actually mad at me too.

"Look, I don't want to talk anymore about... any of this. I just don't. So there's no point in getting a drink."

His eyes are fierce, ready to jump at an argument, but if that's what he wants, then he's going to be disappointed.

"I don't want to talk about anything," Curtis says. "I just want to get a drink with a buddy of mine. He and I used to go out sometimes, and it was fun. I guess if that's over with, I can deal with it, but that would be too bad." He holds his breath, keeping his expression sincere. It seems easy for him to do, maybe because he's actually telling the truth.

I stare for several seconds without speaking, just scrutinizing him. Scratching my jaw just below my ear, I concede, "I, um, guess we could grab a beer, then. I don't want to stay out too long, though."

"You got it," he says, making a point not to smile.

And damn it if a part of me isn't excited at the thought of hanging out with Curtis again. I'm still mad at him for probably sleeping with Lauren – or whatever it was they did – because that was fucked up. *Who does that?* But it's going on seven days of us acting awkward as shit around each other, and it's getting old fast.

"I'll drive," I announce as we leave the house.

Curtis raises an eyebrow. "It's a short walk."

Pretending like I didn't hear him, I pull out the key fob to my truck and unlock it as we approach. It might not be far, but I don't want to risk the uncomfortable quiet on the walk there – that pervasive silence that has plagued so many of our interactions lately.

At the bar, Curtis directs us to a table in the corner, even though I don't understand why it matters because this place is never busy anyway.

"Just one beer," I say, fidgeting with my coaster after we order.

"Sure," he says casually. "Don't worry, I have plans later tonight too."

I know he's lying, but it's so obvious that I think he must have meant it to come off that way.

When the waitress arrives with our beers, we clink them together like we're supposed to and each of us takes a long drink.

"How have you been?" I ask, trying to sound sincere, even though it's a loaded question for more than a few reasons. And it's ironic that I even have to ask, not only because he's staying in the same house with me, but also because an honest answer on his part is neither one that he's willing to give nor one that I'm particularly interested in hearing.

"Good." Curtis shrugs and looks away from me. "Actually, I'm thinking about heading back to Thunder Bay soon."

Resentment creeps into my chest, and my face gets hot. *He's leaving? Just like that?*

Curtis must not like something he sees in my expression, because he adds quickly, "Not because… you're not a good host or anything. But I'm still jobless, and I can't just live off savings much longer. I have to start living my life again."

I release a slow breath. What he's saying is true, but is it really the reason he's leaving? As upset as I've been, I don't want his time here to be a bad memory.

Reacting to my unspoken thoughts, he says quietly, "Come on, Danny boy, it's not like that."

My eyes snap to his. He hasn't called me that since back when we were younger. I try to keep the smile off my face, but I don't do a very good job.

"There he is," Curtis says, grinning back. "You haven't cracked a smile in like a week, you know?"

I wonder why. "Yeah, yeah," I say, ending the line of discussion with a purposeful drink of my beer.

After waiting to see if I say anything else, he ventures, "Why did you decide to move all the way out to the island?"

"I needed a change."

Curtis just watches me like he's trying to figure me out, and I don't like it. Taking a long drink of my beer to finish it off, I motion for the waitress to bring another one while I wait for the questions from Curtis that I know are coming.

Except he doesn't ask a question at all. "I missed you," he says quietly. "After you left for Toronto."

I nod to the waitress as she drops off my second beer. "I missed you too," I say, but my words are guarded. I steal a sip while Curtis watches me. I can see the thoughts moving around in his head, and it makes me nervous.

"What ever happened with swimming?" he asks. "Do you still do it competitively?"

"Not since I left Toronto," I concede. My fingers close around my glass, and I take another long drink. So much for just having one, but I can't handle this trip into the past without a little help.

"Why not?" he presses. "You're still in your twenties and in great shape. You could get back into it."

Trying not to focus on his comment about me being in "great shape," I fight back the rising irritation that he's not relenting.

"Look, man," I say, setting down my beer harder than necessary. "I'm just not *good* enough anymore. I might have been when I was in college, but I fucked up that chance. I really enjoy swimming, but I'm not good enough to compete, and I won't ever be again."

At seeing his intent expression, I try to reel in my frustration as I finish, "Can you just drop it?"

"Yeah," he says quietly. "Sure." The hurt in his voice makes me feel guilty. It's a bad combination, because I'm already mulling over my college days, and going back to those memories never ends with me in a happy place.

Nearly an hour later and our conversation has covered a dozen boringly safe topics – none of which did anything to shake the lingering memories of college that Curtis dredged up. I've also just finished my fourth beer and am well on my way to being plastered.

"Let's get out of here." Curtis shoots me a pointed look, but I refuse to meet his eyes. I raise a swaying hand for another beer.

Curtis grabs my hand with his, practically crushing my fingers in his grip. "Damn it, Danny," he curses. "You trying to get shit-faced or what?"

I shrug, slurring my words. "Wouldn't be the worst thing."

The waitress hasn't even come back to us yet, but Curtis throws a pair of twenties on the counter. "I got it," he says. "We're going."

"You shouldn't," I argue, staring at the bills curling up on the table as I dig in my back pocket for my wallet.

"I said I got it," he snaps. "Now stand up or I'm going to drag you out of here."

I give him a look, and for a moment I consider whether another beer would be worth getting dragged out by Curtis. I'm going to feel like shit tomorrow no matter what, so what's the difference?

His eyes get wide when he sees I'm actually mulling it over. "Jesus, Danny. Can we not do this right now?"

After tipping my glass up to drain the last few drops into my mouth, I slam it down on the table, *hard*. The noise catches the waitress's attention, and a disapproving look gets sent my way. I mumble an apology before stumbling out behind Curtis.

I'm fishing in my front pocket for my keys, but I can't seem to find them. "Hey," I call up to Curtis. "You know where my keys are?"

He's standing beside my truck in front of the driver's door, holding up something in the dark. "These keys?"

"Screw you," I growl. "I didn't say you could drive."

"We'll walk then," he says. "Because you sure as hell aren't going to."

I glare at him before acquiescing to his terms. "Fine, you drive then." Hopping up into the passenger's side, I make a point to scowl as Curtis takes us home.

A short ride later, I jump down onto the gravel of my driveway, catching hold of the truck to balance myself.

"You going to be okay?" he asks, appearing beside me and trying to put his arm around my back to steady me.

Bristling, I shove him away. "I don't need your help."

Walking ahead of me, Curtis doesn't respond as he unlocks the front door and leaves it hanging open for me. I follow him inside and across the wide living room to the kitchen.

He wordlessly pours a glass of water and sets it in front of me. I glare, but I take the glass anyway and drink it down. I know I'm pretty buzzed, but I'm not smashed or anything. Four beers isn't that crazy. Still, I'm going to have to drink quite a bit more water if I'm going to avoid a hangover.

Curtis gets water for himself too, before returning his attention to me. "I didn't... you know... with Lauren."

"I don't care what you did or didn't do," I growl, annoyed that my tongue feels so sluggish.

"Seriously. I didn't."

"You can fuck her if you want. I don't care." My eyes are hard as I stare him down.

"I *didn't*," he says again.

"So what were you doing over there, huh? Sitting out watching the stars? Making brownies? Goddamn, Curtis. If you're going to lie, you might as well try to be convincing about it."

He sighs, dropping his gaze to the counter. "That's why I went over there, but... I didn't. I told her that I'd had too much to drink, and I asked her to take me home."

"And was that true?" My question hangs between us, as though suspended from the ceiling by invisible strings.

Curtis's lips are set into a line, and conflict brews in his expression. But he doesn't answer me.

My voice descends toward spitefulness as I ask, "So you didn't fuck my friend because you didn't think you could get it up, or because you didn't want to be with a woman? It has to be one of those two things, because God knows it wasn't because you wouldn't do it for the sake of our friendship."

As soon as the words are out, I regret them.

His face is tinged with red as his shoulders rise in a shallow breath. "I think you should go to bed before you end up saying more hurtful shit." Before I can respond, he walks away, leaving me alone in the kitchen.

Crap. Even as I was saying that to him, I knew I shouldn't. He's probably going to avoid me for another week now.

Filling up my glass from the sink, I drain it before topping it off once more and carrying it to my room. I want this night to be over.

Stripping down completely and sliding into bed, I flick off the light and try to forget about how the time with Curtis has gotten away from me and gone to shit. Already the buzz in my fingertips is beginning to fade, even though I'd rather it endure and carry me through the night.

It feels hot in my room, although I'm not entirely sure if the alcohol is to blame for that. I throw off the blanket, but it takes me a minute to realize that I'm still sweating. Pushing the sheet down to my waist, I let the air touch my skin. It feels good, and before long, I can feel myself drifting toward sleep.

The first creak on the hardwood would never have woken me on its own. But the second one, slightly louder than the first, is enough to rouse me.

My eyes open and are met by darkness and silence. I don't know how much time has passed since I fell asleep, but the hours at the bar feel distant.

I hear another sound, and as my vision fights to adjust to the darkness, I glimpse movement, close to the bed. It's Curtis, it has to be.

What's he doing here?

Pulse firing through my veins, I consider for a wild moment that he might be here to… I don't know, get back at me for what I said earlier. But Curtis could never do that. He already carries too much guilt over having hurt someone. Far more guilt than any one person should ever possess.

It's dark but not completely devoid of light, so I lower my eyelids as he comes close. Whatever he's doing here, I don't want him thinking I'm awake.

Another sound – right beside me this time, sends my heart racing again. Lying on my back with the sheet around my waist, I feel incredibly exposed. What is he *doing* here?

I can hear his breathing over the sound of my own, but even so, I almost jump when his fingers brush against my skin. Holding my breath steady, I continue to feign sleep as he draws a line up the side of my stomach.

It takes all of my willpower to stop myself from grabbing him and pulling him to me. But I want to know what he's going to do. I'm curious if he'll spook himself and leave as inexplicably as he came, or if he'll just… keep going.

His fingers skim over my exposed chest, hesitant at first, but becoming more daring. He even pauses to touch my nipple. His breathing gets heavier, and it's hard to keep mine from doing the same.

Forcing my stomach to continue its smooth and even pattern moving up and down, I try to somehow keep my dick from going nuts. It's only half hard, but I don't usually wear underwear to bed, so it basically has free reign to do what it wants. It's already pushing up against the sheet, but it hasn't flopped over and charged into the air yet, so that's something I guess.

His touch rises further to my collarbone and then to the base of my neck. He trails his thumb along the edge of my jaw, traversing the light covering of stubble from not having shaven today.

Curtis is *touching* me.

The absurdity of it makes my head swirl, because I don't know what to do about it and I don't know what to think. The only thing I know is that I can't let him keep going, because he's driving me crazy with lust.

Letting my eyes slowly open, I stare up through the darkness to where he's watching me. He freezes, and the pressure on my skin disappears as he attempts to move away.

Before he can, I catch him swiftly around the wrist and hold him tight. He doesn't try to bolt, but he doesn't move toward me either. If it weren't for his pulse – pounding hot and swift through the underside of his wrist – I might have thought he wasn't real at all. Silent and still, he remains completely frozen, his anxious breathing the only betrayal of his presence.

"It's not polite to touch someone while they're sleeping," I whisper.

Eleventh Grade

Almost invisible in the dark, Curtis is leaning over me with his hand resting on the bare skin of my ribs when I awaken. He's so close that I can feel the heat from his chest.

"What are you doing?" I ask, my voice quiet.

In an instant, Curtis recoils, putting distance between us as he stuffs himself back into his sleeping bag.

Stillness pools around us while I wait for a response that doesn't come.

What the hell was he doing? His bed is too small for both of us to fit, so usually we just camp out on the floor together when I stay over. But I've stayed over here dozens of times, and he's never done anything like that before.

"Curtis?"

Unmoving from his sleeping bag, he breathes, "Don't tell my dad."

"What am I supposed to not tell him?" I demand. "I don't even know what you were doing." *Although I do have an idea.*

"I wasn't doing anything," Curtis hisses. "But don't you say a fucking word about this to anyone, or I swear to God, Danny, I'll never talk to you again." His voice is so cold it makes me shiver.

Fear grips my throat with strong fingers, and I swallow hard. Curtis has never spoken to me like that before, not once. And as much as I want to ask him what he was doing before I woke up, I can't bear the thought of losing him.

"Okay," I say.

Chapter Sixteen

Curtis

My heart is pounding, and guilt and embarrassment are burning inside me, but I can't leave because Danny has my wrist in an iron grip. He seemed pretty drunk when he went to sleep, and I never imagined he would actually wake up.

I also didn't bother to think up an explanation if I got caught doing this. *Again*. Even though the other time was years ago.

Not that there could *be* any explanation. At least not one other than the truth. That I'm here because I've been haunted by what we did together. That I haven't been able to get it – or Danny – out of my mind.

Have I always been drawn to him? In high school and before that even? The thought makes me shiver, and I know that he feels it through his grip on my wrist.

"I…" I stall, trying to find words for something that I can't describe or explain or reason with.

Maybe Danny knows that, because he doesn't press me to finish my sentence, not even after that solitary syllable has long since faded into the dark corners of his room. Instead, he tugs me gently toward him as he scoots over to make room on the bed.

Beneath the sheet lying across his waist, I can see the outline of him and know that he's turned on. It makes the arousal coursing through my veins rise even closer to the surface, eroding the voice of inhibition that's frantically telling me to get out of here.

Planting my knee on the edge of the bed, I let him pull me up onto the mattress. The sheet is soft innocence on my skin, a satin deception, because what's about to happen won't be innocent at all. But I don't care.

I want this.

I want *Danny*.

The last time we did this, he was in charge. He took care of me, guiding me as he lavished his affections on me. But even as nervous as I am, I want this time to be different. I'm not going to let my own fears cheat me out of being with him the way I want.

At that moment, the desire inside overcomes my hesitation, and I finally stop resisting. Leaving the sheet covering him, I kneel on either side of his hips and rotate my grip so that I'm the one holding him by the wrists. Forcing his arms back onto the bed, I dip my head downward and press my lips against his.

He still smells vaguely like beer, but that's only an afterthought because he tastes so goddamn good. The roughness of his lips works away on mine, washing away my defenses like waves crush the sand at the rising tide. The inexorable, implacable tide.

For an instant I remember the way Lauren kissed me that night, how she felt too soft and too feminine and too... *not-Danny*.

I force the memory away, and I press my tongue hard against his. He pushes back like I want him to, unapologetic.

I might regret this tomorrow, but fuck if I'm going to lie to myself tonight. Right now, in this second, I need him. More than I've ever needed anyone.

I release his hands, and they roam up my chest before cupping my face to pull me closer. I suppress the irritation that I'm wearing clothes at all, albeit just a t-shirt and gym shorts. Grinding my hips forward, I rub my cock against his, hating that the sheet and the nylon fabric of my shorts are teaming up to keep us apart.

Beneath me, Danny moans. Sensual at first, the timbre changes as I shift a hand to rub his nipple. The sound descends into a throaty growl, and Danny turns his head to the side and breaks the kiss. Staring up at me, the evasive blue of his eyes is gone, replaced with a dark fire that gets its color from the shifting shadows.

Not wanting to be clothed any longer, especially since Danny is already half naked, I tug off my shirt and shorts. Fully exposed, the first ashen twilight of the coming morning touches my skin, lending definition to my body like an artist's charcoal strokes.

I don't mind, because I want Danny to see me. I want him to want me.

My fingers close gently around the edge of the sheet, and I pull it down, uncovering him completely. Sitting back on my heels so my balls are resting just beside his cock, I stare at him.

"What do you want?" he asks, his voice husky.

I lower my gaze and a hand along with it, sliding it down over his chest and stomach before caressing the side of his cock. Unable to hold back any longer, I wrap my fingers around him.

I've known for years that Danny was uncut, but until now, it was never an important detail. Swallowing nervously on account of the boundary that I'm crossing, I focus on his heat as my hand moves up and down. I love the way the skin grows taut around the head when it backs off from the tip.

His hands lie open at his side, like he's letting me do whatever I want. More than anything else so far, that thought turns me on so damn much that I can feel a crystal clear drop of precome appearing at the tip of my dick. Brushing it onto my thumb, I close my fingers around him again and roll the slippery fluid over the dark head of his cock that's sexy as sin.

His lips pull to the side into a smile, because like every guy everywhere, he knows that precome is better than any kind of lube you could ever buy. To give him a drop of mine seems strangely personal, and I like that feeling.

My eyes flash up to his, trying to glean some insight into how he's feeling. Danny is usually easy to read, but in this murky darkness it's tricky. Still, I can sense his desire, mixed with something less savory. Hesitation, I think.

"You don't have to do this," he says quietly.

Unrelenting in the up and down motion of my hand, I breathe, "I want to."

"Really," he presses, his voice softening as he pushes my hand away. "Don't do anything you aren't comfortable with."

If I didn't know him so well, I might think he was trying to dissuade me because he doesn't want to keep going. But even as the filaments of insecurity inside me cast doubt over the meaning of his words, the part of me that's not a complete idiot knows that Danny would never do that. After being friends for so many years, I know him better than I do any other person. The truth is, he's always watched out for me, and he's always tried to protect me. And that's what he's doing now.

What he doesn't know is that… *I want this.*

"I won't," I promise him, holding his eyes with mine for seconds that pass like minutes.

Then I lean down over him, with one hand cupping his balls and the other guiding his cock upward. Wetting my lips, I take him into my mouth. He tastes like heat and sweat and sex, and I love it.

Drawing down my hand around the base, I pull until his skin becomes tight over his head. Still, it won't go all the way down, because his dick is a bit too big for it to stretch over.

Moving my mouth up and down, I roll my tongue around the end, tasting the line where his foreskin meets the softer, more exposed part. I never thought I would ever say or even *think* this, but I let him out of my mouth just long enough to admit, "Your cock is perfect. Fucking. Perfect."

His only response as I take him back in my mouth is to squirm underneath me, turning his head to the side like he can hardly take it anymore. Recognizing where I'm sending him, and not wanting it to happen yet, I back off, leaning in one last time to lick him from base to tip before I move back up to kiss him again.

Tingling with voracity, his tongue grapples with mine like he's trying to start a fight in my mouth. I like that I'm driving him nuts, that I'm the one in the lead this time. It feels more natural, still new and definitely a little weird, but somehow familiar.

His breathing seems to settle a bit as the minutes pass since I had him in my mouth, until I'm confident that he's not going to come right away. I stare down into his vulnerable expression. Danny was always the assertive one… the one who knew the solution to everything, and I love that for once his boundless self-assurance appears to have limits.

"What do you want me to do?" I ask.

"Nothing you don't want to," he says, echoing his words from earlier.

I clench my jaw, and my head buzzes with frustration that he's being so careful around me, treating me as though I'm some small fragile thing. I let the exasperation ring through my voice as I say, "Damn it, Danny. I *want* to, okay?"

He bites his lip, like he doesn't trust himself to say what he wants.

"Spit it out," I command, sitting on his hips as I push his shoulders down. Not too rough, but enough so that he can feel my strength.

His eyes shimmer with reservation as he finally fulfills my demand. "I... I want you inside me."

I pause. I take a breath. I was not expecting that. I figured he'd ask me to finish sucking him off.

I'm not even sure *how* to go about doing what he's asking, at least not in more than a theoretical sense. I've never done that before with a girl. Not like *that*. Thought about it, sure. But never done it.

"Sorry," he says hastily, backpedaling with a voice full of deference. "I shouldn't have said that. You don't have to. We can go back to what we were doing. That's what I'd like." He flashes me a small smile, and he nods reassuringly.

I almost agree with him, almost give in to my nervousness. But then I see past his expression. Into the deeper, concealed desire that *wants* something from me, and that told me what it was when I demanded it of him.

And the more I think about it, the stronger my longing grows. The longing that coils up in the bottom of my stomach like a brooding viper, the longing that caresses the back of my throat with its feather-light touch.

"How?" I ask, my cheeks warming as I confess to my inexperience.

"Are you sure? You don't have–"

"*Danny*," I growl his name like a curse. "How?"

The worry in his eyes is replaced by yearning, and he reaches across the bed to his nightstand and removes a small clear bottle. He watches me carefully as he squeezes a few drops onto his fingers and reaches down, lower than his dick.

Then he takes my hand, guiding me down to the place where he just was. I swallow my embarrassment as he directs me past his balls and the area below until I feel his ass cheeks pressing against my fingertips.

"There," he whispers as I reach a soft spot that feels so... private. The lube he put there makes him slippery smooth, and as my fingers move over the spot, I can make out the circle of muscle and the hole in the center. The awareness that I'm touching Danny in this way makes my mouth dry, but I'm so turned on that I can barely think.

"What am I supposed to do?" I breathe.

"Just touch me. You're doing great."

I do as he says, moving my fingers around the spot and feeling its heat, which is stronger than even his cock. I can feel more precome collecting at the end of my dick, but I'm too enraptured by Danny and this moment we're sharing to even think about touching myself.

Continuing to give him attention with my fingers even as I'm desperately wanting more, I push gently against the hole in the middle of the ring of muscle. Under the slight pressure, it parts obediently, and the tip of my finger slips inside as Danny moans. It feels hot there too, and a little slippery, but I think that's just from the lube.

Slowly pushing my finger deeper, I watch as Danny tosses his head restlessly to the side so his cheek is pressing against the mattress. I love seeing how he's enjoying this, but I'm pretty damn sure that when he said earlier that he wanted me *inside of him*, he didn't mean like this.

I withdraw carefully, but he still flinches the moment that I get pushed out. "Did that hurt?" I ask nervously.

"No," he says reassuringly, and he sets his hand on my wrist as if to show that he's telling the truth. Reaching across the bed once more, he pulls out a small square package. Tearing it open between his teeth, he takes out the condom and rolls it down over my dick. "I'm ready now," he says softly.

Nudging his thighs apart, I walk my knees forward until my dick is hovering above his waist.

Tilting my hips downward, I try to aim for the area where my fingers were a minute ago. Danny extends a hand, guiding me toward him until the head of my cock is pressing lightly against him.

"Are you sure?" he asks one last time. His expression is so full of desire that I can't even guess where his last holdout of hesitation is hiding.

I don't answer him, at least not with my words. Pushing forward, I feel resistance – more than before – but I maintain steady pressure until, like before, he opens up to me.

"*Slowly,*" he cautions me through a hissed breath.

Dialing back, I immediately ask, "Did I hurt you?"

"I'm okay," he assures me. "Just keep going slow."

Resting my hand on the side of his stomach as it softly rises and falls, I use his breathing as a guide as I push farther in, more cautiously now.

He's tight and hot, and it feels fucking amazing. I can't help but thinking that this is *way* different than being with a girl, and I can't wait to be all the way inside him.

It seems like it takes forever, but gradually the resistance decreases and his breathing comes more smoothly. Paying close attention to his nonverbal cues, I pull out just a little before pressing back in. At the movement, Danny makes a muffled noise, but it sounds a lot more like pleasure than pain, so I tip my hips forward and thrust again. *Holy hell that feels good.* I shake my head at the rushing sensation.

I keep going, ramping up carefully in case I go too fast, but Danny seems to be all for it now. When he moans again, it's definitely all pleasure. Reaching across his stomach, he takes his dick into his hand and starts pumping away. Watching him touch himself turns me on even more, and I can feel the telltale stirrings inside me as I push into him again and again.

It seems like it should take longer than this, but I can't fucking help it, because he's so warm and snug around my cock. I watch as he presses his lips into a line and jacks himself off more quickly now. He's close. He has to be.

We both keep going and it feels like I'm on top of a cresting wave and that I should have come a long time ago, but the feeling is still building and my body seems determined not to let the rising heat stop.

The thing that finally pushes me over the edge is Danny flicking his gaze up to my face. In his eyes, I can see his vulnerability and his fondness for our friendship… and his wish for us to be closer, even though at this particular moment that's utterly impossible.

"*Oh God, Danny,*" I try to muffle my voice as I come inside him, but it still comes out as a strangled cry that I have no control over.

Making soft, helpless noises, he comes on his chest.

Our breaths rise and fall in a mismatched cadence, moving in and out of rhythm with one another. Every part of me from my toes to the back of my neck is tingling with the lingering aftershock of what just happened. It was just so fucking good.

"Wow," Danny says, looking at me as he shifts his hips.

The movement reminds me that I'm still buried up to my balls in my best friend. Flushing, I carefully withdraw. He winces again as I do, but I ignore him for the moment. Pulling the condom off, I hop up off the bed and leave the room.

Between the unnaturally slick latex and the glob of come at the end of the condom, the reality of what just happened is forced on me with an acerbic clarity. Refusing to look at it, I whip the condom into the bathroom garbage.

Bracing myself on the sink, I stare at my naked reflection in the mirror as guilt threatens to strangle me. *What the hell am I doing?* It's *Danny*, for Christ's sake. My best buddy all through grade school and high school. And now what? After all this time… I drive out for a visit, we have a few beers, go for a hike or two, and then start fucking each other?

The faucet plinks just a single drop into the sink, but it's enough to break my already waning conviction that I was doing the right thing when I got into bed with Danny. I wanted it so much, but now I just feel like a mess.

Turning the handle for hot, I take the bar of soap from the ledge and grind my hands hard against it to create a lather. I grit my teeth together, rubbing the soap between my fingers and over the back of my hands.

Steam is rising from the flowing water now, but I haven't yet put my hands under it. Determined to scour every bit of uncleanliness from my skin, I rub the soap harder against my hands. As I'm digging my fingernails into the bar to clean beneath them too, the first few tears fall from my eyes.

For the first time in several minutes, I realize what I'm doing and how crazy it is. Refusing to give in to the turbulence hiding just below the surface, I force back my emotion. I set the soap back on the ledge and thrust my hands under the searing water, wishing that it could burn away more than just the suds.

When the water falling from my hands runs clear, I turn the faucet off and take slow steps back to Danny's room. The only light is from the fast approaching dawn, but I still hold my hand in front of my crotch as I stand in the doorway. Not really having moved, Danny is lying against the headboard, watching me.

"You okay?"

I couldn't respond even if I wanted to, because I don't have an answer for myself. So I stay quiet.

Shifting on the bed, he inhales sharply as he realizes I'm *not* okay. "Oh shit. Curtis, I'm so sorry. I shouldn't have pushed you."

Inside, a voice screams at me, *He didn't push you… you wanted this.* But if that's true, why am I so damned conflicted about it now?

Reassuring and masculine, Danny's voice drifts across the space between us. "You can sleep here if you want."

I do want to. I *really* fucking want to. But the thought of it scares me too much. If I stay now, then I'm agreeing that this is really the way I am. *And I'm not.* I'm just... not.

Swaying forward even as I resist the pull to join him beneath those white sheets, I bite down on the inside of my cheek. The pain helps me concentrate on what I have to say. "I can't," I say. "It was just sex. Nothing more."

Danny sighs, and I flinch at the sound.

Silence pours into the room, rushing in through the windows and the door and the gaps in the hardwood as it rises around us like a murky flood. It's trying to drown me, and with any luck, it just might.

When he speaks again, his tone is hard and insulated from any emotion. "Go then."

I wait because I want for him to say more, but he doesn't. His darkened shape and anguished expression turn away, and only then do I drop my hand from in front of my crotch and return to my own bed.

Chapter Seventeen

Curtis

I didn't expect for sleep to come easily, but actually it never arrives at all. Minute by minute as the cold fingers of morning reach even further into the window and crawl into my room, the events of earlier sprint through my head.

The first time we messed around, it was Danny's fault. He made the first move, and the second move. And then... well, I'm a guy. I have a dick, and that thing has a mind of its own sometimes. So when it took over – only after Danny's repeated insistence – it didn't seem like such a crazy thing.

But tonight... I was the one who went to his room. I was the one who touched him. I was the one who... *fucked* him.

The word burns in my mind. And it doesn't even feel like a good descriptor of what we did.

As much as I hate it, my thoughts keep wandering away from the guilt and toward the memory of how good it felt while I was with him... and *in* him, but that's the last thing I want to remember.

And so the minutes pass, stacking on top of each other to form hours. But slowly – always slowly. Until my eyelids have long since grown tired of being closed without sleeping.

Throwing off the covers, I get up and stare out at the cloudy morning. Something in the deep blue of the overcast sky makes me feel like I'm not alone, because the color out there is the same one I feel inside.

Being careful not to make too much noise, I get dressed and pad through the living room. If the late hour of our activities last night was any indication, Danny won't be up for a long time. Shoving my feet into my shoes, I quietly open the front door and slip outside into the brisk island air.

My eyes are scratchy and I'm groggy from not having slept last night at all, but it feels good to be outside. Stuffing my hands into my jean pockets to keep them warm, I set out in the direction of the road. The flowline trail that Danny showed me that first week is my goal. I want to be able to walk without having to think about where I'm going, and what easier way to do that than follow a meandering pipe through the woods?

Twelfth Grade

"Have you seen my Lucky Seven shirt?" I ask for the third time today.

"Sorry, dude."

I flick an annoyed glance toward my bed where Danny is sprawled out on his back and staring at the ceiling. "You could get up and help look," I grumble as I empty a clothesbasket and sift through in search of my favorite green tee.

"It's probably just in the wash," Danny says, briefly glancing away from the ceiling.

"Unlike *some* people," I say, "I do my own laundry. So no, it's not being washed."

"Don't know what to tell you."

I kick the hamper into the corner of the room before joining Danny on the bed. "Scoot over, man," I say before prodding him in the ribs when he doesn't move.

He shuffles over and I flop down beside him. "I can't wait to get out of this place," I muse.

Silence, then: "Yeah."

Something about his voice is off, but I've had too long of a day already to really care. Right now I don't want to think about anything but our impending graduation, and like usual when I'm with Danny, I say exactly what I'm thinking. "I know it's not like we're going that far, but rooming with you is going to be fun as hell. Not to mention that I finally get to leave this shithole behind."

Danny is quiet beside me. It strikes me as odd, but I'm not sure why.

"I've been meaning to talk to you about that," he begins carefully.

"What about it?"

His blond hair brushes against the comforter beneath us as he turns to me. I feel his eyes on the side of my face but I don't move.

"I got accepted to Toronto," he says.

I push myself up on an elbow and stare down at him, knowing that our faces are suddenly very close and not caring at all. "So don't go," I state. There are a dozen reasons why I should congratulate him, but I just can't.

He's still lying on his back as his eyes come to a rest on mine, and barely any space separates us.

"Curtis…" He says it like I'm his little brother or something. Like he's headed off to better things that I can't possibly understand.

"I know it's a good school," I begin, struggling to keep my tone steady. "I know it's an awesome city, and I know your parents are telling you to go there." The more reasons I list, the harder it is to keep my voice from descending into panic. "But don't go. *Please*, don't go, Danny." I sniff to clear the wetness from my nose.

"I already accepted," he whispers, looking away from me for the first time since we started talking.

I can feel my face screwing up with anger as I jump off the bed. "Fuck you, Danny. We promised each other."

I take a breath, stealing a second to try to think this out. But that second isn't enough, and it could never *be* enough.

"We were kids, Curtis," he reasons. "You know that. That's a kid's promise."

"Fuck you," I repeat. "Yeah, we promised that when we were kids. And then a hundred times since then. We've always talked about it. Christ, we discussed it *last month*. When were you going to tell me?" My chest is heaving beneath my rage, and my hands have long since clenched into fists.

"Curtis…" he says my name slowly like before, but this time it's not patronizing. Sitting up, he swings his legs over the edge of the bed.

"How long have you known?" I demand. Whatever he says, it won't make it better, but at least it'll… it'll what?

He shrugs, looking apologetic. "I applied months ago, but I didn't get the acceptance until a couple weeks ago."

In that moment, I realize it doesn't matter how or when or why. All that matters is that Danny is bailing on me. He's the last person I ever expected to do that, but here it is. I want to deck him in the face. I want to hit him so fucking hard, and I think he knows it too, because his gaze keeps moving to my fists.

"Come on, Curtis," he pleads. "You owe it to me to at least hear–"

"I don't owe you a thing," I growl. "Get out."

"Huh?"

"I said, *get out*." I point at the door. Rage burns in my expression, and I hope he recognizes how close he is to getting into a fight with me.

Danny looks sad as hell when he stands up and walks out, and for the briefest second I consider going after him. But then I realize that it's him doing the leaving, not me, and that running after him won't change a damn thing.

At that moment, my dad's words echo silently in my ears. *You should think about why you don't have any other friends besides Danny.* Repeated countless times in countless ways, his message has always been the same. *There's something wrong with you.*

I think he's right after all.

Chapter Eighteen

Danny

For the hundredth time today, I glance at the kitchen clock. I drum my fingers on the counter as I stare through the timber posts that frame the living room. It's a quarter to six in the evening.

I remind myself yet again that Curtis is an adult and he can handle himself, but that doesn't make me any less worried. When I woke up this morning to find that he was gone, I was concerned, but that was more for his mental well-being than anything else. But he's been gone for – I quickly do the calculation in my head – roughly ten hours, depending on how early he left.

Around noon, I started calling him. By mid-afternoon, after hitting his voicemail a dozen times, I searched his room and found his phone beside his wallet and keys. That's when I really started to worry.

What was he thinking? It's like he just took off into the woods.

I get that he needed space after what happened last night, but this is getting a little extreme. Still gazing across the living room, I consider again whether I should go out into the woods. But where would I look? There are a dozen trails near here. The Galloping Goose is the closest, but it passes by several houses, so I can't imagine him getting lost. The flowline trail is a likelier bet, but it goes off in both directions from the road, so even if that's where he went, I'd only have a fifty-fifty shot at getting it right. And that's assuming that he stayed on the trail and didn't wander off.

Pulling out my phone again, I reluctantly scroll through my contacts until coming to Lauren's name. I hold my breath as it rings, unsure if I'm hoping that she'll answer or that she won't.

"Hey Danny," she says.

"Um, hey."

Immediately detecting the tension in my voice, she asks, "What's wrong?"

Without delaying, I explain, "Curtis went for a hike early this morning, and he hasn't come back."

"Huh? So go after him."

"I don't know where he went," I admit. "I don't even know for sure that he's in the woods."

She's quiet for several seconds. "Did you guys fight or something?"

"Not exactly, but he might be... upset."

Exasperation coats the sound of her sigh. "You're not making sense. I'm coming over."

"No, you don't have to," I say, but the line clicks off before I've even finished speaking.

Lauren is staring me down from across the kitchen island. "Out with it," she demands.

"There isn't much to say. When I woke up this morning, he was gone."

Her eyes harden, searching mine for deception. "You said he was upset. Why?"

It occurs to me that her feelings for him have her more concerned than she would normally be about one of my friends going missing for several hours.

I look away, unsure how to lie about this without outing him. Not that he's gay necessarily, I remind myself. It's not going to help anything if I start labeling him, even if it's just in my own head.

"Oh, shit," Lauren exclaims, examining me with a forensic attention to detail. "You guys are like... together or something, aren't you?"

"Um..."

"Oh, fucking hell, you guys," she snaps, closing her eyes and bringing a hand to her forehead.

Eventually she drops her hand and brings her gaze back to me. "Why doesn't this surprise me?"

I shrug. "No idea. I thought you slept together."

"Did he tell you that?" Her tone is sharp, seeming on the verge of an accusation.

"He said you didn't, but I didn't believe him."

Lauren laughs, but she doesn't actually sound amused. "He said that he was afraid of messing stuff up between you guys." She rolls her eyes. "I thought that was weird. What kind of guy thinks of his friend before his dick?"

Despite Curtis being missing, I can't stop the smile from spreading on my face because I know the answer to that question.

"So what are you going to do?" she asks.

"What *can* I do?" I demand as I grind my palms against the edge of my table, like it has some power to guide Curtis back to me. "Drive up and down the road? Report him as missing?"

Lauren glances down at her watch. "Those aren't the worst ideas. Who do you even call for that? BC Parks?"

"I don't think so." Picking up my phone from the counter, I enter the emergency number on the keypad. Staring at the numbers, my thumb hovers over the green call button. I don't know if this is a mistake or not, but I can't wait any longer. Curtis is gone and I need to know that he's okay.

Across the room from us, the front door opens and he steps inside.

"Oh my God," I breathe. I sprint across the distance between us and pull him into my arms, not caring that Lauren is watching this display of affection. His clothes are wet, and his muscled frame is shivering beneath them. Releasing him, I drop my hands to his shoulders and examine him. A dirt-smudged cut above his eyebrow has sent smears of dried blood down the side of his face, but he's not bleeding anymore. His hair is disheveled and he smells like a swamp, but other than that, he's still whole.

"Jesus, Curtis," I say. "Are you okay?"

Through chattering teeth, he gives me a classic Curtis shrug. "I'm cold. And wet."

He doesn't flinch as I place a hand on his face, then touch his hands. He's cold, that's for sure, but his speech isn't slurred and he doesn't look in *that* bad of shape.

"What happened?" I demand. "You scared the shit out of me."

"I got lost. I'm sorry."

Lauren joins us at the door, adding unnecessarily, "You look like hell."

Curtis glances at her before lowering his gaze. He doesn't need to say anything more, because I know him well enough to understand what that means. "Lauren," I begin, not looking away from Curtis for even a moment. "Thanks for coming over, but it's time to go home."

"You're kicking me out?" she huffs, incredulity punctuating the spaces between her words.

"I'll call you tomorrow." I should probably feel guilty about making her leave, but really it was Curtis who wanted that, and I'm not going to deny him anything. Not right now. maybe not ever.

Without responding, she puts on her shoes and leaves, slamming the door behind her.

Curtis lifts his eyes to mine, and in them I can feel every ounce of his vulnerability. "Come on," I whisper. "Let's get you out of those wet clothes."

I don't know if he has hypothermia or not, but if he does, it's a mild case. Being a frequent hiker, it was one of the first things that I took the time to learn about after I moved here. So I want to be careful.

He lets me direct him to the couch, and I begin with unzipping his jacket. He keeps looking at me, but he doesn't speak as I help him strip down piece by piece until he's sitting there in his underwear. Like always, his body is striking, but I force myself to ignore that for the moment.

Digging into the pile of blankets beside the couch, I wrap them around him until he's cocooned and his shivers are subsiding. I move to the fireplace, lighting the paper and cardboard I tossed into it earlier. After building up a fire, I scamper to the kitchen and start heating up soup.

Twenty minutes after he first walked in the door, I have him balled up in blankets in front of a spirited fire with a bowl of chicken noodle soup in front of him. Not too bad, I think.

Sitting down on the couch, I watch him, noticing how he's starting to get his color back. The cut on his forehead is behaving itself, but he's still dirty and covered in dried blood.

He's staring at the serving board that I used to ferry the soup and spoon from the kitchen. "It's beautiful," he says, running his fingers over the rich red of the waterfall woodgrain.

"Eat up," I prompt him, even though I wouldn't mind telling him more about the wood. A year or so ago, I made two of those serving trays from leftover bubinga – an exotic African hardwood that someone wanted a table made from.

Ignoring the spoon, he lifts the bowl from the tray and takes a sip from the edge. "Thanks," he says.

I sit with him as the fire burns down and he warms up. We don't talk, but I don't mind.

As he finishes his soup, he kicks off the top blanket and says, "I think I'm going to take a shower."

"You can use the master bathroom if you want. It has a steam shower."

He glances at me, his expression seemingly lost somewhere between forlorn and hopeful. "That would be nice."

Pushing the rest of the blankets off himself, he stands and follows me through my bedroom to the spacious bathroom. Flicking on the light as he walks in behind me, I kick a pair of my dirty underwear underneath the vanity.

Curtis just stands there beside the shower, and it takes a conscious effort to avert my eyes from his black boxer briefs and how filled out they are in the middle.

He catches me staring, and I blush, forcing myself to make words. "Towels are in the corner, and for the steam, you just push that button on the tile." I point to the wall beside the shower enclosure.

"Thanks."

Awkwardness threatens to fill the space between us, so I force my feet toward the door. "Let me know if you, uh, need anything."

"Thanks," he says again.

Turning away, I step out of the room. As I'm pulling the door shut behind me, he stops me with his voice, "I'm sorry I left this morning."

I look back, feeling a familiar pull toward him. "You're home now, that's what matters."

When I try to shut the door, he interrupts me again. "You... don't have to go."

My heart stands motionless in my chest, and my palm is hot on the doorknob. "If that's what you want."

Curtis squares his shoulders. "I do."

I sit down on the closed lid of the toilet and watch to see what he'll do next. I can't tell if he just wants me to stay and talk, or if he wants me to actually shower with him, but I don't really care. I just want to be here for him.

Reaching an arm into the shower, he turns the faucet toward hot.

Water rushes down, just catching his fingers. Then he taps the steam button on the outside of the enclosure as I instructed.

Curtis turns to face me, holding me with his gaze as he pulls down his underwear – slowly, deliberately. He kicks them off to the side, leaving himself naked in front of me.

I force my nerves to calm down, and I try not to stare.

"You can look if you want," he says, his voice quiet.

I wait fully clothed as he turns away from me and steps into the shower.

After a minute, the question drifts out, "Are you going to join me?"

Without hesitating any longer, I strip down and step into the shower. Curtis is standing under the stream facing me, and the water is dragging his short hair down over his forehead. His eyes lift upward, and he stares at me with an expression full of both regret and desire as the first burst of steam is emitted from the vent at the base of the shower.

We showered together numerous times in the past, but this is nothing like that. It's like I was never seeing him all those other times, because his naked body seems so different from when we were younger. Physically we're pretty much the same, but it's just so much more intimate to see him now. I don't know if it's because we had sex last night or because I know that for the first time, he actually wants me to see him like this, but… it's definitely different.

Steam billows between us, but it doesn't obscure my vision enough to hide the fact that neither of us is hard. I step toward him, and his gaze follows my hand upward as I reach my thumb toward the cut on his forehead. Gently brushing away the dirt there, I follow the streaks of dried blood down his face and wash those off too.

Curtis looks away from me, staring into the billowing eddies of steam. For a second I'm afraid that I made a mistake to join him in here, but then he begins to speak. "When I was out in the woods, I was so furious with myself. The first night we did stuff together, I blamed you. But the second time, it was all on me."

It hurts to hear him say this, but I'm afraid that if I interrupt him, he'll stop sharing.

"And then I fell into one of those swampy mud holes with the stinky yellow flowers."

I know exactly what he's talking about, and I snort out a laugh, even though it's not funny at all. Formed in the holes left when massive trees topple and take their root system with them, the holes are a prime spot for swamp lanterns and their smelly flowers. "Sorry," I say quickly.

Water drips through his hair and down onto his face as he tries to glare, but his expression just comes out full of regret. "Why am I this way?" he whispers.

"Come on, Curtis. There's nothing wrong with being with another guy. If you enjoy it, then…"

"No, no," he cuts me off. "That's not what I'm talking about at all. I mean…" He trails off, and I have no idea where he's going with this. His eyes are red, but it's not from the heat of the shower. "I mean, why do I hurt the people around me? My dad, my ex, you, that woman on the motorcycle…"

The floor falls out from under his voice, and I watch as the haunting events of his past catch up to him once more. He leans forward as he begins to sob. Catching him in my arms, I pull him close as he cries. His wet hair presses against my cheek, and his arms squeeze around me.

Wracked by sobs and held tightly to my chest, he lets everything go for the first time in God knows how long. Surrounded by steam and pounding water, I hold him.

"It wasn't your fault," I breathe into his ear. "What happened was terrible, and it was tragic, and it was an *accident*. It wasn't your fault, Curtis. No matter what your dad says, it wasn't your fault."

He doesn't say anything more and neither do I, not even as he eventually extricates himself from my grasp. Not even as he wipes the redness from his eyes with wet fingers, and not even as he holds my face in his hands and kisses me.

Completely unlike either of our previous encounters, nothing about his touch is hurried as his lips meet mine. His eyes flutter shut as he leans in and his tongue nudges forward. His warm wetness is a stark contrast to the water around us because I know it's Curtis and not anything else.

His hands drop down, caressing my chest before finding their home on my hips. Not once breaking our kiss, he pulls me closer until our chests are pressed together and our cocks are tucked in beside one another. Still we're not hard, which makes sense in a bizarre way, because regardless of the way we're falling into each other right now, what we're doing isn't about sex. Sliding my hands up his arms and then his neck, I push my fingers through his dark hair.

At long last, he ends our kiss and steps back under the stream of water. "Danny, I..." His voice quickly loses strength.

"It's okay," I say. "You don't have to explain anything."

Like so many times tonight, his eyes shine with emotion, but unlike before, the overriding feeling in them is gratitude.

For the first time since he arrived, I'm no longer questioning whether he's about to run out the door. He might be conflicted, and he might be upset, but he's not going to leave.

After we finish showering and dry off, Curtis hesitates. Wearing only briefs, he doesn't move as he watches me. "I think I'm going to crash."

He sounds like he wants to say more, but the air remains still between us.

"Let me know if you need anything," I say.

"I will."

He pushes himself to his feet and leaves the room. As he does, I can feel that familiar tug in my chest, that desire to be close to him. But that's not what Curtis needs from me right now. He needs rest and he needs space.

Exhausted from my own day of worrying, I get ready for bed early, being careful not to make too much noise in my bathroom, which shares a wall with Danny's room. While brushing my teeth, my vision strays across the room until it comes to a rest on the shower.

Being in there with him was so... intimate. Based on my previous failed relationships, I always thought that sex and intimacy were the same thing, but the moments I shared with Curtis earlier proved me wrong. Those two aspects of a relationship might certainly share a strong connection, but they're absolutely different.

From the door, a voice calls softly, "Danny."

Startled, I snap my head in the direction of the sound. It's Curtis, wearing only briefs again and looking gorgeous as ever, despite how exhausted he is.

Turning to spit out my toothpaste, I take a mostly innocent peek downward before returning my eyes to where they belong. "Sorry if I woke you."

He leans into the doorframe, and the muscles of his arms and chest fold obediently beneath his posture. Shadowed circles surround his eyes, and his shoulders seem to have given up on holding themselves straight. "You didn't. I couldn't sleep."

My face grows hot with guilt. "You want to take something?"

"No."

"Is there... something else I can get you?"

Curtis nibbles on the edge of his lip, and conflict plays across his features. "I just don't want to be alone right now. Could you... come back to my room?"

My voice is quiet when I answer him. "Of course."

Setting my toothbrush on the vanity, I follow him back to his room and slide into bed beside him, just like when we were teens after his accident with the motorcycle. Except this time, instead of just putting my hand on his shoulder, I move close to him and sling my arm across his chest. Curtis relaxes into me, and a hand takes hold of mine.

At first I'm not sure if this is what he wants, but after only a few minutes, his breathing deepens. His chest rises and falls under my arm, but I don't want to surrender to sleep because I love being next to him like this. Eventually I let my own eyes close, and his warmth and tenderness begin to drag me to sleep. My thoughts roam, but luckily they don't have to go far to find Curtis.

Chapter Nineteen

Danny

Hours pass into days, and those pile up into weeks. Lauren isn't talking to me at the moment, so I spend a lot of my time in my workshop, finishing the latest batch of cutting boards before powering through a cherry bed frame and a couple other projects.

The new cistern is full from the spring rains, and I've started planting the garden too. All of that keeps me more than busy, but Curtis doesn't seem to mind that we don't spend much time together.

We haven't had sex since the night before Curtis ran off into the woods – or done *anything* like that together, really. I assume he just needs a little space, a chance to feel normal again. Or something. I'm not exactly sure.

As I strip off my clothes and step into the shower, it's impossible to not think about the night we showered together. Rotating the handle toward hot, I step underneath the stream, remembering the way it felt to be pressed up against Curtis, against his bulk of naked muscle. And then I remember how it felt to be there for him in one of his most vulnerable moments and to hold him through his pain and tears.

Water runs over my skin, and my thoughts continue to focus on Curtis. Like the ocean breeze that sweeps into Sooke Basin, they find him, touching his smile and ruffling up his hair and slipping into every corner and contour of his beautiful body.

My hand moves downward, touching myself, and my eyes close.

Before, I wouldn't have allowed myself to do this while caught up thinking about Curtis, but now… I don't think he'd even mind.

"You sure you don't want an apron?" I ask, holding one out to Curtis.

"I told you no already."

"But it would be adorable," I tease.

He glares, but his resolution is already failing, being replaced by a smile. "I'm not really much of a cook," he says.

"Suit yourself," I say, tasting disappointment on my tongue alongside the lingering tomato sauce that I dipped my finger in a minute ago. "It's probably for the best. If you help cook a meal, it never tastes as good."

Sitting down at the table, Curtis raises an eyebrow. "I think you're just worried your lasagna won't turn out right."

"I'm a great cook and you know it," I snap.

Without waiting for his response, I get back to work. Into the pan with sizzling onions I send a half-kilo of Italian sausage and ground beef. The meat hisses when it first touches the pan, but it settles down as I turn my attention to mixing four different cheeses together.

Curtis clears his throat at the table, and when he has my attention, he glances pointedly at the empty space in front of him. "I don't even have a drink," he says with a playful grin.

He's such a cocky shit sometimes, but who could say no to that smile? Not moving my eyes from his, I open the fridge and take out a beer. Still not looking away from him, I carry it across the kitchen. Standing right in front of him, I stare down into his smirking expression as I use the edge of my shirt to get a better grip on the twist-off top.

A hiss of carbonation escapes from the bottle, but still I don't look away from Curtis. Setting the open beer in front of him, I say, "There you go, buddy."

The muscles at the base of his jaw tense as he reaches for the bottle. "Um, thanks." Even in those two words, I can hear the dissonant chords of conflicting desire. And I didn't fail to notice the way his eyes were drawn to the exposed skin of my stomach when I lifted my shirt to open the bottle.

Leaving him with his beer, I return to cooking. While I layer the casserole dish with meat, cheese, and lasagna noodles, Curtis sips his beer in silence. Once the dish is filled, I open the preheated oven and push it inside. Ditching the oven mitt and my apron beside the stove, I reach over to set the timer.

I wouldn't have known that Curtis was behind me if I hadn't heard his breath, barely audible. I straighten and angle my head to the side just a little. It's not enough to see him in my peripheral vision, but I can still sense his presence.

A hand touches my shoulder, then another comes to a rest on my waist. I want to lean back, to feel him against me, but I refuse to make the first move. Or the second.

Curtis pulls me gently toward him until his breath is hot on my neck.

My voice is barely more than a whisper, but I know he can hear me. "I figured you still wanted space."

"Screw that," he says through clenched teeth. "It's been hell, seeing you every day and not touching you."

Warmth rises inside me at his confession, and I turn in his arms to stare him down. Gazing into his brown eyes, I lean forward until my eyebrows graze against his and our foreheads are touching. He looks back without reservation, and I hope he sees the same thing that I do.

"I want you," he growls.

Separating myself from him with a smirk, I lean back against the counter beside the stove. "Then take what you want."

Those dark eyes flash with desire, but the insistent grip I'm expecting isn't what I get. Instead he threads his fingers through mine and pulls me into a kiss. His touch isn't frantic, but it's not slow like in the shower, either.

He's barely tapped his tongue on mine before his mouth moves away, marking a line down my jaw and then my neck. Curtis makes a sound of frustration when he reaches my shirt collar, and without hesitating he pulls off my shirt. Picking up exactly where he left off, he kisses his way down my chest, tongue lapping at my nipple before continuing down the side of my stomach.

I'm horny as hell, but I'm enjoying just letting Curtis do what he wants. That sentiment is redoubled as he breezes past my navel and his fingers begin undoing the button on my jeans. He tugs down the zipper and then pulls my jeans down too.

Is he really going down on me right now? The thought and the wonder associated with it is banished as he frees my dick from my briefs and lowers his mouth onto it.

My eyes close as he takes me to the back of his throat. One hand cupping my balls and the other massaging my ass, he moves his head up and down while his tongue rubs against the underside of my shaft. *Fucking hell, Curtis.*

For a straight guy, he sure knows how to suck a dick.

I almost make a comment, but I'm enjoying this too much to risk spooking him. Instead I let my fingers filter into his thick brown hair. The same hair that I pulled with all my strength when we got into a fight when we were twelve, and the same hair that got him all the girls in high school. And now it's all for me.

"Goddamn, Curtis," I groan as he pulls down on my balls so my dick feels tight everywhere. "That feels so fucking good."

Pulling away, he glances up at me with a smirk before sticking out his tongue to lick the tip once more. "Glad you like it."

"Hell yeah, I do."

"Come on," he says, standing up and taking my hand. "I want somewhere more comfortable."

"For what?" I ask, all innocence as I step out of the jeans and briefs still holding my ankles.

Curtis gives me a wry look as he practically drags me toward my bedroom. Once inside, he shoves my shoulders so I fall back onto the mattress. When we were younger, we used to play rough a lot, but it wasn't *quite* like this. I like it, though.

Clambering on top of me, Curtis goes after my mouth this time. I don't stop him, at least not until forcing him to break the kiss as I pull his shirt off. I've been completely naked since he stripped me down in the kitchen, but even now he still has his jeans on. *That jerk.*

Resolving to fix that problem, I yank off his jeans as he smirks.

Our history and friendship makes being with Curtis feel completely unlike any other time I've been with a guy. From his milk chocolate eyes that I understand perfectly to the subtle changes in his breathing and bearing as we react physically to one another, I've never been so in tune with a lover before.

The word *lover* catches on my lips just as Curtis runs his tongue across my chest again. Are we lovers, or just – quite literally – fuck buddies?

I don't want to be thinking about this right now, and it's hard enough anyway now that his hand is pumping up and down on my dick. But this is important to figure out. If we're lovers, does that mean that he... *loves* me? I'm not sure.

I've never questioned how I feel about Curtis, but what does he feel for me?

"What's wrong?" Curtis has released my cock from his grip, and he's sitting back on his heels, suspended over my hips as he watches me.

"Nothing," I say hastily. "Just got distracted."

He narrows his eyes, but he must believe me because he's starting to grin. "How can you be distracted when you've got me?"

"No idea. I must be nuts." I grab him on either side of his chest and my fingers dig into the meaty muscles underneath his arms. Rotating him around so he's lying on his back, I begin vying for the lead. I fall into him, kissing wet trails down his neck and chest while purposely avoiding his cock. I want to save that.

Kneeling on either side of his hips, I walk my fingers down his abs, dragging my thumb down his dick and over his balls before venturing further. I've been careful not to push this boundary until now, because I know that some guys – especially straight-ish ones – are oftentimes really finicky about getting touched there.

I keep my eyes locked on Curtis and edge my fingers down farther, feeling for the place where he's warmest. I hope he's ready for this. He watches me, and I can detect unease in his expression, but not so much that I'm afraid to keep going. Slowly, cautiously, I move my fingers around in a circle, lightly pressing. Not to get inside but just to give him a sense of what that kind of stimulation feels like.

After a minute, he still hasn't protested, but I can see the unease is starting to spread. "Are you okay?" I ask softly as I move my hand back to the safer territory of his balls.

"Um, yeah," Curtis says even as he blushes. "I'm just not used to being, um, touched there."

"I know," I say. Locking eyes with him, I let my tone resonate with sincerity. "I would never push you to do something you're uncomfortable with."

"I know you wouldn't." He shows me a small smile, and I know that he believes me. "And it felt kind of good, actually," he adds, turning even brighter red.

I smile back at him, but I don't trust myself to keep going down there with him. Not only because he still seems uncomfortable about it, but also because I might have a hard time making good on my promise not to push him. I've done all sorts of things with all sorts of guys, but if I have a choice, I like to top. I just don't know if Curtis is ready for that yet. Or if he will ever be.

When I'm confident that he's eager to move on from what we're doing – shown by the subtle rocking in his hips and the way his hands are holding me tighter at the waist – I take a condom from the nightstand and unroll it over his dick. Not for the first time, and I sure as hell hope not for the last, I revel in how attractive I find him. He's not *huge*, but he's definitely decent sized, and just… good. All around.

Still on his back, Curtis rotates his hips upwards as soon as I've got the latex down over him. He doesn't betray any emotion except with his eyes, which of course give away everything.

God, I enjoy being with him so much.

I make for the lube, but he grabs it away from me. "Let me," he says. Squeezing a few drops onto his fingers, he reaches underneath me. His touch is wet and slippery, but it's also… sensual. He takes his time, working the lube slowly around the area, and then just inside me. Bound by an invisible connection, we hold each other with our eyes, forming a line of communication between us that's at once both more natural and more sturdy than the timber beams this house is built on.

He watches me as his fingers massage. He watches me as my mouth opens ever so slightly. He watches me as I push his hand away, scoot forward over him, and lower myself onto his cock.

Like the last time, I'm relaxed and ready for him. *Unlike* last time, I'm on top of him so I have better control over how fast he enters me. But being relaxed can only take you so far.

The pressure is intense at first, even though I'm expecting it. It's not bad pressure, it's just pressure. Keeping my breaths steady in and out, I let myself relax further as I accept more of him. I love how hot he feels inside me, and I love how full he makes me feel. And I love that he's letting me take control.

I'm playing with myself, but his hand pushes mine out of the way and closes around my cock as I take him deeper inside me. Bracing my hands on my thighs, I move up and down his shaft as he jerks me off.

It feels so amazing to be with Curtis like this, and not only because years of friendship have made me trust him without reservation. It's also because the times I've been with him have been the best sex I've ever had.

Besides his hand jacking me off, Curtis just lies there and lets me do the work. And it *is* a workout. But it's fucking fantastic, since I can move in the way that feels best for me. I might have worried that he's not enjoying it as much as I am, but from his expression of bliss, it's really not even a question how much he's loving this.

Every time I sink down onto him and feel his balls mash against my butt, his cock presses forward and hits that spot that makes it feel like he's stroking me on the inside, forcing heady waves of pleasure through me in ways that don't even seem possible.

My eyes want to shut as the rising energy inside threatens to burst out the tip of my dick, but more than anything, I want to see Curtis finish as *I* finish. I want the mental image of that ecstasy-filled expression to be forever engraved into my memory.

"You're going to make me come," I hiss, knowing that I should have warned him sooner.

"I know," he says. Unable to hold himself back any longer, he begins to thrust harder, and I know he's close too.

His fingers gripping me refuse to change their pace, and the next time that I take him down to the hilt and his dick pushes against that amazing place inside me, the resulting feeling rushes through me like a flash flood. Pouring through every nerve and muscle fiber and washing over every centimeter of my skin, the orgasm sprints to my extremities before bounding back to my center, stronger than when it left. The resulting heat gathers in my abdomen, rolling down through my stomach and collecting in my balls before charging out the end of my cock.

The first shot hits him on the cheek, but his expression is so intent that he doesn't even seem to notice. Teeth clenched with iron resolve through his final thrusts, fierce exhalations come out through this nose as he huffs across the finish line like a champion racehorse.

Goddamn, he's beautiful.

Separating myself from him, I collapse onto the bed beside him, our heavy breaths falling into rhythm together. "That was... really good," he says.

"I didn't know sex could even feel like that."

He grins. "That's because you've only been with inferior guys."

I shake my head. "You're such a cocky shit."

"You like it."

Yeah, I do.

He grabs his briefs and wipes my come off his chest. After throwing the pair of underwear into the dirty clothesbasket, he gets up and walks into the master bathroom, taking off the condom as he goes. I wait while he washes himself off.

Lying down beside me once more, he trails his fingers across my chest as he watches me with tender eyes.

"So," I begin, "you're not going to rush out of here again and disappear for a day, right?"

"I haven't decided yet," he teases.

But as his shoulder presses into my armpit and he cuddles against my chest, I know he's not going anywhere. At least not tonight.

Chapter Twenty

Curtis

The memories of yesterday evening dance around the edges of my mind, slipping away the moment I try to recall exactly what I said or what I was thinking. Nothing has changed since then, but it doesn't make it any easier to swallow the idea that I'm falling in love with… *him*. The pronoun is the hardest part. It's funny how a tiny word can mean so much, but it does. Goddamn it, it does.

It might not have been a surprise for me to think that in the heat of the moment, right when we were getting going and my head was awash with a sea of hormones and lust, but even now I can't shake the thought. Like mist falling out of the island fog, the unspoken conclusion settles over me, kissing my skin in a thousand places at once.

It would have made it so much easier to blame everything on my inhibitions being drowned by a sex-induced flood, but I can't do that, because I didn't come to that traitorous realization until we'd already finished fucking.

For the second time in a minute, a single word sours in my mouth. We weren't fucking. We were making love. To call it anything else would be a blatant lie.

The connection I felt wasn't like anything I'd ever experienced before. Being with Danny was like taking his hand and intertwining my fingers through his, except with our bodies and not just our hands. It was touching his tongue with mine, running my fingers through his hair. It was his breath hot on my neck, a whisper in my ear. It was all of those things woven together, moment by moment, into an experience that can't be compared against or reasoned with or quantified.

That's how I know we were making love, and it's why I'm so scared.

I'm falling in love with him.

But I don't want to be.

That sounds so selfish, but it's not. I don't know if my heart can even explain the rationale to my brain, but I know it's true. Danny is a great guy, and even when the extent of our relationship was a deep and untouchable friendship, I loved him.

But Danny needs someone who can love and be there for him the way he needs. He deserves better than a guy on the fence who's not even sure if he's into guys or not. He deserves someone who will love him unconditionally and never have doubts about it.

I can't promise him that my feelings for him won't change, because I don't know, and that kills me inside. I want to be with him, and I want us to be together – whatever that means. Hell, I've even caught myself thinking about what a future would look like for us. In-laws, holidays, *kids*?

The thought is terrifying, but it has crossed my mind. Despite all of that, I can't promise him that the way I feel now won't ever change. How can I know that in a week or a month I won't feel different?

Stepping for a moment out of my own thoughts, I drum my fingers on the steering wheel of my car. Danny offered to let me take his truck, but I couldn't. My eyes jump from the wheel to the ambulance parked outside the ER.

At first, the thought of taking the classes to become an emergency responder seemed like a crazy dream. I don't want any handouts from Danny, but looking back, I almost wish I had taken him up on the class he tried to register me for.

For the first time, I wonder whether becoming a paramedic might be a real possibility. I always kept the thought to myself, but it was what I wanted to do ever since I graduated high school. My dad told me there was no money in it and that the hours were bad. All that's true, but it doesn't mean it's not what I want to do.

The fact that it was Danny who finally tried to kick me in the right direction after all this time is both funny and a little annoying. He can't read me like I can him, but damn it if he doesn't have a sense for some things. That first night he kissed me, I don't even think I could have predicted that I would go along with it. But somehow he knew.

Thinking about Danny brings me back to the thought-sinkhole of the situation between us. When I came to the island a couple months ago, I was convinced I would only stay a few days, maybe a week at most. But staying longer doesn't seem like such a wild idea anymore. Living with Danny is... good. He can be a little testy sometimes, but I really enjoy spending time with him, even when we're just working. It makes me sad that we haven't done much together in a while.

Dragging my inattentive eyes from the ambulance entrance, I start my car and begin the journey toward home. As I pass the outskirts of Victoria and turn onto Sooke Road that will take me around the bottom of the island, the realization isn't lost on me that *home* no longer means somewhere in Thunder Bay.

Letting myself in the front door, I kick off my shoes and hang my coat beside Danny's. The woodsy scent of smoke is caught in the air, hinting that the fireplace is occupied.

Not disappointed, I find Danny lying on the couch with his laptop. Embers smolder in the fireplace, and he glances up from the screen when he sees me. "You're back."

"Scoot," I say, swatting at his bare feet until he makes room for me. As soon as I sit down, he puts his feet on my lap. I scowl at him, but he acts like he doesn't notice.

Closing his laptop, Danny sets it on the floor and just watches me. He's trying not to smile, but he's doing a bad job of it.

"What?" I demand, glancing down at myself and brushing a self-conscious hand across my lips.

"You're sexy when you're pretending to be mad."

I don't know why that comment makes me blush, but hot blood rushes to my face. And maybe another place too. "Um, thanks." I would love to tell him that I find him attractive as well, that his muscles are sexy as sin, that he's a fucking stud. But despite all that's happened between us, I can't bring myself to say that to another guy, even if that guy is Danny.

"Something wrong?" he asks, scrutinizing my expression.

"I'm fine." My mouth feels dry, and anxiety crawls around the back of my mind.

"Huh, okay," he says, and I can tell he doesn't believe me.

Danny just looks at me, like he's trying to divine what's going on in my head. He won't figure it out because that's not his way. Reading someone was always my gift. His was to be there for someone, unconditionally. Which is something that I've never been able to do.

"You want to get out of here?" I feel silly suggesting it, but I need to get out of the house. Something about being here makes it feel impossible to sort out how I feel. I want to be with Danny, but what if I don't deserve him? The feeling grinds against my insides.

His words are soft when they reach my ears. "How about China Beach?"

"The place you first took me to hike?"

"Yeah."

"At night?"

He gives me a lopsided smile and says, "I'll bring a flashlight."

The night air is cool, and the waves washing up on the beach are agitated. The wind and water speak to one another, warning of rain to come.

But for the moment, it holds back.

Beside me on the surf-worn tree trunk, Danny speaks for the first time since we left the truck. "So what's bothering you?"

The breeze drags cold fingers across my face, and I pull in a full breath of the crisp night. Although barely visible in the dark, I can still feel as Danny's eyes find me. The eyes with that unknowable shade of blue, a color that disappears soundlessly between the fog and the sea whenever I try to identify it.

"I'm just… having a hard time knowing what I want."

Danny sighs, and waves roll up onto the shore. Eventually he says, "That's okay."

"Really?"

"Yeah," he says, but I can tell he's holding back.

"What?"

He stares ahead, his gaze getting lost in the ocean before he finally asks, "Do you really not know what you want, or do you just not want to… want it?"

I don't answer him. Because I can't.

Danny's attention stays fixed on me. "I know you probably don't want to talk about this, but…"

"But?"

He hesitates, and I can feel the unspoken words piling up on his lips. "Did you know when we were… younger?"

"Know what?" I ask guardedly, knowing exactly what he means but hoping all the same that he'll abandon this line of questions. Hoping that he'll abandon it just like he did the night of the thunderstorm when we were fifteen. The night that I could never stop revisiting, no matter how hard I tried to forget it.

Danny's fingers fidget on the dry wood of the trunk. "You know. That you were interested in guys and stuff." Now he glances back to me, and his courage returns. "And don't give me that line that something magically changed when you came out here. The people who believe they can change someone's sexuality like that are just deluding themselves."

"Does it really matter?"

Doubt seeps into his words. "Um yeah, kind of."

"Why?"

I can feel his frown when he presses onward. "Because," he says, lowering his voice, "I *knew* that I wanted to be with you, even back when we were in high school. It was horrible wanting to tell you how I felt and never being able to. And going to college without you? That was hell. I left because it hurt too much to be around you." He pauses as the first rain drops land on us. "I guess… I guess I want to know that I didn't go through that for nothing."

He wants me to tell him that I was clueless, or that I was deluding myself. The second part is true, but not the first. I've only ever lied to Danny a handful of times, and I really don't want to now. Beside me, he watches me expectantly.

Some confessions are never meant to be said aloud. But this can't be one of them. "I knew."

Danny's expression darkens, and when he speaks, his tone is shaky and mired in tension. "You knew *what*?"

I close my eyes for a moment, knowing that this had to come out sometime but hating that it's right now.

"*Goddamn it*, Curtis," Danny growls. His quiet contentedness from just a minute ago has completely evaporated. "Tell me."

My shoulders wilt under the weight of his demand. Somehow I got this far without him ever asking me this specific question. It went so long that I became convinced he wouldn't actually go searching for the answer.

I should have known better.

Better he finally know.

My breath is light on the air, and it's a confession and a betrayal and a truth that I wish were a lie. "I always knew."

Danny shrinks back from me, and I can feel as his confusion crowds alongside the beginning of anger. I should never have told him the truth. Never ever, not even if we spent our whole lives together. Not even as the years passed and our bodies grew frail with age. Not even as one of us laid the other in the ground and whispered heartfelt words meant for us alone.

I should never have dared to let this particular truth escape. I should have spun lies, silken lies that were soft and sweet and warm. He would have believed every saccharine drop and probably loved me more for it.

But I can't do it.

Not this time.

The wind turns cold, and Danny deserves to hear this.

"I always knew," I say again.

This has to come out, or it never will. Ignoring his expression, I continue. "I knew before I met you that I was attracted to guys. I knew it when you pulled me out of the pool, and I knew it when we jacked off in the tent together on that school trip, and I knew... I knew what you were asking when we got caught outside in that thunderstorm." And just like that night, the drops begin to fall.

Danny looks like he's about to cry. "Why?" he asks, and the word is wrapped in a vulnerability that makes me ache.

"I was scared. I didn't have parents like you did."

"Bullshit," he snaps. "You had *me*. I would have kept your secret as long as you wanted me to." He pauses, then demands, "What was the real reason?"

I grit my teeth together, bearing down on the words I have to say. Truth can't be split apart, and it can't be selected. It's either complete or it's nothing at all.

Danny's lower lip trembles as he says, "Tell me, Curtis."

The rain pelts down as I swallow away the hardness in my throat and do as he asks. "When we were teens... I loved you, Danny. God-damn, I loved you so fucking much. And not like the best friend I was supposed to be. More than that, *way* more than that."

I glance to the side and liquid glistens along the bottom of my eyes. But I push forward because Danny deserves to know. "I was scared.

More scared than I've ever been of anything. Being around you drove me nuts, and I hated every second we were together that I didn't touch you or tell you how I felt. But that's what I chose, because I didn't want to be that way. I didn't want to be with a guy."

My heart stands still, but heartbeats thunder onward anyway. Onward into the storm that never managed to end for us.

Danny leans forward across the space between us. He stares into my eyes, and the air is warm on my cheek as he says softly, "*Fuck you,* Curtis." His features blaze with rage, kindled from nearly twenty years of lying to him.

Then he stands up and runs into the woods.

The beach suddenly feels so empty. I follow him because I have to. And because I want to. I can't bear to lose him, not now. Not again.

Rain and darkness are falling heavily from the sky as I push off from the tree and sprint after him. Following the distant flashlight beam as it whips across the path, it takes all my concentration to make sure my footfalls are on flat ground.

I expected him to be sad, and I expected him to be hurt. But not for him to just... run. Danny has never wanted to show me weakness – in fact, I don't know if he ever *has*. He's just... Danny. Impenetrable, untouchable Danny.

He feels pain. I know he does.

He just refuses to let me see it.

Through the pounding rain, I chase after him. I shout his name, but the sound is swallowed by the night. Danny doesn't slow, and neither do I.

Chapter Twenty-one

Danny

My footfalls slam into the earth as I run. As I fight to get as far from Curtis as I can. Because I can't stand to be around him any longer. Not another second.

He lied – at the very least by omission, but probably more than that too. If I had time to think, I could sift through my memories of our shared past, the ones stacked in my mind like dusty books, untouched since I first put them there. I would search through them until I found all the signs I missed.

But I can't. I can't think about *anything*, because a single memory is forcing me to relive a night I've tried so long to forget.

Freshman Year, University of Toronto

The three-story house pounds with music as I push through the crowd surrounding the keg. Holding the two red Solo cups above my head so no one accidentally knocks them out of my hands, I make my way across the sprawling living room and toward the stairs.

Bodies are packed onto the stairs too, but one side remains open for passage. Abandoning caution for a moment, I take a long drink of one of the beers as I climb to the second floor. The music isn't as loud here, but it's still full of drunken students.

Navigating through the sea of bodies, I pause to stabilize myself with a shoulder on the wall as the room sways. I've had a few drinks already but that's probably not the reason I'm a little unsteady. Smoking too much weed an hour ago with Jake is responsible for that one. I should have just stayed in his room, but my mouth was feeling dry so I went to get us a couple beers.

The next staircase is empty, along with the third floor itself. No one bothers to come up here because it's more or less off limits to guests. I don't belong to this frat, but I've been over a couple times and I don't get questioned anymore. Pushing Jake's door open with my elbow, I hand him the extra beer as he sits up on the bed.

"I wasn't sure you were coming back," he says, taking a drink.

I hop onto the bed beside him and lean against the wall. "It was busy down there."

Jake glances over before leaning back too. We're sitting close, and my body buzzes with more than chemical influences. He holds his cup out to me and I tap the rim of mine against it. "Cheers."

He takes a long drink, and I watch him more closely than I should. The shadow of stubble on his cheeks and chin, the way his Adam's apple ducks as he swallows, the stray chest hairs appearing just at the edge of his v-neck shirt.

Jake sets the beer between his outstretched legs, and his eyes stray toward mine. It means he catches me staring, and I blush. Jake is gay. I've known it for a while, but nothing has happened between us. I'm not sure I even want it to, but right now I'm horny as hell.

Maybe it's the weed, maybe it's the alcohol, or maybe it's just that I'm sick of being so stuck on Curtis that I haven't found another guy. Whatever the reason, my hand ventures across the distance between us, trespassing against Jake's chin.

He turns toward me, and surprise twists into his features, but I don't stop. A day doesn't slip past that I don't regret never pushing the boundary with Curtis, and it's that knot of memory that pushes me forward and against his lips. My fingers tighten on his chin, and my heart thuds because he's kissing me back.

Beer spills from his cup as he sets it carelessly on the nightstand, and then he takes my cup from me too. His hands are pulling up on my shirt now, tugging it over my head. I let him, because I want this.

Do I?

He sheds his own shirt and pushes me back onto the bed. Not rough, but not gentle either. He kisses me again, and I go along with it. I don't even know if I *like* Jake that much, but I'm not sure if this is really about him at all.

Jake is struggling with the button on my jeans, but it doesn't put up much of a fight, and he strips me down. Sitting up, he just stares at me for a moment before leaning back down. Bringing his lips close to my ear, he breathes, "I've been waiting weeks to fuck you."

Unease builds inside my mouth, but I swallow it away as he unzips his fly and pushes his jeans down to his knees.

Reaching to his nightstand, he retrieves a small bottle. Unscrewing the top, he takes a quick sip and holds it out to me. "Here."

My heart slams against my ribs. "What is this?"

"Doesn't matter. It'll make you feel good. Take a sip. A *small* sip."

I look from him to the tiny bottle he's holding out. *What the fuck am I thinking?* I barely know this guy. But inside me, a voice says that this is what I need.

I nod, and I do as Jake says. The liquid is salty on my tongue, and I swallow fast. I swallow so the shame can't stand for more than a moment on my lips. Curtis would never have let me do something like this. But that doesn't matter, because he's been gone from my life for a while now.

Jake recaps the bottle and sets it aside, but I don't feel any different.

He pushes me onto my back, and I stare up at him, into the eyes that are nothing like the ones I really want. I feel his tongue against mine once more, and time moves past.

In the span of a single breath, I feel way drunker than I am. When he kisses me again, I can't get enough. Everywhere we touch feels amazing, and I want him pressed against every inch of my skin. The new high pushes further through me, and I want him inside me too. "Fuck me," I growl.

He lubes us up.

I ask again.

And he fucks me.

The door is ajar, and people walk past.

Music pounds.

And it feels good, even though he's being rough.

Really rough.

He finishes, I finish.

And I feel nothing.

Nothing, as the darkness tows me under.

When I wake up, the sour smell of acid hits me. I'm lying on the floor of Jake's room, and a small circle of vomit is spread across the carpet in front of me. I feel like hell.

Wiping my wrist across my face, I sit up. It's still dark outside, but the lamp beside Jake's bed casts a morose light over the room. Jake is passed out in his bed, naked like I am. *Fuck.*

I pull on my clothes. It's a normal action, one that happens every day. But I feel absolutely empty inside as I leave his room, as I push down the stairs and leave the sprawling drunk fest of a house that has calmed down since the last time I was conscious.

Night air touches my face, and I let its cold sink into me. I want the chill to penetrate deep, to make me numb. I don't want to feel right now.

Why did I agree to take what he offered? It was stupid, but I do understand. I wanted to feel *something* besides this ache inside for Curtis. It's an ache that has been with me for far too long, and I want it to wink out of existence. In a blur of color and a flash of dark, I want it to disappear.

Except instead of feeling something when I was with Jake, I didn't feel anything at all. A drunk high and an even briefer rush from the sex. And I feel even emptier than I did before. I wish this was a new feeling, but it's not. In the last semester, I've slept my way up and down the frat houses, and beyond them too. Knowing every time I wake up that another small piece of myself has disappeared.

Against the night air, I can see my breath, a cold purity that's a stark contradiction to the way I've been living since I came to college.

I hate who I've become.

It makes me sick that it's taken me so long to realize that no matter how many guys I'm with, I'm never going to get Curtis back.

My feet continue to carry me toward home, step by step, and I come to a decision. After tonight, I'm going to let go of him. Really, truly, absolutely. And I won't let him hold me back anymore.

I come to a stop in the middle of the sidewalk and stare up into the Toronto sky washed out by streetlights. I take a deep breath, and when I exhale, I force Curtis out of me. Everything that I did for him, everything that I did *because* of him. I'm done with him.

Chapter Twenty-two

Curtis

Rain and wind batter against me as I chase after Danny through the night. Rising up in the woods from the beach, the terrain is slippery and uneven, and most of the time it feels like I'm falling uphill.

It isn't until we reach his truck that I finally catch him. "Goddamn it, Danny," I say through heaving breaths.

We're both sopping wet, and his glare burns across my face.

"You're going to leave, just like that?" I demand. "You don't even want to talk about this?"

"Go fuck yourself," he says over the drum of the storm.

He looks up at me, water dripping down his forehead and into his eyes. "How could you have known all along and never said anything? I spent high school believing that I couldn't tell you half the things I wanted to. Now you're telling me that you *knew*? That you liked guys too, and you never mentioned it, not once?"

He takes a breath and charges on, "Not only that, but you knew I wished we could be more than friends, and even *you* wanted that, but you just… lied about it?"

Danny shakes his head, and water drips from his chin. "Jesus Christ, Curtis. You lied with every breath. Every time you opened your mouth and didn't tell me how you felt."

He stands a little straighter and steps closer to me. Raising his hand, he jabs a finger into my chest, enunciating each word. "*Who the fuck does that?*" His words are a growled curse and a clarion grace, because I deserve every bit of it and a whole lot more after that.

But I won't abandon him. Not again.

Trespassing into the space between us, I bring my fingers to his elbow. Treading lightly, I move up along his arm toward his shoulder.

He knocks my hand away, and pain sinks its teeth into my wrist. "Don't you dare touch me," he hisses.

I stand motionless in front of him, and my eyes sink to the soaking wet ground. He grabs my chin, and forces me to look into his eyes. His grip is firm and his anger so close. I wince preemptively but I don't look away. *Never look away.*

I think he's going to hit me.

I think I want him to.

Then I'll know he still loves me.

Danny steps closer to me, and he drops his hand. "I'm not your dad, Curtis."

Rain falls around us, and in that moment we're back in Thunder Bay in a yard with splotchy grass, finishing a conversation that should have had its ending years ago.

He breathes a question that cuts with every word. "You want to know what's wrong with you, Curtis?"

Tears shimmer along my eyes, mingling with the rain. "What?"

"It's that you let him get to you. And now you're too damn scared to... hell, I don't know, *love yourself.*"

His voice is a whisper as he says, "I don't believe that you never made a move just because you didn't want to be with a guy. I think you were just terrified that you might actually be happy with me."

"And what if I don't deserve to be happy?"

"That's the problem," he snarls. "Right fucking there. But you're the only one who can answer that question. I love you, Curtis, God knows I do. But... I can't be with someone who doesn't think they're good enough to be loved."

He swallows away his own tears before he turns and jams the key into the door of his truck.

Leaving me standing in the rain, he gets in and starts the engine.

"You're just going to leave me here?"

I wouldn't blame him if he did.

He glances darkly at me, and after a moment of indecision, he nods toward the passenger side.

The following minutes are agonizing as Danny drives toward home. His fingers grip the steering wheel too hard and he's driving too fast.

Ahead of us the road curves, and Danny turns dutifully into it. From the headlights of both the truck and the rare passing vehicle, beams of white light charge into the night, hitting a thousand raindrops on their way down. In turn, the rain pounds down across the windshield, obscuring our vision until the wipers temporarily beat it back.

It's a cool night, not helped by the rain, but I wouldn't mind if I weren't drenched. I even have my window cracked a bit, so I can hear the wind and the water as the truck sails through the darkness. I don't know what's going to happen tonight, but I hope it doesn't end with me leaving the island.

Stealing a look at Danny, I allow myself a sorrowful look that he will never see in the dark. I wish I could hold his hand right now, to show him how much I need him. Instead, my fingers tighten around the armrest, but it doesn't squeeze back.

Just ahead, the yellowed headlights of a logging truck barreling through the night catch my attention. We're moving through another curve, but something is wrong about the direction of the truck. It seems like it's coming toward us instead of following the curve in the road.

"DANNY!"

I see him jerk the wheel to the right, but I know it's too late.

Like a sadistic metronome, time all but stops.

The impact comes with the force of a freight train and it roars a crack of thunder.

My eyes tightly shut, I hear the hideous screech of metal meeting metal as the vehicles bite into one another with savage teeth.

The tinkling sounds of shattering glass are an overture to the next moments as the truck spins and I'm flung against the seat belt.

Is this how I die? A whirling descent into darkness – cool, tranquil darkness?

A moment.

Another moment.

A breath.

It's the bitter air that convinces me I'm still alive. Convinces me to open my eyes.

I draw another breath into my lungs, tasting the slick metallic scent on my tongue and in my nose and against my eyes. It smells like iron. Like blood.

My breaths are coming fast as I take in what just happened. My door is smashed in and pressed against my elbow, but the window is open to the air outside. Bits of glass are littered all over the cab, including on top of my legs and a few stuck into my shirt. The windshield has cracks spidering across it, but it's still intact.

Then I remember Danny.

My attention snaps to the driver's seat and to the guy I grew up with. Darkness clings to him, making it almost impossible to see. He's slumped over with his head hanging down and his chin pressed into his chest.

"Danny," I cough his name out through the cloud of dust and fumes and blood in my mouth.

He doesn't move. My fingers are shaking as I unbuckle my seatbelt, and I can feel the adrenaline cascading through my blood. Every sense is force-feeding me information with exceptional clarity, and my brain is sprinting to process everything as it slows down time for me. The feeling makes me want to crawl out of my skin, but I need this right now. I need to use it.

I jam my finger against the cabin light switch, but it doesn't come on. My mind flicks forward. I need to get help.

My phone.

Pulling it out of my pocket, I dial 911.

The spaces between the rings feel like the longest seconds of my life.

"911, what is your emergency?" The voice is calm, masculine.

My hand is shaking on the phone. Why is it so hard to make words right now? "There was... an accident. We need an ambulance."

"I understand. What is your location?"

"Um, just outside of Sooke. On the west side."

"Okay, an ambulance is on its way. Are you on Sooke Road?"

I nod but then remember I'm on the phone. "Yeah."

"Okay. I need you to stay on the phone with me. Are you injured?"

"Not really, but hold on," I say, ignoring the dispatcher's instructions and pulling the phone away from my ear as I turn on the built-in flashlight. Leading with my phone, I scoot toward Danny.

Please God, let him be okay.

The cold white light washes over his unconscious form as I hold my breath. Cuts are scattered across the side of his face, and he has a nasty red mark on his forehead. Grabbing him around the wrist and leaning in as close as I can, I listen for breathing as I feel for his heartbeat.

Both are there. So he's just knocked out, right?

I want to wrap my arms around him and pull him to me, but I don't want to risk hurting him. I can hear the tinny sound of the operator still talking through my phone, but that doesn't matter right now.

Sweeping the light over Danny's chest, I touch the area lightly with my hand. He's still in one piece. I move the light lower, to his crotch and his legs. My eyes snag on something sticking into his jeans, halfway down his thigh.

My breath stops in my throat, and I make several realizations in the span of a single second. The first is that it's not something sticking into his leg – it's sticking *out*. The second is that there's only one bone you can break in your thigh, and if that happens it's always serious. The third is that I've discovered the source of the disgusting metallic scent in the air. All around the bone, the denim of his jeans is stained dark and saturated with blood.

So much blood.

The bone must have sliced through his jeans on its way out. It's the color of cream but streaked with red, and it ends in sharp points of an angled fracture. Broken like it is, I can easily see the hole in the center where dark blood is dribbling out. Christ, I can see his fucking bone marrow. The understanding sends a chill through me, and a wave of nausea washes into my stomach.

Where is the goddamn ambulance?

Bringing my phone back up to my ear, my breath is heavy as I say, "Danny is hurt bad."

"Where is he hurt?"

"Um, his leg. I can see the bone."

"Upper or lower leg?"

I swallow away the rising taste of vomit. "Upper. There's a lot of blood."

"I understand," the reply comes back. "The ambulance is just a few minutes away."

I throw the phone onto the dash and turn my attention back to Danny. Reaching out, I lift his head up from his chest. "Danny," I whisper as I hold him. I don't think it's good that he's unconscious. "Danny," I say again louder, slapping his cheek.

His eyes flutter open, and I can feel them watching me through the silence. "Oh God, it hurts," he whimpers. "Curtis, it hurts." He squirms in his seat but immediately ceases as he sobs in pain.

Dropping my hands from his face, I take his hand in mine and squeeze. "The ambulance is coming. It's going to be okay."

I wish I believed my own words.

His breaths are fast, coming in tight bursts. I can't imagine how much pain he's in, but the part I hate the most is that just like with the woman on the motorcycle, there's still not a damn thing I can do. If I'd started taking emergency tech classes when Danny encouraged me to, I might have been able to do *something*. Maybe not, but now it's impossible to know. I could have been a few weeks into the training already. Instead, I just sat on the couch doing nothing.

"It hurts," he cries again, and he slumps toward me.

I circle my arms around him and hold him in the darkness as the rain pounds against the windshield and his breath pounds against my heart. I hold him through his whimpers. I hold him as hot blood soaks his jeans. I hold him until red and blue lights appear on the road and come to a stop on the shoulder, splashing their colors onto our faces.

Danny is barely conscious as they slide him out onto a stretcher. His jeans are sopping wet with blood, and his face is pale. So pale that it's a wonder he's alive at all.

"Is he going to live?" I demand from one of the paramedics as Danny is loaded into the ambulance.

The guy stops and gives me a sympathetic look. "He's lost a lot of blood and his pulse is thready, but…"

"But *what*?" I plead.

The man sighs. "But he looks like a fighter. That's what he needs to do right now."

From the front of the ambulance, someone shouts that it's time to go, and the paramedic jumps into the back and slams the door.

Down the road I can see a second group of flashing lights surrounding the logging truck. My stomach churns, because the crash was the driver's fault. I should be concerned whether he's okay or not, but I just can't bring myself to care, because Danny is all that matters to me.

Sirens fill the air as the ambulance pulls away, but I stand still.

Heart thudding, I watch the flashing lights paint the night with their colors. I watch them take Danny away. I watch until the sounds fade and darkness surrounds me once more.

Chapter Twenty-three

Curtis

The hospital waiting room is sterile and white, and last night was agonizingly long.

I keep asking the doctor and the nurses how Danny is, but they keep telling me that he's still in the emergency room in critical condition.

It's some kind of cruel joke that Danny got hurt so badly and I escaped with just scratches and cuts. I'm the one who should be busted up right now, not him. Danny didn't do anything wrong. I did. It's like God or fate or whatever is trying to show me something, but I can't figure out for the life of me what it is.

Maybe there isn't a message at all. Maybe shitty things just happen to good people.

For the tenth time this morning, I march up to the nurse's station and ask if there are any updates. The woman at the desk glares at me but checks her computer anyway. "He's been transferred. He's in C208. But you should know that–"

I'm walking briskly away from her before she even finishes, and it's the hardest thing to not break into a run. His room is up a few floors and down a hall, which is actually a pain, because I'm sore all over from the crash. Nevertheless, my feet carry me there swiftly.

Preparing myself, I knock on the door and push it open. Danny is asleep, almost looking peaceful except for the cuts on his face. Then my eyes are dragged toward his parents who are sitting beside the bed. Quickly standing, they usher me out the door with them and into the hallway.

"Curtis," his dad addresses me. The stoicism of his suit matches his expression, and he doesn't sound happy to see me.

"Mr. Somers," I say with a nod. "You guys got here fast. How is Danny?"

His lips press together and he exchanges a look with his wife. "Dan hasn't woken up yet."

My heartbeat thunders in my ears. It's the sound of blood and drums and fear. "You mean, he's just still sleeping, right?" My question is a hope and a plea, because I can't accept the alternative.

Danny's mom steps closer, and her soft hands surround mine. "He's in a coma."

My eyelids flicker, and my fingers curl back tight against my palms. "Can I see him?"

"Of course," his dad says.

The rest of the world blurs as my feet step past the two people in front of me and into the room. Danny is lying on the bed, just like I saw him a minute ago. Except now he looks completely different because that look of repose is a lie and a trick.

I sit beside him, pretending that the clear tube in his arm isn't there. I take his hand, feel his warmth. Feel the roughness of callouses where his fingers meet his palm. Feel the veins running through the back of his hand. I squeeze, as hard as I can. I know Danny can take the pressure because his hands are strong. Stronger than mine.

But he doesn't react.

Heat rises in my throat, and my breaths sound too loud, too close. *Oh God, Danny. Don't do this.*

Once more, a question forces itself to the surface. If I'd started that class when Danny wanted me to, could I have helped him?

What if he dies and it's my fault?

The feeling inside my chest grows more caustic, and acid hurls itself against my insides. Dropping Danny's hand, I sprint three steps into the bathroom and kneel in front of the toilet as I throw up.

I'm still spitting into the toilet when a familiar soft hand comes to a rest on my shoulder. It should be comforting, but it's not. The only thing I want right now is for Danny to be okay, and if I can't have that, I just want to be alone.

I shrug off his mom's hand as I stand and begin washing my face.

Behind me, she takes a breath as if steeling herself. "We are going to be staying with him." Something feels off about her words.

"I will too. As long as it takes, until he... comes back." I say quietly, staring into the mirror at the redness around my eyes.

Danny's dad now joins us in the tiny bathroom. "This isn't the way we wanted to talk to you about this, Curtis, but Dan called us a few weeks ago and explained that you two had become... involved. We're not particularly fond of all the choices Dan has made." He tries to smile but it comes out looking like he's in pain. He reaches out and squeezes my shoulder briefly before dropping his hand. It feels fake, like his words. Danny always hated when his parents called him *Dan*.

"We've always tried to love and support him," Mrs. Somers adds. "But we need to do what's best for him now." Wetness pricks at her eyes.

My hand sneaks up to my forehead, and I press a thumb against my temple. Wedged into a hospital bathroom with Danny's parents, after just throwing up and with Danny in a coma in the next room... it's not the way I imagined having this conversation, either.

Dropping my hand, I let them hear the honesty in my words. "I just want Danny to get better."

Mr. Somers sighs. "That's what we want too." He pauses, before asking, "You moved out here because you lost your job in Thunder Bay. Is that correct?"

"Yeah," I answer, my voice tight. "Why?"

"We know you've been living with Dan, but with the condition he's in, we don't feel comfortable with you staying at his house."

My eyebrows pull together in frustration. Suddenly I get the impression that I'm being forced out of what's happening here. "You can't do anything about it," I say, hating how whiny I sound. "It's his house. I love him, and I'm not going to go unless he asks me to."

Mr. Somers clenches his jaw, like it's hard for him to hear what I just said. "I know that you might not have anywhere else to go, so I want to make it easy for you."

"What are you talking about?"

From inside his jacket he pulls out a piece of paper. "If you need help getting a fresh start back in Thunder Bay, this is yours." He hands me the check, and I stare dumbly at the letters and numbers.

"You can't be serious."

"We are," Danny's mother says.

"Take it," his dad presses. "But please let us take care of our son the way we think is best. He needs us now."

He needs me *now*. But what else can I do? I'm pretty sure they can have me removed if they want. They're family, I'm not.

They don't wait for an answer. Leaving me alone in the bathroom, they disappear into the hallway, like they're giving me one last chance to say goodbye to Danny.

Anger tries to take hold, but there just isn't enough room inside me beside the despair at seeing Danny just lying there.

My throat is dry as I stare down at the check in my hands. Made out to *Curtis Wyatt*, the check is written out for ten thousand dollars. *Ten thousand dollars*, just to disappear? To get in my car and drive back to Thunder Bay. Or anywhere else.

Jesus, it wasn't that long ago I was planning on leaving on my own. And now I've essentially been given months of pay to do exactly that. It doesn't matter, though, because I could never leave Danny after something like this. I abandoned him when we were younger, and I'm not going to do it again.

Approaching his bed, I touch his wrist gently with the back of my fingers. I slide my hand up his arm, detouring around the IV.

"I love you, Danny," I breathe. "I love you so much." I lean over him and brush my fingers through his short hair to straighten it out. He always hates it when his hair is messy.

I can feel the tears rising in my eyes once more, and I know it's time to leave. Pressing my palm against his cheek, I lean down and kiss him on the forehead. *I love you, Danny.*

I glance one more time at the black ink on the check before stuffing it into my pocket and walking out of the hospital.

Chapter Twenty-four

Curtis

Seven days have passed. Danny still hasn't woken up, and I still haven't left.

Most of my days I spend around the hospital, making clandestine passes in front of his room until I see that his parents have left. The first few times that they caught me in his room, they asked me to leave, which I did. That still happens sometimes. Other times they see me and just leave for a while.

Whether or not they approve of what Danny and I had going on between us, I think they're at least partially okay with me being there now. Maybe it's because my visits make it so that someone is always with him. It's an uneasy truce, but as long as I get to spend time around Danny, I don't care.

Lauren visits too. I know she doesn't come to see me, so I clear out when she's around. Not that I would have anything to say to her anyway. Except for maybe an apology.

And when I need to sleep, I make the drive back to Danny's place. Without him, his home is just a house. And an empty one at that. The furniture is still beautiful, and the floors and timber framing are still striking, but it's not the same without him. I started a fire one evening to see if that would coax a little life back into the place, but as it burned down, it just reminded me of the nights that we spent curled up on the couch watching the waning embers.

At the moment, I'm standing at the entrance to Danny's woodshop. My fingers hesitate on the doorknob, wondering about this special part of him that I've never seen. Wondering why he never invited me inside.

The knob turns beneath my grip, and I step inside.

A fine layer of vanilla-colored dust covers every surface, and it smells like... wood. Scents I recognize like cedar, and dozens of others I don't. And all of it coated in this hint of spiciness. I move forward, my eyes catching on numerous machines and saws whose purpose escapes me.

The far end of the room is lined with wooden bins, and I move toward them. One is filled with scraps – odds and ends of cut pieces that he must not be able to use. The next bins are smaller, but likewise they contain raw, unfinished wood and seem to be filled with throwaway scraps too, except these pieces of wood actually tried to become something. There are cutting boards with defects – knots that ran too deep to sand out – and others that seem perfectly fine. Maybe Danny didn't like them for some other reason.

Next to the cutting boards is another kind of object. Flat on the bottom, they're like cylindrical handles with patterns cut into them. From what I learned in high school woods class, I'm pretty sure that Danny made these on a lathe. Picking one up, I run my fingers over the grooves in the dusty brown of the unfinished wood. Feeling the edge of a smile coming on, I realize that it's a tap handle for a bar.

Scanning the rest of the room, something strikes me as odd. I know that Danny was working a lot right up until the accident, but nothing here looks like a project in progress. What was he working on?

It's then that I notice a plate glass window in the back that looks into another area. Following my curiosity, I push through the door and enter a much smaller room.

A large desk dominates this cramped area, and scattered across the surface are sheets of drawings, plans, and scribbled notes. There are so many papers that they cover up the keyboard that accompanies the massive computer screen. I wonder how much drafting he did on the computer and how much by hand. It's just another thing I might never know about him.

Pushing the clutter of papers aside, I sit down at the desk and wiggle the mouse. The screen stays blank, and I sigh, because I'm not *that* much of a snoop that I'm actually going to turn the thing on. But the next moment the screen flares to life, and I have to smile again. His web browser is open to *Pinterest*. I wonder how many hours he spends on there, searching for inspiration.

I glance at the keywords he last searched for, and a knot of regret forms in my throat. I miss Danny. I miss his quirkiness and his kindness and his short temper, and I miss how I felt when I was with him. I sniff, forcing back the thought, because I'm not going to get broken up over a goddamn Pinterest page.

Standing from the desk, I venture out of the office and through another door.

In start contrast, it's immaculately clean in here. A large filtered fan hangs from the ceiling, and another fan is built into the exterior wall. But by far, the most impactful part of the room is the object in the center. It looks like some sort of study desk, built in the same style as the table in Danny's dining room, but the wood itself is completely different. It's some exotic hardwood. In fact, it looks just like the serving board he used the night after I ran off into the woods. The one I told him I loved.

The finish on the surface of the desk is as smooth and clear as glass, and beneath it is a grain pattern that's nothing short of breathtaking. Rich cherry chocolate, the color alternates between light and dark waves, pouring across the wood like water tumbling over a falls. It's absolutely beautiful, and my heart is pulled toward it as I admire Danny's craftsmanship.

Running my hand over the surface, I gaze into the hypnotic pattern. Danny is more than a craftsman, he's an artist.

It's then that I notice an irregularity in the center of the desktop. That seems odd, because I can't imagine that Danny would ever allow such a careless imperfection to persist in his work. Bringing my face close to the wood, my breath catches in my throat as I realize what I'm seeing.

Carved with eloquent strokes into the wood and sealed over by glossy finish are words. *For Curtis, with love – a place to pursue your dreams.*

A cursory glance at the desk would never reveal the message, but seeing it now, it's impossible to miss it. I remember back to when I told Danny I always wished I had a desk.

So he went and built one for me. Out of the wood I admired so much.

Sinking to my knees, I lean my head against the desk, my fingers gripping the edge. Tears leak out of my eyes, and my teeth clench in pain. I love Danny so much. *How am I ever going to survive without him?*

Perched on the edge of the dock, I let my feet sway back and forth as saltwater licks at my toes. My shoes and socks lie in a pile beside me, and the sun is hot on my neck. Somewhere along the way, summer snuck up on me. It rains a lot less now, and the days are warmer but not uncomfortably hot like the summers in Ontario.

In front of me, blue water stretches out across Sooke Basin and a breeze pushes up against me, as if to say hello. This day might be perfect, but it's also the furthest thing from it. Danny is laid up in a hospital bed, unconscious, while people he doesn't know take care of him.

Thinking about Danny draws me back to an earlier time, a time when everything on the island felt unfamiliar. The memory forms slowly at first, and the details surface one by one. The chill in the night air and the sound of Danny's voice as he argued with me that we didn't have to live differently, just because we were older.

Despite everything that's happened, I can't help but smile as I remember his buck-naked butt sprinting past me down the dock. His yelp of exultation as his legs kicked into the empty air.

I should have jumped with him.

In a split-second decision, I'm on my feet, tugging off my shirt and my shorts. I slide my thumbs into the elastic band around my briefs and pull those off too. The breeze is cool against my naked body as I back off from the edge of the dock, my feet leaving wet footprints on the weathered wood.

Sun glinting in my eyes, I steal a breath of the afternoon air. *This is for Danny.*

My bare feet slap against the dock as I run forward. The wind is stronger now, pulling at my legs and my shoulders and my hair. Ahead, the surface of the basin shimmers a unique shade of blue. My heart pauses, and I realize it's Danny's blue. The color I could never understand.

My last footfall touches the edge of the dock, and I leap into open space. Sunlight kisses my eyes, shut tightly, and the air whispers to me, and the moment stretches out as I remember the night that Danny jumped this same jump.

Sun-kissed eyes and whispered air and I'm falling through space.

Danny's color was always the sea.

I'm with him now.

Chapter Twenty-five

Curtis

Nine days since the accident, and Danny's condition still hasn't changed. The doctors don't talk to me about how Danny is doing, but I know from too many Google searches that the best chance of coming out of a coma is in the first two weeks.

It makes me hopeful that he's going to wake up any day now, and it scares the shit out of me, because what if he just... *doesn't?*

I glance up at Danny for the tenth time in the last half hour, but he's still exactly the same. Looking back at the Spider-Man comic I'm holding, I continue reading aloud. "*Some very strange things have been happening lately. Things that don't seem to make much sense. But if you're the clown behind them, pal, it's time we settled the score!*"

I pause and look at Danny again. Still nothing. "Um," I say, narrating the images. "Spider-Man is knocking this guy in the face now. *Zaaat! Bunt!*" I try to make the sound effects not seem ridiculous, but I don't think I'm doing a good job.

"Now he gets spotted by two guys with guns," I explain, moving on to the next frame. "*Aww... one of you musta peeked! Can I borrow those guns, fellas?*"

Feeling silly, I check on Danny once more as I describe somewhat unnecessarily, "He's grabbing their guns with his web stuff." As I watch him, Danny's eyes flutter open. My heart thuds. His gaze lands first on the ceiling and then slides over to me.

"You don't read comics aloud, you dork," he says, his voice hoarse.

My mouth hangs open, and several seconds pass before I can make words. "Oh God, Danny, you're awake!"

He smirks, and then he flinches in pain.

"What's wrong?" I demand.

"Lips are chapped," he croaks.

I grab the lip balm for him off the bedside table. "Shit, sorry. I forgot today." I reach out to put it on for him, but I catch myself and hand it to him instead.

He watches me as he smears the balm over his lips. "How long was I out?"

"Nine days," I say, still amazed that I'm actually *talking* to Danny right now.

"You stayed with me the whole time?"

I shrug. "Not the *whole* time. I went home to sleep and stuff. Your parents are around too."

He doesn't say anything, but his eyes seem to gleam with understanding.

Chapter Twenty-six

Danny

When I get home from the hospital, my mom has to hold the door while I hobble through it on my crutches. Over the two weeks in the hospital, I apparently had three surgeries on my leg, not that I was conscious for any of it.

It feels like barely any time has passed.

And it feels like it's been ages.

The last two days after I woke up were horrible. My parents stayed in a hotel while I endured the nights that devoured me whole. Morphine made the time pass, but only barely. It ushered me into sleep, but the comfort never lasted.

In contrast, Curtis arrived after my parents left, sleeping in the hospital room with me every night, on what looked like the most uncomfortable couch on the island.

I'm not sure that any of it makes sense to me now, especially after everything Curtis said the night of the accident. But he's here now, sitting at the kitchen table and fidgeting as I crutch through the living room to a place on the couch.

"I thought you would have been at the hospital today when they released me," I say to him, sounding more accusatory than I mean to.

My parents seem only now to notice Curtis because they both stiffen.

Curtis stares them down with a decided defiance. "Your parents wanted me to leave." He holds up what used to be a cashier's check, cut neatly in half, and drops the pieces in the center of the table. "They were pretty insistent." Lowering his voice, he adds, "I will, but only if that's what you want."

I sigh and turn to my parents. They look guilty as shit because they are.

It was nice that they stuck around while I was messed up in the hospital, but they're out of their goddamn minds if they think they can take control of my life with a strong arm and a checkbook.

For the first time since buying this house, I'm thankful that it's only one level. Otherwise it would be a nightmare to get around on my crutches. Still, it's not easy as I clunk toward the kitchen where Curtis is making dinner for us. After just a handful of seconds, I can't bear to be on my crutches any longer. Continuing to watch him, I flop down into a seat at the table.

"How are you feeling?" he asks warily.

"Shitty."

"Sorry," he says, and his eyes hold mine. Almost like they used to those times that we made love, but also completely not, because right now they're filled with pity that I don't want.

Maybe he really is sorry, or maybe he's just hiding things like he always has.

He tries again, speaking softly. "Can I help at all?"

I'm about to say *no*, but I change my mind. "Yeah."

"Anything," Curtis says, eyes widening with an annoying look of wanting to help.

Bitterness has become a familiar flavor over the last couple days, and it fills me once again as I say, "I need you to not treat me like I'm going to break if you say the wrong thing. Because you already said all the wrong things, and I'm already broken."

Morosely stirring the pot on the stove, he says a quiet "Okay." He looks miserable, but he can't possibly be feeling worse than I am, so he can just deal with it.

We stare at each other, waiting for something to happen that never does.

"The hospital..." Curtis begins. "They didn't really tell me anything, and your parents didn't either. The only thing I really knew is that you fell into a coma after they got you out of the truck. I didn't ask after you woke up because I figured you'd spent enough time talking about it." He glances at the brace around my leg. "You don't have to tell me if you don't want."

He's right that I don't want to talk about it, but I might as well tell him. "Besides the head injury… there was a compound fracture of my femur, and fractures of the two long bones in my lower leg. When my femur busted out, it just barely nicked the femoral artery, which is why I nearly bled out in the truck."

"Holy shit," Curtis breathes.

I shrug. "I'm still alive." *But it was close.*

"You didn't need a cast?"

"Just this brace. They cut through my knee and bolted rods into my leg to hold everything together."

His face gets screwed up like he wants to come over and give me a hug or something, but I shoot him a look that stops that idea cold. Curtis messed up, big time. I would have been happier if he had never admitted all that shit about knowing he was gay since we were kids, but he came clean about it, and he can't undo that now.

It's nice that he visited me in the hospital and stuff, but I can't just *forget* what he told me. How do I know if he even *wants* to be with me? He didn't when we were younger, so what's changed? If I act like nothing is wrong, will we mess around for a few more months – right up until he scares himself straight again and finds a nice woman? One who will put up with his closeted bullshit and give him the cute little family he so desperately wants? *Fucking coward.*

When he finishes whatever soup he was making, he dishes me up a bowl and sets it on the table. Silence takes a seat at the table with us, and it's so oppressive that I don't even make a comment about what Curtis made. He can't cook for shit.

After dinner, I pop one of the painkillers they gave me and hobble away to my room.

"You need anything?" Curtis calls after me from the kitchen where he's washing dishes.

"No." I slam the door behind me.

Deep in the night, vicious pain in my leg drives me from sleep. My eyes greet the darkness as the feeling takes hold of every one of my senses.

My vision sways as I reach desperately for the bottle of painkillers on the nightstand. It feels like forever before my fingers close around the hard plastic cylinder. I don't have water here, and even if I did, I wouldn't swallow them whole. I can't wait for a slow, measured efficacy. My lips parted, I take two of whatever they gave me, grinding them between my teeth and downing them with saliva.

The acrid taste of the drug fills my mouth, but it's nothing compared to the vengeful fire in my leg. I want to scream, but that won't help anything. So I clench my teeth and wait. The pain swells, growing in intensity. Moving beyond my leg, it spreads through me, scorching every nerve and cell in my body that it touches. It hurts so fucking bad.

Silent tears slip out of my eyes as I lie there, burning.

What's taking so long?

I wish I'd stayed in that coma.

Each second passes, cruelly, individually. Until finally the meds do their job, and the searing acid withdraws from my damaged flesh. My breathing comes easier, but worry quickly fills that gap inside me where the pain just stood. Whatever they sent home with me isn't as strong as the morphine I was getting before.

Am I going to endure this every night?

Chapter Twenty-seven

Danny

Curtis needs to stop being so helpful. I hadn't even gotten up to take a piss yet this morning when he showed up in my room with a tray of food. Eggs and toast and bacon. Even coffee.

Coffee isn't fair.

Neither is bacon.

He's trying his damndest to be there for me whenever and however I need him. I hate it because I don't know if I can forgive him. Maybe he deserves it, or maybe he doesn't. But that doesn't matter if – when it finally comes to it – I can't get over what he did. Or rather, what he didn't do.

Feeling like I couldn't talk to my best friend in high school was a nightmare. College was worse. Those experiences made me stronger, I suppose, but to find out that they never needed to happen... that if Curtis had just stopped being such a chickenshit, our lives would have been so different.

I didn't tell him how I felt, either. But he *knew*. He *knew* we were the same in a way I never could have imagined. His insight into how other people think and feel was always his gift. I never understood it then and I don't now. And I probably shouldn't judge him for using that intuition how he wants, but... how could he not tell me? We were best friends. Better than best friends. I was the one who held him through all the hard times growing up. He was the one who I would have given anything for.

"You getting hungry for lunch yet?" Curtis's voice tugs at my thoughts, and my eyes are drawn slowly away from the hole they were boring in the heavy timber beams over the living room.

"Not really," I say. My appetite has slipped lately. I'm losing weight but I don't see any point in getting on a scale to see how much. That would just depress me even more. "I'll take a beer, though."

Curtis glances at my busted leg propped up with pillows at the end of the couch. "Um, I don't know if you should be drinking. While you're... you know, recovering."

Faster than I can even think, my fingers grab the closest thing – a coffee coaster – and fling it at him as I snap, "Fuck you!" The coaster is ceramic and it nails him square in the chest with a deep thud before falling and breaking apart on the floor. He winces at the impact, but otherwise he stands motionless.

His cheeks burn red, and he bites his lower lip. It looks like he's going to cry, but he stays silent as he gets a beer from the fridge and brings it to the end table beside me.

"I'm sorry," I sputter out my apology. "I don't even know what I was thinking."

He straightens, and the hurt is so visible in his eyes. When he speaks, his voice is guarded. "You were constantly on morphine in the hospital. I have to believe that you're going through some kind of minor withdrawal, because the Danny I know wouldn't do that." Not lingering a single extra moment, he walks away from me and disappears out onto the back deck.

Embarrassment mixes with remorse inside me. I don't know if my sudden outburst was a result of a withdrawal induced mood swing or not, but... I feel like shit as I take my first drink.

Curtis keeps his distance for the rest of the day, which doesn't bother me. At least not until dinnertime rolls around and I still haven't had anything besides breakfast. Unless a beer and pain pills count, and I suspect they don't.

I keep hoping that Curtis will show up and make me a sandwich or something, but when my stomach starts making noises that can be heard across the room, I give up and make myself get up off the couch.

Like always, my crutches feel awkward, wedged under my armpits and pressed against my palms. It doesn't help that my leg is busted up and throwing off my balance. Taking precarious steps into the kitchen,

I try to open the fridge but realize that I'm standing too close for the door to open.

I suppress a growl of frustration and pull the crutches tight against my armpits before moving back a step. This time as I open the door, a swell of lightheadedness presses into me, and my vision blurs at the edges. Acutely aware of my fragile state and shaky balance, I force my tingling fingers to grip the crutches with all the strength I have.

I take a breath, then another, and the fog clears from my eyes. The lightness in my extremities disappears too. Except in my busted leg. Instead of lessening, the uncomfortable sensation there grows more potent, waxing into a painful pressure that demands I stop this whole standing and walking around business.

Crutching back into the living room, I plop down on the couch and elevate my leg once more. My breathing comes out rough, but it's not from the exertion.

With that short jaunt, a nasty truth has been forced on me.

I'm not invincible anymore.

Even though that hasn't been true for years. Not that it was ever true.

For all the hard times I found there, college made me feel like I could take on the world. Even when the world struck me, I could hit back. Even though it hurt, I was still strong.

Now I can't even *stand* for more than a minute or two. And even though the surgeons stitched me up, it's obvious that my body is still all sorts of broken.

My stomach growls obnoxiously, demanding to be fed. I can't get up again, not without risking another brush with low blood pressure.

But I need to eat.

"CURTIS!" I yell, like some baby fucking bird. Like I can't take care of myself.

I wait, feeling horrible for so many reasons that I don't even bother trying to unravel that knot of emotion. "CURTIS!"

The back door opens and he steps inside. "You could have texted me, you know." He glances at my phone on the floor beside me.

"Oh, right." Now I'm not just helpless, I'm an idiot too.

Curtis moves slowly into the living room, and caution follows his steps as he rubs absently at a spot below his collarbone. "You going to throw shit at me again?"

I drop my eyes. "Sorry about that."

He sighs, and the sound is so sad that it almost makes me forget about my own problems.

"So..." he begins, "you needed something?" The way he says it makes me wonder if he's hoping that I *didn't* need anything in particular. That I just wanted to see him.

"I'm kind of starving."

"Kind of starving, huh?" Curtis has the good humor to grin, and this mundane moment we're sharing suddenly seems important. It makes me wish I could grab onto that mischievous smile of his and hold onto it forever.

As darkness slinks through the windows and I retreat to my room for the evening, I make a point to take one of the pain pills right before I slide into bed. Downing it with half the glass of water on my nightstand, I let my head fall into my pillow.

I close my eyes, and my thoughts sneak back to earlier in the evening. Curtis made sandwiches after all – mostly because I insisted that I couldn't wait long enough for him to cook something on the stove. Not only did I get fed, but I learned a valuable bit of information about Curtis. As horrible as his cooking might be, his sandwich making skills are adequate.

Tonight, the drugs seem to take effect quickly, and they pull me under with warm hands. This kind of sleep isn't restful, but it is still sleep, and I'm grateful as my consciousness fades away.

When I awake, my room hasn't yet been freed from the clutches of night, and the cozy touch of narcotics still lingers beneath my skin. But I have to pee. Really damn bad.

I throw the covers off and grope around in the dark for my crutches. Find them. Swing my legs over the edge of the bed.

I grit my teeth to ward off the muted bolts of pain and take hurried steps toward the bathroom, wishing that the painkillers hadn't kept me asleep so long.

Ignoring the light switch, I press on through the dark until I'm standing more or less in front of the toilet. But as I lean into the crutches and plead for them to steady me, a surge of blood rushes from my head, and the room begins unraveling at the edges.

I fight to keep myself upright, but my muscles aren't listening to me. I try to clench my fingers, demand that they steady me, but they won't.

My balance is lost and I'm tipping backwards, falling now, into open space.

My whole body thuds into the floor and my head smacks the tile.

I'm lucky. Nothing bent in a way it shouldn't. I'm in one piece, still broken but still whole, but the fractures in my leg scream anyway. They demand vengeance for my carelessness.

The back of my head throbs, but it's the spiteful hurt in my crippled leg that drags me into unconsciousness.

Distant sound beckons me back from quiet repose. I don't want to wake up.

I hear my name again. "Danny." Too-bright white light stabs at my eyes as I try to open them.

A shadow passes over me, and something flat taps against my cheek. "Danny, wake up."

Curtis sounds anxious, agitated. "*Danny.*"

Blinking away the sensitivity in my eyes, I focus on the face hovering over me. "Curtis," I say. He's only wearing underwear, which strikes me as odd.

"Jesus, Danny. You scared the shit out of me. I heard this huge crash..." His gaze jumps frantically to my arms, my legs. "Are you okay? Should I call an ambulance?"

"*No,*" I growl. Curtis looks conflicted, like he might do it anyway. "Seriously," I say, toning down my voice. "I'm okay. I just fell. I didn't land weird or anything." Everything still hurts like hell, but I'm okay.

"All right..." Curtis says at last. "Let's um, get you cleaned up."

"Huh?"

His eyes are soft as he looks at me. He glances down, and I follow. Only then do I realize that my briefs are soaked and I'm lying in a pool of my own piss.

Heat bursts into my throat and my face burns with embarrassment. Curtis watches as soundless tears slip from my eyes and down my face before dropping onto the tile. I can't do this. *I cannot do this.*

My vision blurs further as my eyes fill while the shape of Curtis moves behind me. His hands slide under my arms, gripping the sides of my ribs, and he pulls me toward him. He pulls me close until I'm sitting up and pressed into his chest. His arms surround me, squeezing me, and I feel his warmth.

His cheek touches mine, and his breath is hot in my ear. "It's okay to let yourself hurt. No matter what you say or do, I'm never going to let you go, Danny. I love you. I love you so goddamn much, and I'm never going to let you go."

Tucked into his arms, I cry. I bawl until my eyes and heart are sore, until the cold tile has turned my skin to cold stone, until the morning light sifts through the glass block window. And still Curtis holds me.

Chapter Twenty-eight

Danny

With each day, I get stronger. The pain is easier to manage, and getting around on the crutches isn't that bad anymore. Curtis helps. A lot. Way more than my dignity would have previously allowed for. He cooks, he cleans, he gets the mail, he helps me in the shower, and he… sleeps beside me.

After he cleaned me up the night I fell, he came back to bed with me. The following night, he did the same thing. I told him no, but he insisted. Our conversation ended with him spouting off that trademark grin and a comment about him not wanting to hit a cripple if I continued to refuse.

I almost don't want to admit it, but I like him sleeping by me. For all the nights after the crash that I was so alone, with the dark pressing in on me… I don't feel that way with Curtis beside me.

And he's warm.

Sometimes if he rolls over too close in the night, I have to throw off the covers before I start sweating. It's worth it, though, because I like knowing that he's close.

"Hey." The subject of my thoughts appears in the living room, leaning a shoulder against one of the two timber posts that support most of the roof.

"What's up?"

"You're doing that thing where you stare off into space with a goofy smile on your face," Curtis says.

I smile wider. "Sorry."

"You sure you didn't take too many of those pills again?" he asks, only half joking. A couple days ago I whacked my leg while getting out of the shower, so I took three pills instead of one and got a little loopy.

"I promise," I assure him.

"So what are you day dreaming about this time?"

I shrug. "Just this cute guy." Part of me can't believe that it's become so easy to be with Curtis again, but it's because... he's changed. He's not the same guy who I grew up with, not even the same guy who came out to the island a couple months ago. Not entirely, anyway.

Curtis smirks and flops down on the couch across from me. "Tell me about this stud."

"I said he was cute, not a stud," I correct him. "And he's a bit of a dick sometimes, but lately he's been kind of awesome."

He raises an eyebrow. "Sounds like a keeper." Then his humor falters and he adds a muted, "Sort of."

"Yeah," I say, not bothering to disguise that I'm checking Curtis out as my eyes flit over his tight t-shirt. "I think so too."

He laughs, but there's a nervous note in it. "So, uh... I have this thing to go to tonight, but there are leftovers from lunch in the fridge for you."

"Sure," I say, shooing him away with a flippant gesture. "Don't worry about me. Lauren is going to stop by, so I won't be alone all that long anyway."

Curtis watches me for several more moments before getting up from the couch. "Okay then. I'll, uh, see you later tonight."

I nod, and then I watch as he puts on his shoes and walks out the door. I listen as his car starts, waiting until the sound of the engine disappears.

I could have asked where he was going, I suppose, but I feel like he didn't want to share. I'm curious, of course, but I'm also glad that Curtis has a life these days outside of taking care of me. It makes me feel less guilty for accepting so much help from him.

"Hey, you," Lauren's voice rouses me from my nap on the couch.

I smirk. "You didn't lose your key, I see."

"Nope," she says, forcing a smile as she sits across from me. Silence. She watches me. "You doing okay?"

I nod, but I'm not sure what else to say.

Lauren sighs. "I'm sorry."

"About?"

"A lot of things." She hesitates, then adds, "I visited you in the hospital."

"Curtis told me."

She tries to smile again, but her words are quiet when she responds. "I thought he might."

"Enough about me," I say, saving her. "How have you been?"

"Well," she says, abandoning her remorseful tone and leaning in conspiratorially. "I finished my living room remodel, and I painted it… lavender."

Hours have passed and I've already brushed my teeth when Curtis gets home. He pokes his head into my room, pausing when he sees me lying on the bed.

"Hey," he says, out of breath. "Sorry I'm home late. The, uh… thing ran long."

"It's fine." Curiosity sticks to my words, but I don't ask him where he was. "Are you coming to bed?" The question still sounds presumptuous, but he's spent the last several nights with me, so I ignore my unease.

"You bet," he says. "Just give me a few minutes."

Once more I'm alone, but for the first time in a long time, it's not an unwelcome feeling. I pull in a full breath of the quiet evening, letting my chest puff out and my shoulders rise to accept the air. I shouldn't be as okay with everything as I am right now, but I can't help it. And even if I could, I wouldn't, because the last few days have been sort of amazing.

Somewhere above my knee, a sudden itch beneath my leg brace demands my attention, and despite the crawling sensation tickling my skin, it's with careful fingers that I undo the Velcro straps. My leg is puffy and red, but it looks better than when I took the brace off for the first time the other night.

Slowly, cautiously, I slide my hand down my thigh, avoiding the bandage that covers the hole where my femur broke out. In defiance of the meds, everything is sore, and I'm afraid that even my own fingers might somehow prove injurious.

But the nerves are desperate for contact, for connection with something other than the lifeless brace.

"You've got that old piece of meat out again?" Curtis jokes, staring at my unwrapped leg like it's some kind of creature that washed up on the beach.

I scowl at him as he moves onto the bed and comes close. He leans in and nuzzles his nose against my neck before pecking me on the cheek.

I raise an eyebrow. "Someone is in a good mood." And feeling courageous, because that's the first time he's shown that kind of affection since before the crash.

"You're cute when you're playing leg doctor." His words taste like cinnamon rolls and melted butter, and it takes every ounce of my willpower not to smile back at him. I'm still pretending to be annoyed.

"So," he presses, "what exactly are you doing?"

"I'm not sure," I say, and it's the truth.

"That feels good?" he asks, whisking skeptical eyes over where I'm lightly touching my leg.

"Really good, actually. It's like it's itchy and sore all at once." I bite my lip, toying with an idea. "Do you, uh, think maybe you could do this? It's hard to reach past my knee."

He raises his eyebrows at me. "Like... massage your leg like that?"

"Yeah."

He snorts a laugh. "That's weird, Danny. But for you? Absolutely."

Chapter Twenty-nine

Danny

Tonight is one of the few nights that Curtis is free. He still hasn't shared where he's been going in the evenings, and I haven't asked either. But that doesn't stop me from taking advantage of his presence and suggesting that we get out of the house. I was hoping for dinner or something, but he brought me to the gym instead.

My doctor did clear me for swimming – encouraged it, actually. So even though I didn't want to come here, Curtis insisted.

My legs hang over the edge as Curtis dog paddles in the lane. "Take your time," he says as he rolls over into a back float. His eyes land on me, and they don't move.

"Stop that," I tell him.

"Stop what?" he asks, full of innocence.

Irritation creeps over the hairs on my neck. "You're checking me out."

Curtis plants his feet on the bottom of the pool and straightens up before shrugging pointedly. "You're hot."

I frown, because it's not true. Despite the robust summer sun that Curtis has been enjoying lately, my skin is pallid and I generally feel like hell. Like I've been through the wash too many times. I'm sure that everything is to blame – the injury, the drugs, the lack of appetite.

I've lost nearly twenty pounds in the weeks since the accident. I'm still not eating enough, and I definitely haven't been able to work out.

But still Curtis looks at me like… *that*. Like he is now, sort of just… beaming. Like he's observing a perfect sunrise or something equally far removed from what I am.

As he watches me, his positive expression frays at the edges. "Come on in," he says smoothly, moving toward me through the water that fights to hold him back.

"I never said I would get in," I point out.

"I know," he breathes, coming closer yet. "But you want to."

"Maybe."

The corners of his lips pull ever so slightly upward. "Don't worry. The water will catch you."

"Screw that." I'd probably bust up my leg all over again if I just jumped in.

"Then *I'll* catch you." He holds his arms up.

I suppose I can handle that.

Scooting to the edge, I lean forward until his hands press hard against the sides of my chest. He lowers me down into the water, and instantly the scent of chlorine feels that much more present.

"You doing okay?" Curtis asks as my feet touch the bottom of the pool.

I nod, and he releases his hands. The surface of the water sits still around my shoulders, waiting for me. Expecting something from me. Curtis is watching me too.

Leaning into the water, I let it hold me like I know it can. Like it wants to.

The muscles in my arms tense, working together to draw me forward through the water as my feet flutter kick. Or at least they try. My broken leg hurts less each day, but it's still weak and the movement is strained.

I make it all the way down the lane before stopping to steady myself on the pool ledge.

"You're doing great," Curtis says as he joins me at the edge.

I want to tell him that I'm swimming like shit. That I'm afraid I'll never be able to move like I used to – in the water or out of it. But right now, he looks… happy, and I don't want to bring him down. "Thanks, Curtis."

He smiles, and in that moment, I feel like I'm actually going to get through this. My body will heal in time, and my life will return to normal. And Curtis will be there with me. I think. I hope.

He must see this insecurity play out in my expression, because the brightness in his eyes fades to a cool sobriety. "I'm sorry I was such a coward when we were teens," he says softly. "I can't tell you how often I wish I'd told you the truth." Liquid shimmers beneath his eyes. "I fucked up, and I am so, *so* sorry." Curtis swallows, and I can tell he's about to cry.

Maybe I should let him cry, to make him pay penance for his years of deception. But I can't. God knows I can't.

I let out a breath, and with it I forgive. I forgive him for everything he did. "It's okay," I whisper, confessing my secret to the silence between us.

Curtis still looks like he's going to cry, but the choked up noise he makes next is one of relief. Not looking away, he moves closer. His arms encircle me, holding me tight, and his face presses against my shoulder. I hope he never lets go.

Chapter Thirty

Danny

Days tick past and my strength continues to improve. At my doctor's orders, Curtis begins taking me to physical therapy twice a week. My biggest problem is that after weeks of having my leg straight in the brace, my knee will barely bend anymore. So basically the therapist guy just cranks away on my ankle every day I go, and the range of motion begins to come back. Slowly, painfully.

Letting go of my memories from the day, I stare up at the ceiling of my bedroom and wonder when Curtis will be done brushing his teeth. It always takes him forever, and I'm beginning to suspect he has a bit of an obsession with oral hygiene.

It takes me a moment to realize that Curtis is standing in the bathroom doorway, just watching me. His expression is soft, skirting along the edge of amusement. His eyes are beautiful, and I wish I could fall into them right now. At the very least, I want a taste.

"What is it?" I demand.

"Nothing," he says, coming close to the bed. Maneuvering around my feet, he lies down beside me and his chest presses against mine. "Oof," I say. "You're heavy."

"Shut up," he commands just before he kisses me.

I kiss him back through his smile, and it makes me want him to take me right here. As he slides a hand beneath my shirt, I can feel myself getting hard, but before he's made it halfway up my chest, I push him away.

"I can't."

"Sure you can."

"Seriously," I say. "My leg is all busted up and I can barely bend my knee. I'm not sure what you expect me to do besides just lie here."

He raises an eyebrow. "Maybe that's all I want you to do."

I swallow. "You mean like…"

Instead of answering my question, he gives me a look that makes my dick really stiffen up.

He lifts my shirt and leans down to brush his lips against my stomach. I suppress a shiver at his light touch, but he doesn't withdraw and I don't try to stop him. His fingers slide under the elastic band of both my gym shorts and my briefs, and he tugs them downward until they're sitting around my knees.

He leans over my midsection once more, and I bite my lip as he takes me in his mouth. My fingers slide through his hair as my eyes shut. His tongue dances on the underside of my dick, and I can't stop myself from releasing a groan of pleasure. I haven't even jerked off in weeks.

Curtis sits back, trying not to smile. "You like that?"

"Hell yes," I say, wanting him more than I ever have before. Wanting to be with him in a way I've never been before. Wanting to be *inside* him.

I stare at him and he stares right back. I can't wait any longer.

Reaching to the nightstand, I pull out the lube and a condom.

"You don't need that," he says.

I look at him like he's crazy. "The lube?"

He rolls his eyes. "No, the condom. I trust you."

My tone is harder than it should be, but I can't stop myself. "Damn Curtis, you've got to be smarter than that."

"Huh?" he says, bristling. "I just said I trust you. Should I not?"

I sigh, trying to figure out how to explain this to him. "It's not that. But… if you're going to have sex with guys, you *have* to be careful. Unless you've got the other guy's test results in hand – along with your own – and you're absolutely certain that he's not sleeping around on you, then you use a condom. Always. Every time."

He sits up against the headboard, shifting away from me as he does. "Are you fucking around with other guys?"

"What? Of course not. Are you?"

"No," he says defiantly. "I'm clean. Are you?"

I hesitate, even though there's nothing wrong with the honest answer. "Yeah, I am."

"So what's the big deal?" he counters.

Frowning, I sit up beside him. "I just..." My voice stalls out as I search for the right words. "I just want to be sure that if you do go back to Thunder Bay, that you're careful and you watch out for yourself. Just because it's safe with me doesn't mean it's safe with other guys, no matter what they tell you."

Curtis closes his eyes for a moment and releases a long breath. When he opens them, he looks at me hard. "You can be really, *really* dense, Danny. You know that?"

"Um..."

He pauses, takes a breath. "I feel stupid saying this, but I've... I've fallen in love with you."

My eyes widen. I never expected him to be so forthright with his feelings, whether he really felt that way or not.

"I'm okay not using a condom because it's you," he says as he jabs a finger in my direction. "I don't know if it's because I feel more comfortable around you than anyone else I've ever met, or whether it's just the world's fucked up way of showing me that none of us have as much control over our lives as we think. But damn, Danny. I fell in love with you. *You*, and no one else."

He hesitates before charging onward. "You know me better than anyone, so I just don't get why you think I could just drive back across the country and start picking up guys in bars. Like, *seriously*?"

My cheeks are red, both from his confession and his chastising tone. "I guess I didn't know. I hoped, but..."

Curtis doesn't wait for me to stumble through my sentence. "When I said I trusted you, I meant exactly that. I trust *you*, not someone else. I would run blindfolded along a cliff if you had my hand, and I would hold a gun to my head if you told me the chamber was empty, and I would trust you with my beating heart in your hands. Because that's what you've got."

In that moment there's nothing I want to do more than make love to him. To show him how much I care, to make him really know that he's *worth* it, that he deserves every kiss and soft touch.

"Come here," I say.

Chapter Thirty-one

Curtis

The seconds stretch and twist, growing longer, but Danny's loving eyes don't move from mine. My confession of a moment ago continues to resonate through me, reinforcing the truth of the words I've just uttered. It scares me, but it's also a relief to tell Danny how I feel without holding anything back.

"Come here," he repeats himself, his voice soft just like before.

And finally I do as he asks. Leaning over him, I bring my lips to his. As we kiss, his hands become more frantic, pulling at my shirt and fighting with the button on my shorts. He's already naked, so it's only fair, I suppose.

Once Danny has managed to pull the last of my clothes off, he tugs on the sides of my chest. His expression is beautiful as I move closer to him, and I feel like I'm clinging to a thread of ecstasy. Danny is my everything. Maybe he always was, and I just never knew it. But the past doesn't matter, because I know now.

Being careful of his injured leg, I kneel on either side of his hips and stare down at him.

"I want you," he breathes, and the elusive oceanic blue of his eyes finds me, scales the walls I put up to keep him out. He sees everything. Maybe he's even figured out that I've started taking paramedic classes in the evenings. He hasn't said anything about it, but the way he's looking at me right now… how could he not know? Those eyes of his, they strip me down, lay me out, open me up. For Danny alone to see inside.

In that moment, I don't have any secrets from him. He sees into me, from the darkest places to the parts of my life I'm actually proud of.

And that makes me want him too. More than anything.

He's been complaining that he's lost weight, that he's fading away, but all I see is the most handsome man I've ever met. I tell him that.

Danny flushes, his cheeks tinged with pink. "Liar," he says, but there's no bite in his voice.

I smile, and I take the lube from where he abandoned it earlier. Popping the cap on the bottle, I squeeze the clear liquid onto my fingers. Too much of it.

The overflow glops through my fingers and falls onto Danny's stomach, and he laughs. I wrap my fingers around his cock, and then he shuts up. Reaching beneath myself, I make sure I have lube where I need it before wiping my hand on the sheets.

"You want me to do anything to get you ready?" Danny asks. His expression is hopeful, and for a moment I wonder whether he *wants* to get his fingers inside me first. To feel me.

But whether or not that's true, I don't want to wait for him. I want him inside me, and not just his finger. I can't wait another fucking second, even if it hurts.

I hold his dick as I lower myself down. The tip of him is hot against my underside, and he feels bigger than he is.

"Relax," he says, his hands resting gently on my hips.

Despite my rising nerves, something in his tone makes it possible for me to do as he says. Breathing evenly in and out, I find my way to his eyes. Those eyes I've wanted to disappear into for so long.

My mouth parts slightly, but I don't look away from him as part of Danny becomes part of me. I feel so tight and full, and it hurts a bit too, but Danny is right here with me, and it's okay.

I sink lower, accepting him fully and loving the look on his face as I do.

His blue eyes shine, and his voice is a whisper and a prayer. "You're beautiful."

The warmth in my chest swells, and the pain from below subsides. Danny encircles my cock with his hand and begins to pump up and down. With Danny inside me, what he's doing feels so fucking good. It's only then that I remember that he doesn't have the strength to move underneath me.

Tensing the muscles in my thighs, I rise off him before coming back down. I can feel how he moves inside me, and it's nothing like anything I've ever experienced before. It makes me wish I could melt into him, to just hold him through the hours and never let him go. But it just feels too damn good to stop.

As I continue, Danny's expression is overtaken by a look of bliss, but still he doesn't stop with his hand. It's almost embarrassing how quickly the heat is building inside me.

Except I could never be embarrassed in front of Danny.

I want to hold out longer, but I just *can't*. From his muffled whimpers I think he's getting close too. He bites his lip and tenses beneath me. I can't stop myself either, and I come on his stomach and chest as he comes inside me.

Collapsing beside him, I exhale heavily. "Damn."

Danny turns his head, smirking. Then he kisses me, and I know without the slightest hint of doubt that this kiss isn't the end to something but the beginning. Danny isn't going anywhere, and neither am I.

It might have been over quickly, but I don't mind, because I know I'm going to experience this again, and again. And I'm going to love it more every time.

Finally responding to my earlier declaration, he says, "I love you too."

Chapter Thirty-two

Curtis

Four months later

"You're still in here," Danny says as he flops down on the bed in my room. A bed I haven't used in months. "I thought you were hungry."

"I am," I say, trying to summon a smile as I look up from the handcrafted desk spread out before me. The desk with the message engraved into the waterfall grain of the bubinga heartwood. After Danny presented me with the desk – yet another secret that I knew about beforehand – I made a point to learn more about his craft.

The last few weeks have been hell as I've waited to hear back on my paramedic licensing exams. My fingers rest on the surface of the desk as my thoughts try to sink toward the exam. I spent months studying at this desk, reviewing the material from class. Now that it's over, I think I retreat here more out of habit than anything else.

Jerking my eyes back to Danny and his patient expression, I fight to ignore my stress so I can give him the attention he deserves. I've been going through the motions, but I haven't been myself lately, and that's not fair to him.

"I'm hungry," I begin.

"Oh yeah?" he sounds interested, but he's also holding something back.

"But not for dinner." Perhaps sensing the impending change of plans, my stomach rumbles.

"Lies." Danny grabs me under the armpits and heaves me up out of my chair. "I'm taking you to dinner. And then we can do whatever you'd like." He winks.

"If you insist."

"Put on something nice." He gives me a meaningful look.

Danny's eyes flash up at me from across the tablecloth of the purest white, and his subtle smile drags my attention away from the pair of flickering candles at our table.

"What?" I demand.

"You're sexy when you're nervous," he says, dropping his voice as the waiter approaches our table.

I flush and lower my gaze to the menu, even though I'm not really seeing the words. My button-up feels tight around my neck and my wrists, and sweat is conspiring to make my shirt wet beneath my arms. Even the menu feels slick under my fingers. It's not hot outside, but clearly they need to turn up the air conditioning.

"And for you, sir?" the waiter's voice cuts through my thoughts.

"Huh?" I feel like an idiot the moment that the sound escapes my mouth.

"Your wine selection?"

"Uh…" I stumble, wishing the menu had an option for *I have no fucking clue what to order at a place this nice.* "I'll have what Danny is having."

"Very well – the Chateau Leoville." He nods and leaves us alone once more.

I've never been to such an upscale place. Even though I know that there are plenty of more expensive restaurants than this, it still makes me feel uncomfortable.

Glancing away from the street outside, Danny reaches across the table. I don't resist as he finds my hand and pushes his fingers through mine, pulling lightly. Like always, his palm is warm, and it helps to calm my nerves. For a moment, the restaurant falls away. The tables and the chairs and the other patrons and even the candles, all of it fades into black until the only thing left is Danny and me.

The waiter returns to pour the wine, and I watch as he tips the bottle toward the top of Danny's glass. Just a taste is all he pours. Danny samples it and nods, and the waiter pours the rest. The wine tumbles gently into the glass, and for the tiniest second, the sound reminds me of the ocean. That first day when Danny took me into the woods and down the coast. The perfect disorder as the waves tripped over one another to climb onto the beach. The color of Danny's eyes and the solemn clouds overhead.

After both glasses are poured, the waiter asks what we'll have to eat. I can't pronounce half the things on the menu, and Danny must know it, because he orders for both of us without bothering to ask me. Usually I hate that we're so different, but times like these make me really appreciate it. And they make me really appreciate *him*.

Snapping me out of my thoughts, Danny holds his glass up. It still feels a little weird to be doing this with another guy, but I lift mine anyway and clink it against his, toasting to an evening with the man I love.

I've been trying to convince myself that nothing is up tonight, but Danny has had this glint in his eye since we got here. Maybe that's why I've been so on edge.

"What?" I finally ask.

The corner of his mouth pulls up into a sly smile, and I don't need any more confirmation that he's hiding something.

"*Tell me,*" I demand. When he doesn't answer, my eyes narrow and I stare him down.

"You're no fun," he complains. Leaning to the side, he stuffs his hand in his pocket and pulls out an envelope. As he hands it to me, he says, "I didn't even realize it was made out to you when I opened it. I'm still not used to getting mail for you..."

I hate that my fingers shake as I take the envelope with the torn top and withdraw the letter. *Dear Mr. Wyatt...* My eyes flit down the page, racing over the words as my heart stands still. *We are pleased to inform you that you have passed the Primary Care Paramedic licensing exam.*

And then everything makes sense. Danny's bubbly mood earlier, this restaurant, the smile he's wearing now.

"Holy shit," I say, and my voice feels empty and full all at once. "I did it."

"Damn straight, you did," Danny says, beaming as he gets to his feet and pulls me up from my chair. The restaurant isn't crowded, but the attention of other patrons feels hot on my skin as Danny's eyes gaze into mine. "I'm so proud of you," he whispers as he pulls me into a kiss.

My tongue tastes the wine and it tastes Danny, and suddenly I don't care anymore that we're in a public place. All that matters is that we managed to find each other the way we needed. I don't even care that it took almost twenty years for that to happen, because we're here now.

A polite cough from behind us makes me pull away, and I glance to our waiter and the plates he's waiting to place at our table. Warmth fills me, but it's not because I'm embarrassed. Still, I separate myself from Danny and take a seat again. The waiter serves us, and Danny sends a smirk meant just for me. A smirk confessing that he'd be willing to do it on the table right now if I wanted.

And I smile back, because maybe part of me *does* want that.

Chapter Thirty-three

Curtis

The hot and sunny days of summer are long past, and autumn has swept over the island. Other than the new crispness in the air, only the scattered deciduous trees admit to the changing seasons.

I take a deep breath, feeling the cool day fill my chest as I lean back into the dock piling. Danny is across from me against the opposite post, and our gazes stretch out across the glassy water. It was today's rare sun that drew us out to the water's edge, but I think we might have come out here anyway. Something about this day feels like change. The temperature maybe, on the cusp of cold but refusing to relinquish its grasp on the heat of summer. Or maybe it's just the scent of fall carried in on the light breeze.

"I've started looking for an ambulance job," I say.

Danny shifts his position, and his jeans brush against the dock. "I figured." He pauses, and I know he wants to say more.

"What?"

"You don't have to. Not right away, I mean."

My stomach turns, and now I understand his hesitation. "I don't need you to support me." *Any longer than you already have been,* my mind fills in the rest of my sentence.

"I know," he says hastily. "I just meant, if you wanted to, you could wait."

I don't answer him. Danny is wicked talented, and I'm sure his business could support us both and then some. But I don't want anyone to think that I'm with him for any reason but the real one. Namely, that I love him so goddamn much that I can't imagine spending a day without him anymore.

"I want to get a job. You know, be old and boring."

Danny laughs at that. Even after the sound ends, it seems slow to fade away. "Get up," he says, standing up himself.

"Huh?"

He looks down at me, waiting. So I do as he asks, and I get to my feet.

We stand beside one another, and we look out over the basin. Sun pours over the water, coating it in layers of silver and gold.

"You never jumped," Danny says softly.

"No," I say. Even though I did. This is a lie that will never hurt him.

I follow his gaze downward, and I find his hand, palm open and fingers spread just a little.

The day feels cooler than before, and a shiver breathes down my neck. I slide my fingers through his, and our palms press together.

I'm going to jump with Danny.

"The water will catch you," he says. It's an inside joke, and it's a promise.

"And if it doesn't?"

"Then I will."

I believe him.

When I look at Danny, he's got this look like he knows this moment intimately and perfectly, from the stillness between us to the sunlight streaming down. And he flashes me a subtle smile that reaches all the way to his eyes. I stare right back, and in those eyes I taste the color of the sea.

We're running now, our hands our bond. Feet striking wooden planks, Danny's stride wavers. He's not fully healed yet, but I'm ready for that. I hold him steady, just a few more steps now.

A perfect moment, the taste of the sea, and we leap into space.

---The End---

The Water Will Catch You

ACKNOWLEDGEMENTS

I would be absolutely lost without my beta readers, so I would like to say a very heartfelt thank you to Brian Gumm, Nick Pageant, and Sunne Manello. You guys are the best.

Chase Potter lives in St. Paul, Minnesota with his husband Mitchell and their dog Alex. The Water Will Catch You is his third novel. Raised in rural Minnesota, Chase has also lived in Germany and Austria. The experiences growing up in a small town and his struggles to adapt to foreign culture and language have served as inspiration in his writing.

Made in the USA
Middletown, DE
31 May 2021